# The CHOSEN®

## BOOK TWO COME AND SEE

JERRY B. JENKINS



FOCUS ON THE FAMILY.
BroadStreet PUBLISHING

**Come and See**



A Focus on the Family book published by BroadStreet Publishing®.

*Focus on the Family* and the accompanying logo and design are federally registered trademarks of Focus on the Family, 8605 Explorer Drive, Colorado Springs, CO 80920.



Editors: Larry Weeden and Leilani Squires

Cover design by Michael Harrigan



978-1-64607-021-3 (hardcover)
978-1-64607-085-5 (paperback)

Library of Congress Cataloging-in-Publication Data can be found at www.loc.gov.

Printed in China

26 25 24 23 22 5 4 3 2 1

**PRAISE FOR THE CHOSEN:** *I HAVE CALLED YOU BY NAME*

"For over 70 years I have heard the redemptive stories of the Bible told without the emotion and passion that would indicate real people actually experienced these events. Who drained the life blood from the hearts of these men and women? Jerry Jenkins's account of *The Chosen: I Have Called You by Name* is a refreshing transfusion that restores life to the people of the Bible and to its redemptive story. You will feel like you are there. You will hear the Messiah call YOU by name."

—**Ken Davis**, award-winning author, speaker, and communication consultant

The only thing better than the film is the book, and the only thing better than the book is the film. Jerry B. Jenkins has taken the brilliant project of Dallas Jenkins—this look into the lives of those Jesus *chose* to be his followers, his friends, and his "family"—and gone a step (or more) deeper. Readers will be drawn as quickly into the pages as viewers were into the theatrical moments of *The Chosen* film project. I cannot say enough about both.

—**Eva Marie Everson**, president, Word Weavers International, and bestselling author

The movie series brought me to tears, but Jerry's book showed me the Jesus I wanted to know. *The Chosen: I Have Called You by Name* draws the reader into the humanity of Jesus. This story captures authentic insight into his personality. His love, humor, wisdom, and compassion are revealed for every person he encountered. Through Jesus' interaction with the real-life characters, I too experienced the Savior who calls the lost, poor, needy, and forsaken into an authentic relationship.

—**DiAnn Mills**, Christy Award winner and director, Blue Ridge Mountain Christian Writers Conference

Jerry Jenkins is a master storyteller who has captured the action, drama, and emotion of *The Chosen* video series in written form. Far more than a mere synopsis of season 1, Jerry has shaped and developed the first eight episodes into a fast-paced novel. If you enjoyed the videos, you will savor the story again as Jerry brings each character to life. And if you haven't watched the video series, this novel will make you want to start … just as soon as you've finished reading the book, of course!

—**Dr. Charlie Dyer**, professor-at-large of Bible, host of *The Land and the Book* radio program

Writing with accuracy and immediacy, Jerry Jenkins immerses us in the greatest story ever told in a fresh and powerful way. Jenkins is a master of taking profound scenes and themes from the Bible and weaving them into captivating journeys, whether they are centered on the time of Jesus or the end times. *The Chosen: I Have Called You by Name* expands on the amazing TV series and will move readers through its unique retelling of the gospel story.

—**Travis Thrasher**, bestselling author and publishing industry veteran

To a girl who cut her teeth on Bible stories, it's no easy task to transform all-too-familiar characters into an experience that is fresh and alive. That is precisely what Jerry Jenkins has done with his newest novel, *The Chosen: I Have Called You by Name*. From the first chapter, I was enamored. And by the second and third, I started to see the Jesus I've long loved with new eyes and a more open heart. This book offers the reader more than mere diversion. It offers the possibility of true transformation.

—**Michele Cushatt**, author of *Relentless: The Unshakeable Presence of a God Who Never Leaves*

What better way to bring the gospel to life than to explore the impact Jesus had upon those with whom he came into contact. And what better encouragement for those of us today who hunger for his life-changing presence. I heartily recommend both the video and the book for any who long to experience his transforming love more deeply.

—**Bill Myers**, author of the bestselling novel *Eli*

The story of Jesus has been told and re-told, but with this beautiful novelization, Jerry Jenkins brings unique and compelling perspectives to the biblical accounts of Jesus and his followers, echoing those in the acclaimed *The Chosen* video series created by Dallas Jenkins. As someone who always thinks the book was better than the movie, I was delighted to discover a book and film series that are equally enthralling and even life-changing.

—**Deborah Raney**, author of *A Nest of Sparrows* and *A Vow to Cherish*

*The Chosen: Come and See* is Jesus in present tense. The story engages the heart and allows you to experience what people see and feel and taste. Get your feet dirty with them. It will transform *your* present tense.

—**Chris Fabry**, bestselling author of *The War Room* and the *Left Behind: The Kids* series

To Arthur Taylor,
an example of the believer in word and deed,
and Chaplain of the Welland Canal Mission,
St. Catharines, Ontario, Canada

Based on *The Chosen,* a multi-season TV show
created and directed by Dallas Jenkins
and written by Ryan M. Swanson,
Dallas Jenkins, and Tyler Thompson.

# NOTE

*The Chosen* was created by lovers of and believers in the Bible and Jesus Christ. Our deepest desire is that you delve into the New Testament Gospels for yourself and discover Jesus.

*“Nathanael said to him,*
*‘Can anything good*
*come out of Nazareth?’*
*Philip said to him,*
*‘Come and see.’”*

**JOHN 1:46**

# PART 1
# Thunder

Chapter 1

# "...BEFORE HE KNEW ME"

*John's home, Ephesus, AD 44*

Grief.

On the fifth day of sitting shiva for his brother, Big James, slain by the sword at the direction of King Herod Agrippa of Judea, John tries to distract himself from his heartache. The disciple who believes he was most favored by Jesus has dug out the scant notes he's kept since his days with the Rabbi. Spurred by this latest tragedy, he's eager to flesh them out before he and his mates risk the same fate. Fretting over getting his account just right, John has invited his friends to share their memories, those who had been with him and his brother with Jesus for three years no mortal could ever forget. The churches, the world, must know.

John has filled the main room of his unassuming home with chairs and benches. But will his mates come, especially on a night like this? They had attended Big James's funeral, of course, and sat with Jesus' mother and John the first evening.

They aren't required or expected to return a second time during the seven-day mourning period, but in truth he has asked them for more than just comfort and support this time.

Black clouds rolled in late this afternoon, and now distant flashes appear on the horizon. If his beloved compatriots don't arrive soon, they will be caught in a downpour. John cracks open the front door, and a cold wind forces him to hold it tight to keep it from banging the wall.

"Patience," Mother Mary says, raising her shawl to cover her head. "They'll be here. You know they will. It's barely the first hour of the night."

The radiant woman has lived with John since the crucifixion of her son so long ago. From the cross, Jesus told her, "Woman, behold, your son!" And he told John, "Behold, your mother!"

Indeed, Mary immediately became like a mother to John, and he cherishes her—and feels cherished. The years—and sorrow—have grayed her, yet he values every line in her serene face.

"Close the door," she says, her hand gentle on his shoulder.

As he presses it shut, a gust through the window extinguishes a candle on the sill, and the rain begins.

"Oh, no," he says.

"Don't fret," Mary says. "These men have endured all kinds of weather ..."

"But young Mary will be with them—"

"A grown woman!" she says with a smile. "And no doubt prepared. Just make sure the fire is roaring and be ready to wash muddy feet."

An hour later, everyone has arrived—shaken the rain from their garments, had their feet washed, and taken their turn by the fire. Regretting that he has put them through this, John is relieved and warmed. The mood is only slightly different from what it had been the first night of shiva, but clearly his friends feel awkward, unsure what to say, how to act.

"Tonight I just want to talk," he says, trying to put them at ease.

The mood is somber, but he must raise his voice over the crackling fire and howling wind. He sits at a table before them, his pages illuminated by candles flickering in the draft. "I'll ask questions, take some notes."

"About your brother?" Matthew blurts.

"He's on my heart and mind, of course," John says, "but no. I want to talk about Jesus. Let me start with you, Peter, if you don't mind. Tell me about when you first met him."

Peter smiles through a graying beard. "Long before he changed my name. Hmm. The first time? You *know* the first time, John. You were there."

"Humor me."

Peter sighs. "I was out on Andrew's old sloop. I'd had a bad night." He gazes up. "At first I didn't even know it was him. Remember? I thought he was a Roman about to ruin my life." He chuckles and shakes his head.

"And what happened next?"

Simon Peter recounts the whole story, how he resisted the man's help, finally acceded to his advice, and was soon nearly capsized by a haul of fish from nowhere. He fell at Jesus' feet and pleaded, "Depart from me! I am a sinful man." But Jesus told him not to be afraid, but to follow him and become a fisher of men.

Next, it's Thomas's turn. He tells John, "It was at a moment when I thought my career and my reputation were about to be destroyed." He can't keep from laughing, and John finds this somehow comforting at a time reserved for grief. recording Thomas's account of Jesus saving a wedding feast, and Thomas and Ramah's reputation, by turning water to wine.

Nathanael says, "My first time? Philip simply said, 'Come and see.' And I did." He sits staring at John. "And look, I don't know how to describe it other than … He knew me before he knew me." Nathanael had sat alone in anguish under a fig tree, and the Rabbi said he'd seen him there and knew him by name.

"Me?" Andrew says, smiling. "I was standing next to John the Baptizer …"

"Creepy John," Simon Peter interjects, perhaps forgetting where he is and why.

"… And he walked by. I got to know him. And John freaked out. He said, 'Behold!'"

"'I'm eating a new bug,'" Peter teases.

Andrew pushes him.

*Only Simon Peter,* John thinks.

Thaddeus sits before John and next to Little James. "For me, the first time—Jesus was just sitting there eating lunch with all the construction workers, cracking jokes." The memory amuses him, then appears to grieve him.

Little James says, "I was on my way to Jerusalem." But suddenly he breaks down. "I'm sorry. All of this is just—it's difficult to talk about. It reminds me of how much I miss him."

"But we have to," John says.

"I know. I just—I talk about him to others every day. But with all of you, who knew him, it's difficult."

Sitting across from the younger Mary, now a mature woman herself—bearing the same docile beauty he has seen in her since her deliverance from demons—John says, "Just tell me about the first time you actually saw him."

She smiles self-consciously. "It was in a tavern." Mary nods. "He set his hand on mine." She looks up quickly. "Which isn't what it sounds like. Maybe leave that part out. People will get confused."

"I don't know yet what I'll be including," John says. "I'm just writing it all down."

"Good," she says, and recounts the story of the stranger who revealed himself as her creator and redeemer by knowing her name and transforming her life.

John is struck by the contrast between the Matthew who sits before him and the tax collector he had been when Jesus called him. Back then, he wore finery he could easily afford, and his youthful face was bare and smooth. Now he sports a full beard, and his clothes are as plain and ragged as the others'.

"It was the fourth morning of the third week of the month of Adar ..." Matthew begins. "Sometime during the second hour."

The same old Matthew. "It doesn't have to be precise," John says.

Matthew recoils. "Why wouldn't it have to be precise? Mine will be precise."

This surprises John not a bit. He is aware Matthew is working on his own record, and he can't wait to see how it reflects the meticulously obsessive author. For now, he relishes the story of Matthew responding in wonder to the call of the Master and astounding his Roman guard by simply leaving everything to follow Jesus.

John saves Mother Mary till the end. She settles across from him, looking weary. He asks her the same question he has posed to the others.

"My answer might not make sense," she says.

"Try me, Mother."

"I can hardly remember a time when I didn't know him." She pauses and seems to study John. "There was one little kick."

John rustles a clean sheet of papyrus from his stack and scribbles with his reed pen. "Go on."

Mary hesitates, gazing at him. "My son, why are you doing all this? Why now?"

"Because we're getting older, and our memories are—"

"I mean why now, during shiva?"

"Because everyone is here. I need to get their memories, so—"

"You need to mourn Big James."

John can't meet her eyes. "He won't be the last of us this happens to. Who knows when I will see the others again, or if? I'm not in a hurry to write a whole book, but I do want to get the eyewitness stories now, while we're together."

"Isn't Matthew going to write something?"

"He's writing only about what he saw and what Jesus told him directly. But I was there for things that Matthew doesn't know about. I was in Jesus' inmost circle. He loved me."

"He loved all of you." She smiles. "You just feel the need to talk about it more often."

John can't deny that.

Wistfully, Mary says, "I prefer to treasure these things in my heart," and John scribbles even that. "You know that if you try to write every single thing he did, the world itself could not contain the books that would be written."

John looks at her in wonder. "Hmm. A disclaimer. That's good. I'm going to say that. You see, Mother, if I do not write these things down, they will be lost to history. James would agree."

She falls silent again. Finally, she says, "Where will you start?"

"In the beginning, naturally. I'm just not sure which beginning."

"His birth," she suggests.

"Earlier."

"His ancestry?"

"I'm pretty sure Matthew has that covered."

"Maybe the prophecies?" she says. "The promise to Abraham?"

John nods. "I thought about starting with Abraham. But still, so much came before him."

"What was before Abraham?"

"Noah."

"And before him?"

"The garden."

"Well," she says, "you could start there."

"But I want it to be known that he was much more than what could be seen or touched. What was before the garden? 'In the beginning, the earth was formless and void …'"

A clap of thunder makes John look out the window. Mary says, "I cannot hear that without thinking of you two." Jesus had often referred to John and his brother as the Sons of Thunder.

John shakes his head. "I cannot believe how much he put up with. Others. They will not even remember the sound of his voice. They'll be just words."

"He said they weren't just words, remember?" she says. "'Heaven and earth will pass away'—"

"'But my words will never pass away.'"

"They're eternal," she says.

At more rumbling from the sky, Mary slowly rises. "You'll think of something." She makes her away around the table and massages his shoulders. "Take your time." She kisses the back of his head. "I'm off to bed."

And as John gazes out the window, his friends move to gather their cloaks. The weight of the day and the memory of his brother overwhelms him to speechlessness as everyone leaves. He merely embraces them and nods.

John sits back down to his sheets of papyrus, unable to stem the tide of memories. He finds himself in despised Samaria, of all places, years before, trailing his big brother over stony, unforgiving terrain. A thick rope around his waist, he's straining to pull a rock-laden wood pallet bearing long spikes in an attempt to break up the soil.

Chapter 2

# LOST

*Samaria, 13 years earlier*

Every step proves an ordeal as John and James sweat through their tunics in the unrelenting sun. Why are they even here, tilling who-knows-whose meager plot that seems to resist their every effort? On the one hand, John feels special, having been assigned this mysterious task by Jesus himself. But on the other, he's still unable to comprehend why the Master is even in this godforsaken area—anathema to Jews for generations. Everyone had warned him, questioned him, and advised him to circle wide around it.

John marvels at his own thinking—his mind has been taken to new horizons ever since he began following the Rabbi. He shakes his head at having referred to this region as godforsaken. *It no longer is, is it?* he tells himself, given what he—what they all—believe about Jesus. The Messiah is here, and so the Divine has some purpose, even in this place. And as usual, eventually Jesus will clarify why.

But for now, John follows James, who manhandles a crudely

constructed crossbar that drags a single plow with yet another heavy stone roped to it, forcing it into the ground. And as much as he'd love to continue pondering deep thoughts—the kind Jesus spurs within him—all John can think about is where he'd rather be: anywhere but here. "I'd rather clean out the hold after a long weekend of fishing!"

"Yuck!" James says. "You'd reek for a month! I'd rather mend every hole in Abba's sails."

John chuckles. "And probably sew your hands together in the process." He bends to clear rocks from his path, tossing them beyond the narrow strip they've spent more than an hour tilling. "I'd rather wrestle a swordfish."

James sets down his cumbersome tiller and tosses a few rocks away. "Just get in the water with it?"

"I meant on a hook. But I'd snatch it out of the water with my bare hand if it meant not spending a night with—these people."

"You know it has a sword on its face, right?" Big James says, and they both stoop to plant seeds.

"We lucked out, brother." John laughs. "Planting while the others try to keep up with Rabbi in Sychar."

"It wasn't luck," James says, suddenly serious. "He chose us. You going two thumbs deep with those seeds?"

"Yeah, yeah, rows three handbreadths apart." John rises. "Why do you think he did that, choosing us for this?"

James seems to study John. "Because we're good workers? And maybe he knows we don't like Samaritans."

John considers this. "Maybe Jesus just likes us best."

James smiles. "Yes, that must be it."

John tries to maintain a light tone, but he's serious. "So why *do* you think he likes me best?"

"For the same reasons I like you best—you pose no threat to anyone, intellectually or physically."

"Thank you, brother.... Wait a second ..."

"What I want to know is who we are planting this for. Jesus said it would feed generations."

"I assume travelers," John says. "People passing through, like us." He imitates Jesus: "'Hospitality isn't just for those with homes, John.'"

This makes James smile. "Don't quit your day job."

"It's too late for that."

"Ha! Yeah, me too. Come on, let's pick it up. I don't want to lose this job."

As they return to pulling and straining, John says, "I'd rather talk with Matthew for a whole minute."

"I'd rather listen to Andrew's jokes."

• • •

Thomas, his wedding vintner girlfriend Ramah, and her father, Kafni, stop at a fork in the road in rural Samaria. The three are on foot, Kafni leading a heavily laden donkey. Ramah studies the map. "Sychar is on the other side of Mount Ebal," she says.

They debate the best route, and Thomas concludes they have to veer south, "because if we keep going westward, we'll encounter the hostile city of Sebaste."

Kafni says, "It's faster to go between Mount Gerizim and Mount Ebal."

"But more dangerous," Thomas says.

"Not if we avoid the cities," Ramah says.

Thomas smiles. "There's no avoiding cities on a road. That's what roads do—they connect cities."

"You're not taking my daughter off-road."

"Kafni, I have given you my word that I will protect Ramah from harm."

"Can you even protect yourself?"

Thomas sighs. How to put this? "With due respect—"

"You are walking *toward* Samaria," the older man says, "to find a group of men you do not know."

"And a woman," Ramah says.

"A woman who would be with a group of men. Do not talk back to me, young lady. This is foolishness."

Thomas gives Ramah a long look. She points to a group of Samaritan women washing clothes in a creek. "Maybe they know the way."

"Shalom!" Thomas calls out.

Two teen boys approach. One hollers, "Hey! What are you doing talking to our mother, Jew!"

Not looking for trouble, the three move on.

• • •

*Late the next morning*

At an inn on the main square of Sychar, Simon has news for Andrew, Little James, Mary Magdalene, and Matthew. "Thaddeus counted fifty, with more arriving every minute. Is Jesus ready?"

"He's in the back storeroom," Andrew says.

"He needed a moment," Mary says.

Simon shakes his head. "But many are begging to hear more."

"He's been talking to people since dawn," Little James says. "He needs a break."

Andrew says he'll take Jesus some water.

"I thought most people had left after the first sermon," Mary says.

"They left to go get their families and friends," Simon says. "And now they're back threefold."

Matthew sits by himself, using a stylus to maneuver beads on a small counting frame. "The population of Sychar is approximately two thousand."

"Not including women and children," Mary says.

"There are twelve hours of light per day at this time of year," Matthew continues. "And he said we would stay here two days, which means over twenty-four hours, so the number of men we need to reach per hour is eight-point-three-three-three-three …"

"And what," Simon says, "is point-three-three of a man, Matthew?"

"Simon!" Andrew scolds.

"There's a crowd growing out there, and we need to know what to do."

Mary says, "Why don't we just tell him the situation and let him decide?"

"It's what he's going to do anyway," Little James says.

"I'll tell him," Andrew says, heading off with a cup of water.

"How many stadia wide is the city?" Matthew says, making Simon laugh. "It will give us a rubric for how many square cubits we need to cover per hour."

*This guy,* Simon thinks, shaking his head. "Rubrics? Cubits per hour?"

"His ministry deserves careful thought," Matthew says.

Simon faces him, dead serious now—still battling his resentment of the man and his former occupation. "No one's thinking about it more carefully than me."

Andrew returns. "He's gone."

"What are you talking about?" Simon says.

"He's not in his room or anywhere in the house. I checked the alley—"

"We *lost* him?"

"He's probably not lost," Andrew says with a glance at Little James.

"Okay, James," Simon says, "you search the southern side. Andrew and I will search the north. Mary, tell Thaddeus to keep an eye on the crowd."

Matthew rises. "What about me?"

*Yes,* Simon thinks. *What about you, who not so long ago kept fellow Jews in bondage to merciless taxes?* "Stay here," he says. "In case he comes back."

"I will be back soon, Matthew," Mary says, making Simon wonder why she's so unfailingly kind to him. "And I won't be far," she adds.

As she turns to leave, Matthew says, "Staying here gives me the greatest likelihood of locating Jesus first."

She smiles. "Well, there you go."

Chapter 3

# FINDING JESUS

Simon wonders how it could have come to this. Can one actually lose the Messiah? Oh, he is independent, sure, and unruffled by whatever comes his way. He will, no doubt, be found and no worse for wear, but that makes Simon no less frantic to find him. Simon and Andrew dash through the teeming Sychar market, asking everyone, "Have you seen the teacher from Galilee, the man who arrived here yesterday? He was in the square. My Master, about yay high, beard, long hair? No? The Teacher?"

Elsewhere in the square, Little James limps about. "The one called Jesus of Nazareth, has he passed this way?"

"Have you seen the teacher, Jesus?"

Simon recognizes a woman merchant who had been in the crowd the day before. "You wouldn't happen to have seen the Teacher up this way?"

"He passed by earlier," she says. "Is he going to be back in the town square?"

Andrew carefully chooses his words. "He's on—an errand. Where did he go?"

She points. "Down toward that alley."

As they hurry off, she calls after them, "I was just about to go see him again and bring my friend!"

"He'll be there," Simon assures her. "He'll teach more. You won't be disappointed."

• • •

In the alley, Jesus lies on his back beneath a cart jacked up on rocks, tinkering with the underside. The owner, an African, peers down. Jesus presses the parts, testing their tautness. "There," he says. "All tightened up."

"So it *was* the axle," the African says. "I told my brother it was the axle."

"Sometimes all you need is a fresh set of eyes. Now hand me some pitch and it will be as good as new."

The man gives Jesus a bucket and a brush. "You're good at this. You should stay in town and open up a shop."

Jesus imagines it, amused. "Should I?" He nods. "A shop."

A beaming woman enters the alley with a couple of friends. "Rabbi!" she calls. She turns to her companions and shoos them back. "Quickly, get the others!"

Jesus recognizes Photina, the woman he met at the Well of Jacob, the first person to whom he revealed his true identity. She laughs, obviously thrilled to see him.

"That woman," the African says, "is going to introduce you to every Samaritan in the country."

Jesus chuckles. "I hope so."

He smiles at her, and it's clear she doesn't know what to say or do. She cocks her head, claps her palms against her skirt, then wipes her face and neck. "It's hot," she says.

• • •

Back at the inn, Matthew sits alone, fidgeting, compelled to run his fingers up and down the elaborate tunic that reminds him of his days of plenty. Someone knocks at the gate, and he leaps to his feet. Jesus?

He hurries over and swings it open, only to find three people he doesn't recognize—a young man, a beautiful young woman, and an older man. The young man says, "Shalom."

Matthew furrows his brow. It's only polite to respond. "Shalom," he says without emotion.

The young man studies him. "I don't know you," he says.

"Maybe you're in the wrong place," Matthew says, and begins to shut the gate.

The young man pushes it back open. "Ah, we are looking for Jesus."

"Everyone is," Matthew says and closes the gate, heading back to his bench.

But from the other side of the gate, he hears Mary Magdalene. "Oh, you're here! Thomas! And Ramah, yes?"

Matthew opens the gate yet again, this time to find the young woman smiling. "Yes, Mary?" she says.

"Good memory," Mary says, embracing Ramah. "It's so good to have you!"

"It's good to see you again, Mary," Thomas says, bowing.

Kafni clears his throat.

"This is Ramah's father, Kafni."

Mary smiles at him, but he ignores her and enters the inn.

Thomas mouths, "I'm sorry."

Kafni seems to examine the place, eyeballing Matthew but not greeting him. When they're all inside, Ramah says, "Where is everyone?"

"They're out looking for Jesus," Mary says.

"Is he lost?" Thomas says.

"He's never lost," she says. "He probably just needed a moment. The townspeople have been clamoring to see him. He's been changing many hearts."

"I know how that works," Thomas says. "So, your friend here wasn't just being rude."

Mary introduces them. Matthew says, "You approached a strange home, and when the occupant answered, you said, 'I don't know you.' Isn't *that* being rude?"

Thomas appears taken aback. "We had a brutal journey," he says at last. "It wasn't easy. And the Samaritans! Whew! I thought we'd be torn apart."

"Samaritans and Jews are historical enemies," Matthew says.

"I'm aware," Thomas says evenly. "We knew the journey would be fraught, but it's like Jesus is actively making it difficult to follow him."

"I'd have come," Kafni says, "just because of his saving the reputation of my vineyard—and your careers. Not that you care about that."

Thomas addresses Matthew and Mary. "I'm glad we found you at least. But why aren't you—"

"Out looking for him?" Matthew says. "I stayed. It's likely he'll return to the last place he was seen."

"—a little farther from the city is what I was going to say. But what do you base that on, this returning to the last place he was seen? Isn't it most likely that he's gone on to his next appointment?"

"He does not keep a schedule."

"Oh!" Thomas says. "Perhaps I can be useful as an organizer then. I'm good with figures, times." He glances at Ramah, who nods. "Precision is my specialty."

Matthew is about to counter with his own credentials

when Big James and John arrive, filthy head to toe and sweating through their clothes. "Ah, you made it!" James says, shaking hands with Thomas.

"Good to see you again," John says, also shaking hands.

Thomas recoils and stares at his hand.

"Oh, sorry," John says. "It's been a long day."

"We were working," Big James says.

• • •

By now Jesus has returned to the square where he is surrounded by a crowd. Some sit on stairs, others mill about on catwalks above. From a small, shaded booth high overhead, Photina's fifth husband, Nedim—the one she tried to divorce so she could marry yet a new lover, before Jesus met her at the well—watches and listens.

"We know," Jesus is saying, "that God pursues the sick more than the healthy. Think of it this way—are there any sheepherders in the crowd?"

A longhaired young man bearing a tall staff says, "I am."

"Ah!" Jesus says. "We are honored you are here. I have a very warm place in my heart for shepherds."

Little James limps into view, smiling. Across the square, Simon and Andrew arrive, breathless, with Thaddeus. Simon is greatly relieved.

"Who is tending your flock now?" Jesus asks the young shepherd.

"My brother. We're taking turns."

"How many sheep?"

"One hundred, Teacher."

"Say one of them goes astray. What would you do?"

"I'd go look for it, of course."

"Of course! But what about the other ninety-nine?"

"I'd have to leave them behind. I can't lose the one sheep."

"Hmm. And if you find it?"

The young man beams. "I'd lay it over my shoulders and bring it home. And I would probably do a little dance!"

Jesus laughs. "And what would you say to your friends—who have been worried for you?"

"I would tell them to rejoice with me, for I have found my lost sheep!"

Jesus turns back to the rest of the crowd. "Do you see what he just said there? He rejoices more for one sheep than over the ninety-nine who never went astray. So it is not the will of my Father that one of these should perish. In the same way, I tell you, there will be more joy in heaven over one sinner who repents, than over ninety-nine righteous persons who need no repentance."

Simon is fascinated by the rapt attention of the crowd. Andrew whispers, "Look at them …"

Simon says, "You couldn't tell Jew from Samaritan, the way they're listening."

• • •

As dusk slowly settles in the outskirts of Samaria, Melech, the owner of the gravelly field Big James and John spent the day tilling, tells his wife and seven-year-old daughter he must try to exercise his badly broken leg. "Where will you go?" his wife asks.

"I'll just walk the property, Chedva," he tells her, setting out from their ramshackle farmhouse on his homemade crutch.

"Are you sure you can make it, Father?"

"I'll be fine, Rebecca. I'll take it slow."

Overcome by the shame of his poverty and now his inability to do anything about it, Melech hobbles a half step at a time, his leg wrapped ankle to thigh in a makeshift wood and leather splint he and his wife fashioned. Feeling helpless and worthless, he wonders if this is what the end feels like. He can't imagine what Chedva will do for meals the next day, let alone after that. Surely their paltry supper has depleted her stores of flour and other essentials. *They would be better off without me.*

But what's this? In the waning light he doesn't trust his eyes. The last bare patch of ground with even a hope of growing anything looks nothing like it had the day before, when he wondered if he had a prayer of hiring someone to work it—unable to pay them unless and until it produced a crop. Melech squints and shambles closer.

He cannot make sense of it! What had been a sketchy strip of unyielding dry dirt now stretches out before him, rich in moist, black soil someone has expertly furrowed. He forces himself closer yet. If he is not mistaken, the ground—now appearing fertile—has also actually been planted! Who would do such a thing?

He glances heavenward. *What did I do to deserve this? Nothing! Less than nothing!* And tears roll. Dare he say anything to his wife and daughter? No. What if it turns out to have been a cruel dream?

• • •

*The inn at Sychar*

Thomas, Ramah, and her father sit in awkward silence, sipping water at a table in the anteroom when Jesus and several disciples enter, fresh from the long day of preaching. They're exulting over all they've seen. Thaddeus is saying, "Did you see the woman and her little girl though?"

"I know Simon did," Little James says.

Simon shrugs. "I always get emotional."

"I know," Andrew says. "You think you won't, and then—"

The three at the table rise, and Thomas calls out, "Shalom!"

"Hey, you came through!" Simon says. "You made it."

"Of course he did," Jesus says, smiling, rushing to embrace Thomas. "It's good to see you."

"You too, Rabbi. You remember Ramah?"

"How could I forget? So you will be joining us also?"

She hesitates. "Well, Rabbi, this is my father, Kafni."

"Oh, yes, the owner of the vineyard that produced such fine wine for my friends! Shalom."

Kafni clearly struggles to remain cordial. "Very kind of you to say."

"I imagine you'll want to speak to me, yes?"

"If you have some time, I would like to ask you some questions."

"You wouldn't be a good father if you didn't. Here's what I'd like to propose, if you approve. We've both had very long days, yes? This establishment has rooms available for you. So, why don't we get some rest, and tomorrow morning we'll talk about everything. Sound good?"

"I-I'm—I suppose we could."

"It's a plan," Jesus says. "Thank you." He places a hand on Kafni's shoulder, and the man stiffens. "We're delighted that you are with us. Now if you'll all excuse me for a moment, I must go speak with a couple of men who performed a truly remarkable act of service today."

Simon steps forward. "Let us escort you, Rabbi."

Jesus appears to stifle a smile. "If you like." He steps through a curtain to the kitchen, Simon, Andrew, Little James, and Thaddeus behind him. There he finds John and Big James at a table full of food, still sweaty and filthy, stuffing their mouths. They look up with alarm. "We've arrived," Jesus announces.

"What happened?" Big James manages, mouth full.

"I was just telling everybody that work you boys did today, how remarkable it was. You must be famished."

"Uh, yes, um," John says, clearly embarrassed. "We were hungry."

Jesus chuckles. "Eat. Restore your strength. And when you're done, please describe the work to the others. I hope everyone takes note of what John and Big James did here. Good night, friends."

On his way out past the other disciples, Jesus claps Simon on the shoulder. Simon steals a glance at Andrew and sighs. These guys have been singled out again. The brothers raise their cups and affect looks of humble pride, as if to tell Simon, "That's right. Did you hear that?"

The last thing Simon wants is to hear all about it. The truth is, he knows he'll likely never hear the end of it.

Chapter 4

# THE ERRAND

*Sychar, the next morning*

Jesus has given John and Big James another assignment, instructing them to take the entire rest of his entourage along. Simon, none too pleased to be in the dark—and frankly miffed that he's not in charge—finds himself among the gaggle of disciples. They follow the brothers up and down stone city steps, through alleyways, and into narrow streets.

"Where are we going?" Matthew asks Andrew.

"I don't know any more than you. Jesus gave them an errand and said to come with. I don't get it either."

"They described moving stones and digging. Are they leaders now?"

"I don't know," Andrew says with a smile. "Didn't sound all that much harder than fishing, but …"

"I have never performed hard labor," Matthew announces.

Andrew stares at him, appearing unable to imagine it. "Guess you'll just have to tag along like the rest of us."

Simon tells Thomas, "The list of things he might do is long.

First, there's a leper colony to the west, and they're begging him to come."

From behind Simon, Mary explains, "They're not allowed into the city, so they have no way to hear him."

Andrew calls back, "Both Jewish and Samaritan purity laws forbid coming within four cubits of a leper."

Big James, leading the way with John, barks over his shoulder, "What distance do we have to keep from these Samaritans?"

John says, "We've been within four cubits of a leper before, Andrew."

"I'm just saying, if he breaks their law, it might cause a stir."

"And for dinner," Simon tells Thomas, "we've been invited to the home of the town treasurer. And we have to juggle that invitation with another one, to have dinner at the home of the high priest of Sychar, which could get messy."

"Why messy?" Matthew says, covering his mouth with a kerchief as they move through the bustling city.

Andrew says, "Samaritan beliefs are so at odds with Jewish beliefs. He might want to trap Jesus in his words."

"I don't think he's afraid of being trapped by his words," Big James says.

"I'm just saying ..."

Mary gives Ramah a knowing look and says, "We could be somewhere else, with people who actually *want* to listen to him and not argue."

"If he convinces the rabbi of the town," Matthew says, "his message will be preached long after we leave this village."

"Leave it to the Boss, eh?" Simon says. He turns to Thomas. "What do you think? Dinner at the treasurer's or the high priest?"

"Neither!" John says.

"Dinner with whom, then?" Thomas says.

"You know," Simon says, "there are a lot of people who want to talk to him."

"Yes, but," John says, turning to face the rest, "*he* wants to make dinner."

"That's the errand," Big James proclaims as the rest gather around.

"Oh, yeah?" Simon says, amused and crossing his arms. "That's the errand? You guys are really enjoying this, being in the know, huh?"

"Ha!" John says, pointing at him. "Coming from you, Simon?"

"What does that mean?"

Big James says, "He told *us* his plans, so … Matthew, distribute the money accordingly; Thaddeus, buy bread enough for twelve—"

"Thirteen," John says.

"Thirteen people."

"Leavened?" Thaddeus says. "Unleavened, rye, sprouted, spelt?"

"An assortment," John says. "Your choice."

As Matthew hands him coins, Simon says, "Thirteen? Who are the others?"

"Little James," Big James continues, "buy a leg of lamb, including the knuckle and the fillet—no, no, two legs of lamb."

Matthew says, "We only have—"

"Andrew! Grapes, currants, cherries if you can find them."

"At this rate," Matthew insists, "we won't have enough for—"

"At the start of this trip," John tells him, "we didn't expect to find a bag of gold, did we? We're putting it to good use! Simon …"

"Yes, Master," he says, dripping with sarcasm that gives John pause.

"… three skins of wine."

Simon thinks of a retort but stifles it. "Done."

Matthew holds out coins to him, but Simon stalls before accepting them. *Receiving* money from Matthew for once? He still can't comprehend why Jesus wants this man as part of the group.

"Matthew, black pepper, chives, salt, olive oil."

"At this cost," Matthew says, "we will not make it to Judea."

"Have faith, Matthew," John says, "in him. Mary, look for leeks, garlic, and onions, okay?"

When the others set off on their assignments, Simon remains. "And what are you guys going to do?"

"We are going to get out of the streets," John says.

"Why?"

"Samaria's biggest problem …"

Big James finishes John's thought. "… Too many Samaritans."

• • •

Simon heads for a vintner's booth and asks for three skins of wine.

"What kind?" she says.

He pauses. "Red? Something with cloves, I guess."

"Simon!"

He turns to find Photina approaching. "There you are!" she says. "I've been looking for all of you."

"Lucky for you, we're all in this market."

"What are you doing? Is he going to teach here?"

"Just shopping, if you can believe it."

She turns to the vintner. "This man, he told me—"

"Everything you ever did, yes, we've heard him for ourselves. It's because of his words we believe he is the Anointed One. You don't have to keep telling us, Photina."

Looking embarrassed, as if she can't help herself, Photina shrugs at Simon.

The vintner hands Simon his wineskins, then reaches out with a fourth. "No," he says, "I need only three."

"It's on the house," she says. "Anything for him."

Photina says, "Simon, I need to deliver a message." She chuckles as she hands him a small scroll and urges him to read it.

It's an invitation to dinner with her and her husband, Nedim. She's beaming.

"Everyone?" Simon says.

"Yes!" She's near tears.

"But there's ten of us."

She shakes her head as if that's inconsequential. "Please?"

## Chapter 5

# HONESTY

*Later the same morning*

Kafni sits alone in the common kitchen area of the inn, keeping a despairing eye on the shadows outside. He needs to be on his way home soon and feels rudely treated by the traveling preacher. The man had promised a morning conversation, though Kafni has to admit they never settled on an exact time.

His daughter left early with the other devotees of the so-called rabbi, venturing into the town square on some mysterious errand. And so he waits, hungry and yet ignoring breads and bowls of fruit. He has a priority, and eating is not it. Ramah has been his heart since the day she was born. And while she is of age, he feels no less responsibility for her. Clearly she's enamored of Thomas and also this celebrated prophet, and Kafni can't decide which relationship troubles him most. Thomas he knows, and in many ways admires, and yet he is really the one intent on following this Jesus. Why couldn't the young man stay home and plan a conventional future for Ramah?

Kafni cannot, must not, leave before doing what he came

here to do, but it's all he can do to sit still. It is long past time to get on the road, and yet here he sits, idle, fuming.

Finally Ramah appears. He's relieved, but that had better mean Jesus is not far behind. Normally he would rise at her entrance, but he just sits gazing expectantly at her.

"Sorry, Abba," she says. "It was a busy morning. I'll make you some porridge."

As she sets to work, Kafni says, "What do you think he's doing? I just need a few moments with him."

"He said it was a short walk. I'm sure he'll be here soon, Abba."

Kafni raises his voice. "I have things to say. You're lucky I came all this way with you. I could have just decided no. I can't decide what Thomas does. He can make his own bad decisions. But you … I have things to say."

"I know," she says, mixing ingredients. "I'm very grateful."

He studies her. "Porridge," he says flatly. "Soon you will know every way to make it, because that is what you eat when you don't have a job or live with your family."

She raises a brow as if she wants to respond, but Jesus appears in the doorway. "Kafni, good morning. Thank you for your patience."

Kafni rises, feeling anything but patient.

"I had a few people to meet," Jesus continues, "before our important talk. Were you comfortable last night?"

How to answer? "Yes. Although I must say, I didn't sleep very well." He steals a glance at his daughter.

"Mm," Jesus says. "I know what it's like to be concerned about someone you feel responsible for. But I am not a father. I imagine all of this makes you nervous."

Kafni would rather have this conversation in private. He nods to the door. "Could we …?"

"Sure." Jesus offers Ramah a reassuring look as he and Kafni move into the next room.

"Allow me to first say why I am here," the older man says. "I want to thank you for whatever you did at the wedding. You kept the reputation of my business, and of my daughter and Thomas, from suffering. Ramah and Thomas have insisted that you performed a miracle. Now, I am an old man. I need to leave for my journey, and I don't have time to be unclear. I believe this to be the edge of blasphemy, and I am not in the habit of believing a man from Naz—a man performed a miracle. And I am not in the habit of giving my blessing for my daughter to leave our home. But I am in your debt, and that is why we are in this room with you now."

"Thank you for your honesty."

"I cannot give you my belief or my devotion," Kafni continues, "so I'm afraid my honesty is all I have to give after giving up my daughter." His voice catches at this, and he looks away, lips quivering.

Jesus nods, his own eyes filling. "I understand. I ask a lot of those who follow me. But I ask little of those who do not."

Kafni gathers himself. "I don't want to be rude, but I have said all I want to say."

He turns and heads back into the kitchen, where he presses a small bag of coins into Ramah's hand. She tries to refuse it, but he insists. Kafni holds her hands, presses his forehead against hers, grips her shoulder, then pulls away to find his pack and walking stick.

Ramah follows him out of the inn and into the square, where Thomas stands with the man's already packed donkey. Kafni adds his sack and faces Thomas. "I have long admired you for your hard work," he tells the young man. "And you have done well in spite of the loss of your father. But this is foolishness, and

I won't pretend it isn't. I will see you next when you ask for my daughter's hand."

Thomas shakes his head. "Kafni, I—"

"No, I am not stupid. You may be," he adds, chuckling. "But I am not. But when that day comes, I don't know what I will say." He pauses, overcome. "Keep her safe."

Thomas nods.

"Shalom," Kafni says, pulling the donkey past Thomas and then Ramah, who looks longingly after him and then at Thomas. And she weeps.

Chapter 6

# THE BAD SAMARITAN

*The outskirts of Sychar, dusk*

While Simon painfully misses his wife, Eden, back in Capernaum, he does not miss fishing—at least fishing for fish. It was unending, backbreaking, not to mention smelly work. And regardless of how expert he'd become at it, success seemed to depend on the whims of nature.

Jesus promised to make him a fisher of men, and he can't deny the adventure has been all he could have dreamed of—and more. Oh, it's had its moments, and this foray into Samaria has in many ways rocked him to his core.

As the Rabbi leads the disciples, Mary Magdalene, and Ramah to the plot of ground the brothers John and Big James worked the day before, Simon has mixed feelings. On the one hand, he's still reveling in the teaching the Master conducted in the city square—deftly getting a local shepherd involved in his lesson on how one lost sinner means as much to God as one lost sheep does to a herder. Brilliant. But on the other, Simon finds it difficult to reconcile a couple of things: why Jesus seems to favor Big James and John when Simon himself is obviously the most committed to the cause. And Jesus' seemingly blithe acceptance of a filthy dog, the tax collector.

Yes, Matthew surprised everyone—including the Romans—by instantly giving up his lavish life, somehow recognizing Jesus as someone worthy of his devotion. But has the man truly repented of his heinous treatment of fellow Jews, conspiring with Rome to tax them within inches of their lives? How could a man even call himself a Jew, treating his own people like scum for the sake of his own pocketbook?

Still, Jesus has to know best. Simon bears zero doubt that he is the Messiah, so he just hopes everything will soon become clear—including Matthew's being held to account. Is Simon being hypocritical? He doesn't think so. He acknowledges who he was and what he has done. He even knelt before Jesus and pleaded, "Depart from me! I am a sinful man!"

Has Matthew done anything like that? Surely he is as much a sinner as Simon, if not more so. Simon can wish only to be as forgiving as Jesus, and it leaves him out of sorts. With the thrilling miracles he witnessed and the divine teaching he has enjoyed, he should be above petty rivalries with the brothers and comparing himself to a former tax collector.

Now here they all stand with Jesus—eight disciples and the two women laden with all the foodstuffs they'd gathered that morning—gazing over a beautifully tilled plot of earth.

Jesus lets out a low whistle. "This is some expert work, my boys. Exceptional."

"You should have seen this place," Big James says. "Weeds and branches piled everywhere."

"We cleared and sowed it in a single afternoon," John adds.

"So you've told us," Andrew says wryly.

Jesus pats Big James on the chest. "Well done." He grips John's arm. "Very well done." It appears to Simon the brothers are about to burst.

Jesus walks away, and Simon signals the others to follow. He leads them beyond some overgrowth into a clearing where a dilapidated farmhouse looks as if it's on its last legs.

"Uh, what are we doing here, Rabbi?" Simon says.

"This is where we'll be dining tonight."

"Someone lives here?" John says.

Simon thinks Jesus has to be kidding.

As they draw within fifty feet of the place, a man in rags hobbles out on a crutch.

"You must be Melech!" Jesus calls out.

It seems he knows everyone.

"I am," the man says, clearly wary. "You're the teacher?"

"I'm Jesus of Nazareth. These are my students." Jesus stops before the man.

"I believe I owe you a debt of gratitude," Melech says. "I would bow, but as you can see …"

Jesus points. "It's John and Big James here who put in the sweat."

"Thank you."

Big James stares. "*You* own the field?"

"I do."

*A Samaritan!* John can't hide his disgust. "We thought it was for travelers."

Jesus smiles at them, as if to remind them to get used to different.

A look of realization comes over Melech. "Okay, so spit it out," he says. "What's the catch?"

"Catch?" Jesus says.

The man appears frustrated now, having to explain himself. "You don't know me from Adam. You're a Jew. You come all the way from Galilee to preach in town. You send your students to work my land …"

"Photina told us you were in need."

"Mm-hm, she told me all about you. So what do you want from me?"

Jesus merely gazes at him.

Melech shakes his head and gestures. "I don't have any money. I can't make a donation to you. Can't even feed my family."

Jesus points at him. "That's what I want."

"What?"

"I would love for you to share a meal with me and my friends."

Melech looks crestfallen. "I'm really so very sorry, but we don't have any food. Not even for ourselves."

Jesus smiles. "We've got that covered," he says, turning to those behind him. Simon and the rest—except John and Big James, of course—hold up their food supplies. Jesus covers his own chest with his hand. "Please. I would be honored."

*Honored to treat a Samaritan to a bountiful feast? After having already plowed the man's field for free?* Simon shakes his head.

• • •

Simon is amused at the nonplussed Melech who shyly introduces his wife, Chedva, and young daughter. The three of them seem to relish the spread and eat their fill at tables outside near a roaring fire. Jesus has asked Simon to tell the family about the day he and Simon met. Simon recounts every detail, all the way up to, "The boat almost flipped! Then the net strained so hard I thought my arms would come out of their sockets."

The others chuckle, and Andrew adds, "And James and John took their sweet time coming to help us!" He steals a glance at them, but they are clearly not amused. He mimics them straining and grunting.

"Yeah!" Simon says. "I had to call for help five times before you moved!"

Jesus and the others seem to enjoy the repartee, but John abruptly stands and leaves, carrying his plate.

The others tell their stories of meeting Jesus. Melech appears stunned. "So you followed him all the way into Samaria?"

Matthew, as usual, feels the need to explain. "We did suggest the alternate route along the Jordan."

Melech asks Jesus, "You didn't think it could be dangerous for you?"

"Of course."

Melech seems on the verge of a story himself, but Chedva clears her throat. "When I was a little girl, my father told me the Messiah would bring an end to pain and suffering. If you are who people are saying you are, when will you do that?"

After a long pause, Jesus says, "I'm here to preach the good news of the kingdom of heaven, a kingdom that is not of this world, a kingdom that is coming soon—where yes, sorrow and sighing will flee away. I make a way for people to access that kingdom. But, in this world, bones will still break, hearts will still break, but in the end, the light will overcome darkness."

Chedva appears overcome and meets her husband's gaze.

Jesus smiles at her and then turns to Melech. "Speaking of broken bones, what's the story?"

"I fell off a horse."

"I didn't see a pasture."

"It, uh, it wasn't mine."

"Aah, a friend's horse. That's always dangerous."

"No, not—not exactly."

"Oh."

"Look," Melech says, whispering now, "you've already done so much for me that I didn't deserve ..."

"Come, Rebecca," Chedva says, "it's time for bed. Say good-night to your new friends."

The little girl shyly says good night, and everyone responds in kind. Chedva gives her husband a knowing look—a warning?—as she departs. Melech looks troubled, and Simon realizes that only the crackling fire and chirp of crickets can be heard.

Melech leans toward Jesus and whispers, "If you knew who I am, you would never have helped me."

Jesus appears to be looking into the man's soul. "That's not true. This is what we Jews do. We tell and listen to stories. Our stories connect us." He nods to the man. "Tell me your story."

Melech appears to consider this, studying Jesus' face, then scanning Simon and the others. He lowers his head. "We ran out of money," he begins. "And food. My little Rebecca, I could see her ribs through her skin. And Chedva, her eyes turned gray. There had been a drought, so there was no work in town. I had a friend in Tirathana who was also in bad straits. We traveled south past Ephraim and laid in wait along the road from Jerusalem to Jericho.

"We attacked a Jew who was traveling alone. Pulled him down from his horse, took all his money and all his clothes. He fought back, so Dishon knocked him down, hit his head on a rock. I thought he was dead. Dishon was to take the Jew's belongings and sell them to pawn traders in Anatoth. I was to ride north and sell the horse at a Roman outpost. But I wasn't on for ten minutes when she reared up, threw me, and broke my leg.

"I had to crawl, pulling myself along by my elbows and forearms to the nearest town and beg for a ride back to Sychar, worse off than before." He falls silent and gazes at Jesus. "So now you know what you've done—the kind of man you've helped. Every day I think about that Jew, naked and alone on the road, probably dead. I could be a murderer."

Jesus looks at him with compassion. "He didn't die."

The man stares, speechless.

Jesus shakes his head. "Somebody came along and helped him."

Melech grimaces, tears flowing. "How do you know?"

"Melech, I know. I promise you, he did not die."

The man holds his head in his hands and sobs, panting in relief. He looks to Jesus again. "Why me? Why did you come all the way out here? Isn't everyone in town falling at your feet?"

"The shepherd leaves the ninety-nine on the mountain to search for the one that went astray."

"What do you want?"

"Believe my words. Return to synagogue. Search Torah."

"I never learned to read."

"Then listen to the Word read aloud, and let it affect your heart. See what happens."

"And then what?"

"Tell others."

"You know the crime I committed in cold blood. You'd help someone like me?"

"He would," Simon says.

"Sleep on it," Jesus says, rising. "We'll be in town for one more day."

Chedva reappears. "She is asleep."

Simon says, "We'd better go back into town before it gets too late."

"Yes," Jesus says with a twinkle. "We never know what sort of men may lie in wait along the side of the road, huh?"

Melech and Chedva look stricken.

"Too soon?" Jesus says, laughing, and Melech laughs with him.

"You told him," Chedva says.

"I think he already knew."

"May I?" Jesus says, gathering Melech in an embrace. "Sleep well tonight, my friend," he whispers.

Chapter 7

# SONS OF THUNDER

*Sychar*

Simon can't deny that possessing the scrolled invitation from Photina makes him feel somewhat in charge again, if only temporarily. It's obvious, at least to him, that Jesus tends to favor John—if anyone—and Big James benefits from that too. But Simon leads the little throng all the way back into town and to a house that appears modest outside but seems to cover a lot of ground.

The weary travelers assemble behind Simon as he looks at the scroll and studies the front door, flanked by wall torches, then timidly knocks. *Please be the right place.*

Thaddeus sidles up to him. "You're sure this is it?"

Simon cranes his neck to assess the height of the dwelling. "I don't know. This is the address I was given."

Presently the massive door swings open. Photina's husband, resplendent in an evening robe, fills the frame, taking in all the men and two women gathered in his courtyard. "I'll be honest upfront," he says. "I only have five extra bedrooms, and two of them are drafty."

Photina appears at his side. "Nedim!" she scolds. She peers out, smiling as if about to burst. "They usually sleep on the ground. I think they'll be fine."

Simon says, "You're sure this isn't a problem?"

"I'm dying anyways," Nedim announces. "I don't need the house anymore." His lifts his chin. "Where is Jesus?"

From the back row, Jesus raises a hand.

"You have certainly livened things up around here," Nedim says. "You have *me* in a good mood just to fit in."

Photina laughs.

"Come in!" Nedim adds.

As they file past the couple, Nedim says, "One of the rooms is haunted—by my dead grandmother."

"Ooh," Jesus says. "I'll take that one!"

Photina leans into Nedim. "Do you know who he is? He's not afraid of ghosts."

Andrew steps in. "*I* might be."

• • •

*Melech's home, dawn*

Little Rebecca is startled awake by a thump from her parents' bedroom. Her father cries out, "Oh!" and pants.

Rebecca rushes over to see her father writhing on the floor at the foot of the bed.

"Melech?" Chedva says, leaping from the bed. "What's wrong?"

"Abba?" Rebecca whines.

"What is wrong?" Chedva insists, reaching for him.

"My leg!" he exults. "No pain! No, no, no, no!"

He struggles to his feet and repeatedly jumps, making his

wife and daughter scream. He bounces to Rebecca and lifts her off the floor, twirling her. "No pain! No pain!"

He sets down the girl and rushes to his wife. She stares at his leg that just the night before remained horribly broken and twisted, so tender that he could barely put any weight on it. He pulls her into a tight embrace, giggly.

Chedva pushes him back. "Melech, Melech! It was him!" She's weeping now. "It was him!"

Rebecca joins them, laughing aloud.

• • •

*When did it come to this?* John wonders as he rouses in one of the large guest rooms in Photina's home. He and Big James have spent the night in the same room as the Messiah, each having his own luxurious bed and blankets. James remains asleep beyond where Jesus lies on his back, staring at the ceiling, chuckling. John props himself on one elbow, and when Jesus chuckles again, John says, "What's so funny?"

Jesus says, "Oh, I just know of a family that's having an unexpectedly good morning."

John can't hide a puzzled look. Jesus uses two fingers to mimic walking down his forearm.

"Who?" John says. "Melech?"

Big James awakens as Jesus nods. "What's happening?" James says.

John says, "You don't even have to be there to perform miracles?"

"Don't sound so surprised, John," Jesus says. "One day you'll be given authority to do the things I do. Even greater."

Big James is fully engaged now. "Wait, I'm sorry," he says. "Can you say that again?"

Jesus laughs. "So, how did you sleep?"

"Well, it took me a while," John says. "I was a little scared about what Nedim said about this room being haunted."

"Oh, come on," Jesus says. "It's not haunted."

James says, "Why didn't you correct him when he said it was?"

"I don't address everything at once with new converts, Big James. Well, I'm ready for breakfast."

The three sit on the edges of their beds and open their hands in their laps. Jesus says, "I am thankful before You, living and enduring King …" and the brothers mouth the prayer along with him. "For You have mercifully restored my soul within me. Great is Your faithfulness."

• • •

At breakfast, Simon silently chastises himself for caring that the brothers got to share a room with Jesus. He's pleased when the Rabbi sits directly across from him at Photina's huge dining table where everyone has gathered, some milling about at a buffet filled with fruit, bread, and vegetables. Glad to be at least somewhat in the know, he tells Jesus, "The invitation from the treasurer stands."

"And the priest," Andrew says.

John speaks up. "The priest is a high risk."

With a grape tucked in his cheek, Andrew says, "Only if he wants to fight over whose Torah is better."

Matthew turns from the buffet. "But a great reward if he believes."

It's all Simon can do to look at Matthew. Being able to stomach Samaritans is one thing, but he's trying, especially under Jesus' example. But a tax collector? A follower of Jesus or not, the man has yet to acknowledge the grievous betrayal of his people.

"Don't forget the leper colony," Mary adds.

Jesus suddenly leaves the table.

John looks alarmed. "Where are you going?"

"For a walk."

Frustrated, Simon says, "But we haven't made our plans yet."

"Whatever the plans will be," Jesus says, "I'm sure it will be a long day, and I need some time alone."

Big James rises. "You need protection."

Jesus stops and turns. "Enough with the protection. I'll be fine. I won't be long."

"But where can we find you?" Simon says.

Jesus stops at the door. "Seek and you will find." And with that, he is gone.

Big James, looking embarrassed, sits back down.

Simon shakes his head at the others. "His riddles," Simon says.

"It didn't sound like a riddle to me," Ramah says.

"If you look for him, you will find him," Little James says.

"That's not what I heard," John says.

*This guy,* Simon thinks. "Oh, yeah? What'd you hear?"

John faces Simon, dead serious. "I heard you looked and *couldn't* find him."

"Matthew says you guys lost him for practically a whole day," Big James says.

Simon slowly turns to glare at Matthew, who appears to be pretending to be preoccupied with something on the ceiling.

Unable to throttle his anger, Simon says, "He goes where he wants when he wants."

"Yeah, well," Big James says, "we need to do better."

Simon looks aghast at his brother, Andrew. "Can you believe these guys? They dig in the mud and suddenly they're running the show."

"We just think we need some leadership," John says. "Okay? Security concerns aside, we need a plan."

"No matter what happens today," Big James says, "the real question is where will we be after we leave here?"

"We'll get to that," Simon says.

"That's why James and I have outlined a plan for the next month," John says.

"Month!" Simon says.

"Beginning with a visit to the Temple," John continues. "His first appearance there since performing public signs."

"Whoa, whoa, whoa!"

"A visit to the scribes at Qumran," Big James says.

"Two days preaching at Hebron," John adds.

"Hold on!" Simon says.

Big James leans toward Simon. "He said we were excellent planners."

Little James says, "I'm pretty sure he said 'planters.'"

"He applauded our execution!" John says.

"He sent you to the farm," Simon says with a smile, "to teach you a lesson."

"And we made an impression," Big James says.

"Let's vote on it!" Andrew says.

"Sure," John says. "Okay."

"All in favor of John and Big James's plan?"

John and Big James look expectant, hopeful. When no one responds, Simon snickers.

Suddenly Matthew raises a hand, and Simon knows it's intended to spite him. "I agree an agenda would be prudent," Matthew says.

Mary says, "I'm not voting."

Thomas says, "Me either."

"Why not?" John demands.

"Huh-uh, new guy," Thomas says.

"Look," Mary explains, "it doesn't matter what I think he should do or what you think."

"All opposed?" Andrew says.

Simon, Little James, Thaddeus, and Andrew raise their hands. The rest look awkward, embarrassed.

John shrugs. "I'm sorry you feel that way. But I, for one, am not okay losing him for long periods of time. I'm not okay arguing about where we're going every day."

"So don't argue," Thaddeus says.

John slaps down his napkin and leaves the table. Big James quickly follows him out.

• • •

"Hey!" Big James says. "Where are you going?"

"To tell Jesus our plan!" John says.

"The group said to leave it alone."

"They also said he gets to make his own decisions. So, let's let him. Why do you think he picked us to plant that field?"

"I'm starting to wonder about that. If I had known it was a Samaritan's field—"

"Come on," John says. "Jesus will sort it out."

They find Jesus outside the city, and John approaches. "Rabbi!"

He looks none too pleased. "Ah, you couldn't wait, could you?"

"We're sorry. We just wanted to clear a few things up, if that's okay."

"By all means."

But before John can continue, a caravan of Samaritan traders approaches. One hollers, "You Jewish boys are far from home!"

"Yes, as a matter of fact, we are," Jesus says. "Shalom to you too."

"Here's our traditional Jewish greeting for you," the man

says, and two others fire rocks at the three men. They duck out of the way.

John and Big James start to rush them, but Jesus holds them back. "Don't lift a finger," he says.

"That was a warning," the man says.

"Try it again and see what happens!"

"Quiet, Big James," Jesus says.

"Shalom to you too!" the man says as they pass, and he spits on John.

"You filthy dogs!" John shouts.

"I said, Quiet!"

The traders grin as they move on.

John faces Jesus. "Let us do something!"

"And what would that achieve?"

"Defend your honor," John says.

"They reviled and humiliated you," Big James adds.

John points at him. "They deserve to have bolts of lightning rain down and incinerate them!"

"Yes!" James says. "Fire from the heavens!"

"Fire?" Jesus says.

"You said we could do things like that," John says. "Say the word and it will happen."

"Why not?" James demands. "We knew we couldn't trust these people. We shouldn't have come here in the first place. They don't deserve you!"

Jesus appears to study them. "Why do you think I had you work Melech's field? What was I trying to teach you?"

John and James look at each other and shrug. "To help?" James tries.

"You think it was just to be more helpful? Or to be better farmers? It was to show you that what we are doing here will last for generations. What I told Photina at the well, and what she then told so many others, it's sowing seeds that will have a lasting impact for lifetimes. Can you not see what's happening here? These people whom you hate so much are believing in me without even seeing miracles. It's the message, the truth that we're giving them. And you're going to get in the way of that because a few people, from a region you don't like, were mean to you? That they're not worthy? What? You're so much better? You're more worthy? Well, let me tell you something: you're not. That's the whole point! It's why I'm here."

John and Big James hang their heads, peek at each other. "I'm sorry," James says.

"I'm sorry, Rabbi," John says.

"As we gather others," Jesus says, "I need you to help show the way. To be humble."

James punches John's arm. "We will."

Jesus nods, looking pleased at their response. But he fixes them with a wry gaze. "You wanted to use the power of God to bring down *fire* to burn these people up?"

The brothers look miserably at each other. "Well," John says, "it sounds a lot worse when you say it that way."

Jesus chuckles. "You two are like a storm on the sea. Come on." He turns back toward town and drapes an arm around each of them. "Thunder exploding out of your chests at every turn. In fact, that's what I'm going to call you from now on—James and John, the Sons of Thunder."

John grimaces. "Is that a good thing or a bad thing?"

"Today it was not good. But strong passion can be a good thing when channeled for righteousness. I just may have to delay giving you that authority we discussed earlier, or in smaller doses until you two calm down a bit."

As they near town, they come upon the rest of the disciples and the women with a stranger in tow.

"James, John," Simon says. "You look terrible. What happened?"

"What happened," Jesus says, "is that James and John needed to be reminded we're here in Samaria to plant seeds, not to burn bridges."

"Master," Simon says, "we've brought a guest who wanted to deliver an invitation to you personally."

"Rabbi," Matthew says, "this is Gershon, the priest of Sychar."

"Ah, yes," Jesus says as a dark-skinned, handsome man steps forward. "I've heard a lot about you."

"And I've heard a lot about you," the priest says. "You have blessed this village beyond our deserving."

"The pleasure is ours to be here."

"But we got word today might be your last day in Sychar."

"Word travels fast."

"Indeed, Rabbi, indeed. Would you do us the great honor of giving a reading from the scroll of Moses in our humble synagogue?"

"Of course."

• • •

John is ashamed and feels conspicuous among his compatriots. *A Son of Thunder indeed*, he thinks. *Guilty*. Jesus had been clearly disappointed in him. Will he now fall out of favor with the Rabbi—as he knows he deserves? Jesus has made him feel so special, so honored. And John had flaunted his status among his peers. They didn't deserve that, and now he deserves to have been brought down to size. Having felt part of Jesus' inner circle, along with his brother and the impetuous Simon, he will not be surprised to lose whatever status he imagined.

He and the rest find the Sychar synagogue jammed with locals. All the disciples and the women are pressed into guiding the crowd to their seats—the men in their section, the women in theirs. John is pleased to see Photina and Nedim, he appearing strangely shy and uncertain for such a large, imposing man. His wife urges him on, and Andrew leads him in. Photina, as usual, radiates with glee in the presence of Jesus.

Gershon leads Jesus into the Torah study room but soon reemerges and beckons John with a finger. "I have shown your master our holy scrolls, from Beresheit—which, as you know, means 'In the Beginning'—to Shemot ('Names'), Vakira ('And He Called'), Bamidar ('In the Desert'), and Devarim ('Words'). He is deciding on his text and requests your presence."

"Me, really?"

Gershon gestures toward the room.

Hesitantly, John quietly enters and steps next to Jesus.

"The five books of Moses and no more," Jesus says, sadness in his voice.

"They're missing out on so much," John says, "limiting themselves to just these."

"Yes," Jesus says. "But we have to start somewhere. What do *you* think I should read?"

*What do* I *think?* What a question! Not that long ago, John was a fisherman, almost as far from a scholar as a shepherd. He had studied the Torah like all Jewish boys, but he certainly hadn't devoted his adult life to the memorizing and all the rest. And he had so recently embarrassed himself in front of Jesus, disappointing him.

"Maybe," Jesus continues, seeming to sense John's hesitation, "Moses striking the rock instead of speaking to it? Or Balaam hitting his donkey when he was mad."

*As if I should advise him!* John scoffs with a smile. "Don't torment me."

"How about when Moses broke the tablets? Jonathan

storming away from the dinner table. Samson striking down the men of Ashkelon. Oh, wait, they don't have those scrolls."

"I get it, I get it," John says, making Jesus laugh.

He grows serious again. "I really am open to suggestions for the reading."

John stares at him. "I couldn't. After today. After yesterday. I do not feel very much worthy."

"Ah," Jesus says. "Who is worthy of anything?"

A question for the ages. "You," John says simply. "But no man, apparently."

"I'm a man, John."

*Well, sure, but ...* "And yet ..."

Jesus faces him and waits for eye contact. "I am Who I am."

Somehow this makes John feel loved anew and he falls silent.

The priest calls from outside the room, "Have you made your selection, Rabbi?" After a pause, "Rabbi?"

"Almost!" John calls out, perturbed.

Jesus' look reminds him to tone it down.

"Sorry," he whispers, and tries a more pleasant-sounding, "Almost." He tells Jesus the crowd must be getting restless.

"So, do you have a favorite passage from the first five?"

*Why couldn't he have asked me about sails, nets, bait?* "Um, do *you*?"

"I don't know. I like them all."

John chuckles. "You don't say. I suppose I love the beginning. I love how God simply spoke and the world came into being."

"Yes. As David wrote, 'By the word of the Lord the heavens were made.'"

"You know," John says, "the Greeks use *word* to describe divine reason—'what gives the world form and meaning.'"

"I like that," Jesus says. "And it is a favorite memory." He reaches for the scroll.

*Who else anywhere,* John wonders, *could refer to creating the world as a memory?*

• • •

John leads Jesus into the sanctuary, where he takes his place at the lectern. Melech arrives without even the hint of a limp, and Matthew leaps from his seat so the man can sit. Jesus winks at Melech.

Jesus uses the ornate yad to point at the text, and as John listens—his heart full and tears streaming—the master begins.

"A reading," he says, "from the first scroll of Moses. 'In the beginning, God created the heavens and the earth. And the earth was void, and without form, and the darkness covered the face of the deep. And God said, "Let there be light," and there was light. God called the light Day and the dark Night.'"

• • •

*John's home, Ephesus, AD 44*

The beloved disciple holds the first pages of his Gospel toward the light of the candles. He is alone now, Mother Mary already off to her bed, and his precious friends gone. The rain continues.

He studies what he has written and reads aloud softly.

"In the beginning was the Word, and the Word was with God, and the Word was God. He was in the beginning with God. All things were made through him, and without him was not any thing made that was made. In him was life, and the life was the light of men. The light shines in the darkness, and the darkness has not overcome it …"

# PART 2

# "I Saw You"

Chapter 8

# RUINED

*Caesarea Philippi*

Nathanael knows he should be thrilled, blessed in his early twenties to have landed an architectural commission—from the Romans, no less—in a major city. He has designed a magnificent structure, if he says so himself, the first on his own since studying under and working with some of the best designers in the empire.

His parents and siblings, devout Jews from Cana in Galilee, seem ambivalent about all this. He knows they're thrilled with his accomplishments, but to work for the Romans? Will not any structure they build somehow pay homage to their pantheon of so-called gods? Nathanael has assured them he remains committed to his dream—the life's work he longs for—to display his love and devotion to God by fashioning stunning synagogues, houses of worship that thrill the hearts of the faithful and draw them closer to the Lord. Naturally, he's had to keep that longing to himself. His mentors would be anything but sympathetic to his belief in the one true God of Abraham, Isaac, and Jacob.

While Nathanael considers this building neutral at best, he believes it will establish him as an expert, someone religious leaders can trust with their edifices. But as the youngest man on this job—and the only non-Roman—he has so far found it mostly a nightmare. The laborers seem to resent his youth, but the foreman—ugh, the foreman—Leontes obviously considers him a nuisance.

Can't the man see that what's already been raised matches Nathanael's beautiful drawings? His request is anything but out of the ordinary—seawater to add to the cement, a no-brainer. Leontes is dismissive, saying it will take three days to transport that to the building site.

"You can't stop construction for three days!" Nathanael says. "Is it because I'm Jewish?"

They walk the site, Nathanael trailing the bigger man and dodging men carrying huge stones and buckets of mortar. Leontes denies the charge.

*Then why?* "I've been telling you and any I can get to listen. I even told the Primi. I need that saltwater or the cement won't set to full strength!"

He follows Leontes into his office, and they stand across from each other at the foreman's desk, Leontes busying himself as if he wishes Nathanael would leave. The man speaks slowly, as if educating a child. "Seawater's heavy. It's hard to move. Understand?"

"Plans are hard to draw," Nathanael says, "bedrock hard to reach. It's all hard, but your incompetence is making it harder!"

Leontes points at him. "Careful."

"Hey, I'm just telling it like it is."

It's obvious the man has heard enough. He gives Nathanael his full attention at last. "Three days. You're in no position to make demands. You're lucky enough to have this job."

*Lucky?* "That's why I have to demand what I need, Leontes. Do you know how hard I had to work to earn a Roman commission? As a Jew!"

"You're a child who skipped the line! The men don't respect you for that."

Nathanael flinches. "Skipped the line? Just because I was smart enough to go to school instead of carrying mud."

"Twenty men show up every day," Leontes says. "Who cares what they think?"

"I care! They need to share my vision."

"They need to each do their jobs. The day laborers, the craftsmen"—he points to himself—"the foreman, and the architect."

There it is, the man's true view of Nathanael. Just a cog in the wheel. "Yes," Nathanael says, "in concert with me."

"Who do you think you are?" Leontes says. "I am the foreman here. You think if everyone would just do it your way, it will all turn out?"

*Exactly, as a matter of fact.* "I do."

"Well, people have their own ideas!"

Leontes is about to continue his tirade when a loud creak and groan outside causes men to scream, and a huge crash sends smoke and dust billowing through the window. Leontes races out, Nathanael on his heels.

Nathanael skids to a stop, horrified at the collapse of the entire structure—the pillars, scaffolding, all of it. Leontes helps pull a man from under the wreckage and yells for help. He spots Nathanael frozen in place and points. "You're ruined," he growls. "Do you hear me? It's over!"

Relieved beyond measure to learn no one has been killed, Nathanael soon realizes Leontes is right. Such a project was merely an audition. Success would surely have resulted in more and more such work, a sterling reputation, a long, successful career doing what he loved. But failure—especially as egregious as this—means the opposite. Everyone will know the designer of a structure that couldn't even survive construction.

How can God allow this when Nathanael's ultimate desire is only to please Him? In an instant, he has gone from a young man with a limitless future to one with nothing before him but heartache. With his pure motives, he believed God was with him, would favor him, bless him. Now it feels as if the Lord has turned His back and doesn't even see him.

Nathanael finds it impossible to pray. What is there to say? All he can do is demand why, but God is not to be questioned. Just yesterday, even that very morning, it had been easy to praise the Lord and to seek His face—even with the frustrations on the job. But those seem like nothing now. *Ruined* is the perfect word for what has transpired. With the fall of everything that had gone into that structure went Nathanael's hopes and dreams—and devotion.

Chapter 9

# THE STRANGER

*Bashan countryside*

Watching Jesus interact with people, Simon decides, is the fun part of all this—preaching, healing, telling parables, surprising everyone with his wisdom. The way he seems to peer into people's very souls and listen, really hearing them, clearly warms them. Most leave his presence reluctantly, but they go away smiling or even weeping with joy.

As energizing and inspiring as witnessing such encounters can be, they do not assuage Simon's longing for his beloved Eden—her precious smile, her embraces and kisses, and yes, even her direct talk. One thing he's never had to wonder was what his wife was thinking. She's the first thing on his mind every morning and the last thing on his heart every night.

The days between Jesus' dramatic ministering to throngs, however, have proved mundane, even tedious. Today Simon's on an errand with Thomas, John, and Big James, searching for firewood. If he is to be assigned boring manual labor—which is fine;

he's more than willing to do it in service of his Rabbi—he'd just as soon be fishing. At least that's a trade he knows.

He has come to appreciate Thomas, a smart, plainspoken young man with a head for precision—sort of a Matthew without the ugly baggage. John and Big James he has known forever but strangely feels estranged from them now. Close as they were for years, fishing the Sea of Galilee, Simon finds himself resenting their status with Jesus. It's as if the Master doesn't even try to hide his favoritism. He even invited John into the Torah study room at the synagogue in Sychar.

That's why Simon had been more than amused when Big James admitted he and his brother had been chagrined—humiliated, really—to have been chastised by Jesus for something they'd said and done in Samaria. Simon feels petty for reveling in their discipline and for feeling as if he's constantly jockeying with them for position with the Messiah. They are friends, after all, compatriots in a cause for the ages. But still, he wishes Jesus would recognize his fierce loyalty, his absolute commitment to the Rabbi's safety and well-being.

As they move into the sparse wilderness from their temporary camp, Simon looks over his shoulder, expecting Andrew to catch up with them soon. The wheelbarrow Big James pushes lies only half full of kindling and a single ax.

Thomas asks what Simon thinks Jesus meant by "two days' worth."

"He said to leave enough firewood for the next weary traveler. You heard that, John?"

"Mm-hm."

"What if it isn't enough?" Thomas says. "We used up all the dry stuff."

*Ah,* Simon thinks. *Another chance to needle the brothers.*

"That's why it's good to have some strong bodies around. Like the Sons of Thunder here."

John smacks James's arm. "What, you told him?"

"Don't worry," Simon says with a grin. "His account made him look just as bad as you did."

John shakes his head, but James suddenly stops and stares. "Hey," he says.

A man has emerged from the woods and approaches across the dry, weedy plain. To Simon he resembles Jesus, but perhaps not as tall, and more shabbily dressed. James pulls the ax from the wheelbarrow.

"Who is that?" John says.

Simon says, "Maybe it's a scout from—where are we? Seleucia?"

Thomas stays behind Simon, arms folded. "Maybe he's just walking."

"No one just walks in the Bashan," John says.

"No one but us," Thomas says.

As the man comes within earshot, Simon shushes the others and steps forward. "Don't come any closer!" he shouts, making a show of reaching for the knife sheathed at his waist. John does the same.

The stranger stops, a stalk of wheat in his mouth. He waves and calls out, "Shalom!"

Big James says, "He's Jewish."

John says, "You think?"

The man begins to approach again.

"What do you want?" Simon demands.

"For the Romans to go away," he says wryly. "For a pretty wife some day. I ate a fattened goose once! I'd love that again." He's smiling now. "Are you followers of the Rabbi Jesus of Nazareth?"

"Don't say anything," Simon whispers. "He could be a spy."

"Spying for whom?" Thomas says. "For what?"

"There are spies," the man says, stopping a few yards away and pulling the stalk from his mouth. He gestures with it. "But they're not smart enough to dress like this. Are you Simon? Son of Jonah?"

*How could he possibly . . . ?* "Who are you?"

"You're new at this," the man says. "I get it. Once you've followed your rabbi for long enough, you won't even blink when a strange man, such as myself, walks out of the woods with a message he can give only to Jesus directly."

"Yeah," James says, "we are pretty new."

"Doesn't make us dumb," John mutters.

"We can't let you see the Rabbi," Simon says, "without knowing your business."

"I can't say. If you want to send me away, fine. Say hello to my friend Andrew for me though."

That stops Simon. This man knows his brother? Who must he be?

Thomas says to the others, "What do you think?"

John says, "I don't know. Bring him in, I guess? Let Jesus figure it out."

James shakes his head. "Something's not sitting right with Simon."

"Andrew has friends?" Simon says, making John snicker and the stranger shrug and smile.

"Philip!" Andrew calls, running up from behind them. He flies past Simon as Philip shouts, "Hey! There he is!" and the two embrace, laughing.

"Whoa!" Andrew says. "You smell terrible."

"Well, what did you expect, huh?"

"Come on!" Andrew says, dragging him past the others and back toward the camp. "What are you doing here?"

"Ah, well, wait till you find out."

Back at camp, Simon pulls Andrew aside and learns that this friend is from Bethsaida, a disciple of the Baptizer. "You never mentioned a Philip when we were there."

"You'll find this shocking," Andrew says, pouring a cup of water, "but I have a whole life that doesn't revolve around you."

"What's your problem? I'm just asking about this kook."

"He's not a kook! You know, you could be a little less—*you* all the time."

Guilty, and Simon knows it. Maybe he has overreacted. "Fair enough."

Andrew raises the cup and hands it to Simon. "You take this to him. Make nice."

Simon knows that's the right thing to do.

But as he approaches the newcomer, he finds him sitting with his back to a fire pit, dozing. Mary and Ramah gaze curiously at him, as do Thomas and the brothers. How could he be asleep already? "We've been back five minutes," Simon says. "Philip?"

Nothing.

"Philip!"

The man slowly opens his eyes, and Simon hands him the cup.

"Ahh," he says, "you never know when you get to sleep next." He drinks. "Or when you'll have clean water. Take advantage when you've got either one. Thank you."

"Sounds like you're in a war out there with Creepy—with John the Baptizer."

"Ah, no. War has rules."

• • •

Philip is there to meet Jesus, of course, but he's also relieved to find that he might just like these people, and he can hardly wait to get to know them. What made them choose to follow Jesus—or did they have a choice? When he first heard John the Baptizer preach, Philip had no idea what to think. All he knew was that he was once again playing hooky from the hook—wanting to do something, anything, with his life but fish the Galilee.

That sea was crowded with men and their sons, or brothers whose fathers had already passed, who had been raised on boats, mending nets, casting lines, and dropping anchors. They lived for this stuff. Philip simply didn't. He tried to tell himself he didn't even like the odors, but the truth was, he did. The smell of fresh fish drew him, especially if it were being fried.

What he loved most was memorizing the Torah. Becoming a priest or rabbi was not his goal, but the Scriptures made him introspective, forced him to want to do something significant with his life for God. But what?

The last thing he wanted was to become an itinerant preacher, someone people laughed at and talked about behind his back. Until he heard there was such a man worth listening to.

Many referred to the Baptizer with derogatory names, epithets, and made him the butt of jokes. Philip first followed a small crowd just to see what all the fuss was about. He made the mistake of standing downwind from the man, who preached at the top of his lungs before a small body of water. Philip could smell the man from twenty paces—but at least he could hear him.

John, as he called himself, harangued the crowd with memorized passages from the Holy Book—passages Philip also knew. John called people to repentance and persuaded them to be baptized. The man's attire, such as it was, consisted of animal skins, and he was twig thin, as if he barely ate.

But passionate? He spoke with authority and called sin sin. Philip forgot where he was, what he was supposed to be doing.

He didn't miss a syllable and found himself edging closer and closer to the strange man.

Someone hollered and asked if John claimed to be the Messiah.

"I am not!" he shouted back. "I come to prepare the way for him! You will know him when you see him!"

When the preaching and the baptizing were finished, Philip timidly approached.

"The curious one," John said, quieter. "I could tell." He pulled from a rucksack a honeycomb covered with dead locusts and held it out. "Care for a bite?"

"Hardly," Philip said. "I just want to talk."

"Suit yourself," the Baptizer said, popping the comb in his mouth. "Never know when you might get a meal."

*All I have to do is go home if I want to eat,* Philip thought.

But after a lengthy conversation with John, he went home only once more—to break the news to his parents and siblings that he was becoming a disciple of John the Baptist. Despite their obvious misgivings, he could tell from their looks that they knew he could not be dissuaded. They wished him Godspeed and assured him he would always be welcome if the man proved to be a charlatan.

"If he does," Philip said, "I am the worst judge of character alive."

Following John brought him a new set of friends, fellow acolytes who wanted nothing more than to spend their lives helping John set the stage for the Messiah and his kingdom. Andrew, a fisherman himself from only a few miles south, became a fast friend. And while Andrew still fished, Philip and he were there the day Jesus of Nazareth came to be baptized and John identified him as the Son of God.

The memory was burned into Philip's mind. He was jealous

when John freed Andrew to follow Jesus. But now, much later, John had finally sent Philip to become a disciple of the Nazarene. The question was, naturally, would Jesus accept him?

• • •

Matthew approaches from his own wood-gathering chore, gingerly carrying an ax.

"What did you find?" Big James says.

Matthew looks embarrassed. "Nothing suitable."

"Of course he didn't find any," Simon says. "Where did you look?"

"To the east, one mile."

*Typical. Idiot.* "That's the ravine. Anything you find there would be—"

"Wet," Matthew says. "Yes. I discovered that."

"But there was wood?" Philip says.

"It was wet," Simon says. "That's Matthew. He checks the ravines for wood. Probably fishes in the desert too."

Others chuckle, but Philip does not. "Mm," he says. "Good work, Matthew."

"Thank you. Who are you?"

"Well," Philip says, standing, "I'm the guy who dries wood. Now if only you had an arsenal of weapons, we could do it in the manner of Ezekiel."

"How did Ezekiel dry his wood?" Matthew says.

"No," Andrew says, "it's—"

"The prophecy against Gog and Magog," John says.

Philip begins to quote, "'And then those who dwell in the cities of Israel will go out and make fires of the weapons and burn them.'" Suddenly the others—Andrew and Big James and John and Thomas and Simon—join him and recite in unison: "'Shields and bucklers, bows and arrows, clubs and spears; and they will make fires of them for seven years, so that they will not need to take wood out of the fields or cut down any out of the forests….'"

Mary and Ramah and Matthew look on in wonder. Philip finishes alone, "'… for they will make their fires out of the weapons.'" He smiles at Matthew and beckons him to walk with him back toward the ravine. "Hey," he says to the others. "Keep the fire going."

Chapter 10

# RIDDLES

*Caesarea, that afternoon*

Nathanael has never been so low. At the end of himself, he does something he has never done before. He visits a tavern in the middle of the day. Small, dark, dingy, it fits his mood perfectly. He trudges to the bar, slapping down his cloak and his leather bag of drawings.

"Your strongest," he tells the bartender. "And cheapest."

The man pours him a cup. "Is something wrong, friend?"

"Yes."

"Did someone die?"

"Yes."

"I'm sorry for your loss. Was it sudden?"

"I think—it was a long time coming for him. But it felt sudden."

"Hmm. Tell me about him."

The pain—the devastation, really—is so fresh Nathanael has not considered ever telling anyone. He could have kept this to himself for the rest of his days. Yet this man, this stranger, looks upon him with such compassion, he genuinely seems to care. Perhaps such an approach with customers is merely good for business, yet Nathanael needs a sympathetic ear.

"He was an architect," he says, and pauses. "It was what he wanted to be his whole life."

"Sad."

"He came from nothing. Worked his way up. Loved God." Expressing this very sentiment nearly stops him. He remains in a Roman city, after all. But his love of the one true God of Israel is what makes this so bleak. Where is God in all this? He looks away, but the bartender is clearly not put off. Nathanael finds his voice. "He wanted to build synagogues eventually. I know that's not very popular around here." The very thought of his dreams, and yes, probably the alcohol that fires the back of his throat, inspire him. "Ones with colonnades that sing. Parapets that practically pray. Vaulted halls that draw the soul upward to God. That's what God made him for—or so he thought."

"He sounds like an ambitious guy. What did he die of?"

The question of the ages, but the answer comes immediately to Nathanael. "Hubris." He takes a sip. "It's me, by the way. I'm the dead man in the story."

"Yeah," the man says. "Yeah, I got that."

"I just wanted to be clear."

• • •

*Bashan countryside*

Matthew still feels self-conscious, but he is intrigued by this newcomer, Philip, who does not seem repelled by him. They have set off for the ravine, Matthew carrying an ax. He no longer feels so out of place, so over-dressed. His outfit of luxurious imported fabrics has frayed from all the time in the sun and wilderness, so unlike his days in Capernaum ensconced in a collection booth.

Still, he's better dressed than Philip, whose odor proves the man has not taken advantage of all the water that must have been prevalent when he was a disciple of the Baptizer. "Did you learn how to dry wood before or after you started following John?"

Philip's silence tells Matthew he has apparently misunderstood something again. Had the drying wood comment been metaphorical? Deciphering such was not one of his skills.

Philip abruptly changes the subject. "What's up with you and Simon?"

So it's that obvious, even to new people. "He doesn't like me. He sees me as his enemy."

"Why?"

"I was a tax collector."

"Mm-hm …"

"I was everyone's enemy. That doesn't shock you?"

"I *was* something else once too. Once you've met the Messiah, *am* is all that matters. Next time Simon rides you, remind him that the people out there, they want to define us by our past. Our sins."

"Out there, where?"

"With the sleepers. But we're different. We're awake."

Matthew is frustrated. Here's a man who plainly accepts him, doesn't look down on him. He speaks to Matthew as if to a friend, but Matthew can't get his mind around what Philip is saying. "I don't understand."

"Well, you haven't felt any relief except with him, your rabbi, have you?"

The man certainly has that right. "No."

Philip smiles. "Don't expect to."

Matthew senses some helpful wisdom there for him, but still it eludes him. He raises what happened back at the camp before they left. "How did you memorize prophecy?"

"In Hebrew school. Like all Jewish boys. Didn't you?"

"I started," Matthew says, "but then I skipped ahead."

"Skipped ahead? Never heard of anyone skipping ahead. What did they do that for?"

"I was sent to apprentice under a bookkeeper."

"Were you that good with numbers or that bad with Torah?"

As usual, Matthew takes the question at face value. "I was proficient at both."

"No, I'm kidding. How old were you when you skipped ahead?"

"Eight."

"Eight!"

"I showed unusual promise."

Philip chuckles. "I'll bet you did. How come you never circled back to Torah?"

"I was paraded before the magistrate. Rome offered me higher wages than the annual income of my father and three of his brothers combined. Bought my first house when I was thirteen."

"Why did you need to buy a house?"

The painful memory floods back. "My father—"

"Kicked you out."

Matthew nods.

"I don't blame him," Philip says.

Matthew is taken aback. "I thought you said …"

"He's a man. He acted by man's standards. Everybody in your old life is playing a different game than you now. Do you get it?"

Matthew starts to nod, wanting so badly to understand. But he blurts the truth. "No!"

This causes Philip to stop and face him, looking as if he is ready for Matthew to speak his mind.

"Everyone speaks in riddles!" Matthew says, louder than he intended. "I can understand esoteric ideas! They're not beyond me!"

"Of course not," Philip says. "You'll probably pick it up faster than the rest of us. I'm sorry, man, I don't mean to sound like an oracle here. It's a force of habit. Spend all your time with a rogue preacher in the wilderness and you get to be a little—obtuse. They're simple ideas for complicated people."

This is not helping. The man sounds obtuse while explaining why he's obtuse! "I just—" Matthew sighs and looks away. "In your obtuse language …" He draws on the ground with his ax. "Here's a circle. It represents everything in the world and all the people that have ever been." He drives the ax into the ground outside the circle. "And that's me. That's how I feel."

He winces, squints, avoiding Philip's eyes until the man says, "Well said. Good for you. And yes, I've been living literally outside this circle with John the outcast for a couple of years. So, I can relate." Philip closes the gap between them and speaks softly. "You're fine, Matthew. Stick around." He gently punches Matthew's shoulder. "You're gonna be all right."

Philip starts off again toward the ravine. Matthew still feels somewhat in the dark, yet also somehow encouraged.

Chapter 11

# ASHES

*Caesarea Philippi*

Never a man of strong drink, Nathanael dutifully stops at one cup. He thanks the bartender for his kind ear and trudges out into the sunlight. As he makes his way from the bustling town and into the wilderness, he wonders if another cup or two might have been just what he needs.

He shakes his head at the memory of his mother's last letter, telling him of the rumors in his hometown. She said people at a local wedding feast were abuzz with talk of a stranger who had somehow produced delicious wine from plain water. "Of course I don't believe it," she had written, "but someday I would like to witness a real miracle. Not that I need one like the patriarchs of old to maintain my faith in Yahweh."

*Yahweh.* Where *is* God in all this? Nathanael has never felt so alone.

How long has it been since he has so starkly felt no destination? He's on the move but aimless. His whole life he's felt momentum—learning, growing, achieving, aiming at a future of promise and accomplishment. Nathanael now cannot even conjure an alternative to the career he had envisioned for himself.

If only he could talk to his old friend Philip. He always knew what to say. But he's gone too, seeming to have abandoned his Bethsaida family and their fishing trade to roam the Galilean wilderness with some crazy vagabond who claims to be paving the way for the coming of the Messiah.

Nathanael has always known Philip to be a man of uncommon sense, articulate, thoughtful. Devout. Will something like what he has done become Nathanael's fate now—no choice but to become the sycophant of a traveling showman? He's too smart for that, even if he is a failure. And yet, Philip …

The weeds and plains stretch before Nathanael. The barren landscape is a picture of his own soul. He finds himself suddenly exhausted in the rising heat of the day, but what has he done to bring on such fatigue? Even his argument with Leontes was all in a day's work.

At the top of a rise looms a leafy fig tree. At least he can get out of the sun. He longs to talk with God, but he senses the Lord has already said what He wants to say—allowing what happened for what reason? If it's to teach Nathanael some lesson, he's not getting it. Unless it's that God has removed His hand of blessing.

It strikes Nathanael that a day earlier he might have appreciated the beauty of this place, with its low mountains in the distance and just enough fluffy clouds to offset the brilliant blue of the sky. But what is all that to a former artist, yesterday an appreciator of pristine scenery but today just a layman?

Nathanael settles wearily beneath the tree, his back to the trunk. He pulls from his satchel the drawings for a now-razed building that was to be the key to his limitless future. He stares. That the renderings are exquisite—for he invested all of himself in each—only deepens his agony. He looks to the heavens and lifts the pages. "This was done for You," he whispers, weeping. "Blessed are You," he tries, tears pouring now. "Blessed are You, Lord our God, King of the universe." He looks back at the pages. "Hear, Israel, the Lord is our God, the Lord is One."

Nathanael is horrified at his own thoughts, even as he prays, but he cannot stop himself. He sets the pages in the dirt—the best work he has ever done—and pulls a flint and rock from his bag. "Hear my prayer, O Lord," he sobs as he scrapes a spark onto the parchments and they burst into flames. "Let my cry come to You." He looks again to the sky as the drawings burn. "Do not hide Your face from me in the day of my distress." He sees nothing but dark clouds now. "Incline Your ear to me," he cries out. "Answer me speedily in the day when I call."

Yet Nathanael hears nothing but the crackling of the fire, not even a breeze.

"No? This was done for you! Do not hide Your face from me!" And now he shouts to the heavens. "Do You see me?"

Nathanael is so far into the wilds that his voice finds nowhere even to echo.

"Do You see me?" he whispers.

• • •

*The Bashan camp*

Matthew can't deny this feeling—though he has trouble labeling it. Pride? How long has it been since he's felt that? When he finally leads Philip to the ravine, where he had earlier despaired over finding only wet wood, his new friend exults. "This will work! And look how much you've found!"

"But Simon says that wood this wet is—"

"And I told you it can be made to work. But look at our lack of faith! We're going to need a wheelbarrow. Leave me the ax and go get it. There's so much here that once we've loaded it, one will have to push and the other steady the load."

All the way back, Matthew anticipates telling the others—bragging?—that he and Philip will be bringing back a supply of tinder as big as, if not bigger than, anyone else's. But the only ones around are Thomas, who doesn't seem to care for Matthew much more than Simon does, and Mary and Thomas's beloved Ramah. Boasting to them does not seem prudent, so Matthew is just grateful to find the barrow and head back to the ravine.

He finds the going rough. He has been teased unmercifully for what Andrew described as his "indoor hands." At least Andrew seems good-natured about it, adding, "A few more weeks roughing it and you'll start developing some callouses."

Matthew wishes he had those callouses, not to mention more muscle, as he runs the cart back to Philip. Even empty he finds it unwieldy and heavier than he expects. It keeps wanting to veer off the path, and it takes all his strength to keep it straight.

By the time he arrives, Philip has chopped a load of firewood that will more than fill the contrivance, and Philip immediately begins loading it in. Matthew knows he should do something, but again he feels conspicuous, trying to keep his flowing cloak out of the way as he tries to match Philip's movements. His friend easily works three times faster, stacking log after log while Matthew gingerly hefts one, sets it in place, and returns for another. Philip appears amused at this, and Matthew is grateful he says nothing.

When the barrow is filled to overflowing, Philip says, "You want to push or steady the load?"

"Oh, I could not push," Matthew says. "And I don't know if you can trust me to keep the stack in place."

"Well, you have to do one or the other," Philip says with a smile.

So all the way back, Philip bends and grunts forcing the cart along as Matthew mince-steps beside it and tries to keep the logs from tipping. Twice he fails and they have to replace several logs, but thankfully Philip does not scold him.

Matthew is disappointed that still no one is at the camp to see them bring in their load. Thomas is busy with something, and the women are chatting in a tent.

Philip finds two machetes and shows Matthew how to sit near the fire, propping each log against a heavy stump, holding it between his knees, stripping off the bark and tossing it into the fire between them. It should be easy—at least Philip makes it look so, reaching to the bottom of each log and deftly pulling back on the blade.

But Matthew struggles. He can't make the blade dig into the bark more than superficially, regardless of whether he uses one hand or two, scrapes toward himself or away. The effort makes him sweat, and he fears he'll soon smell as bad as the others. He grunts and sighs, frustrated. Why is everything so much easier for everyone else?

Philip, he knows, can't help but notice. The newcomer stabs his machete into the stump before him and pulls from his satchel a strip of burlap.

"What's that for?" Matthew says.

"It turns a blade into a razor for logs." He wraps it around each palm, picks up his machete, and scrapes with vigor. "Protects your hands." He takes it off and tosses it to Matthew.

As Matthew tries to mimic Philip's wrapping of the cloth, Philip says, "Twice."

Applying it to his machete, Matthew tries pulling the blade toward him and slices a huge piece of bark in one swoop. Success! He smiles broadly. "I have never done manual labor before."

"You must have worked pretty hard to avoid it. But that's

behind you now too. You have to lean into it. Let someone teach you a thing. Laugh at someone's jokes. And then tell jokes. Do you know any?"

"Any what?"

"Jokes."

Matthew doesn't know what to say. They are working almost in unison now.

"So," Philip says, "was it difficult to leave it all behind?"

"No," Matthew says. "It should have been. I was comfortable. I had a dog."

"Bold," Philip says. "I like it."

"That was a source of amusement for others—who often referred to me as a dog. My house was bought with blood money. My parents and I haven't spoken much in years. And numbers didn't make the world clear anymore."

"You gave everything away …"

"But it's uncomfortable when nobody likes me."

Philip pauses, appearing to think. "If this rabbi, Jesus of Nazareth, called you, it means you already have everything you need for right now. And he'll give you the rest in time."

"I just don't know what he sees in me. He's a religious teacher and I know very little about religion."

"From what I understand," Philip says, "Jesus doesn't love everything about religion. Matthew, what you think you know, it doesn't matter. Only that Jesus chose you. That's where your confidence comes from now."

"I know he knows what he's doing. I just wish I did."

"Skipped out of Hebrew school at eight—I think you'll catch on."

Matthew chuckles.

Philip changes the subject. "Here's an easy one. If somebody asks you to tell a joke, tell them you have a vegetable joke, but it's corny."

Matthew looks blankly at him.

Philip chuckles. "We'll work on it."

• • •

*Caesarea Philippi, dusk*

Nathanael has no more tears. He has sat with his back to the fig tree for hours, his drawings a pile of ash next to him. He scoops a handful and raises it over his head, releasing it into his hair. *Fitting,* he thinks, the grit mixing with his sweat and wafting down onto his once-pristine garments.

Again and again he lets the ashes fill his hair. At long last, he labors to his feet, fetches his empty leathern bag, and slowly hikes away—to where, he has no idea.

• • •

*Bashan camp, that night*

As the new man, Philip has drawn first watch and sits tending the fire. He had hoped to get to talk with Jesus by now, having seen him only once while following John the Baptizer. But the others have told him the Rabbi has been away for a few days, a common practice of his.

As Philip pokes a twig into the embers and sparks fly, he hears only crickets and the wind through an acacia tree. Everyone else must be sound asleep after a long day, but only Matthew slumbers outside.

Philip startles at footsteps in the dark and rises quickly, ready to do whatever is necessary to protect his new mates. But the man approaching makes no attempt to be stealthy, and as he comes into the firelight, Philip recognizes him. To his surprise,

Jesus seems to recognize him, too—showing no fear at a stranger so close to his followers. "Shalom," Jesus whispers. "I'm glad to see you here."

"I'm Philip."

Jesus nods, as if he already knew.

"Wait, John told you?"

"No. I remember your face. You were standing with Andrew the day I was baptized by John."

"Ah."

"How is my old cousin? I shouldn't call him old. We're the same age."

"Uh, his reputation with Rome is down, but his spirits are up."

Jesus smiles. "Sounds about right."

"He sends me with a message. Wants me to tell you something—on my behalf."

"That's good, because I have something to say to you too."

"It's a very short message," Philip says. "Only two words."

Jesus says, "Mine is also short—follow me."

Philip says, "I will."

They stand smiling at each other. "So," Jesus says, "John thinks you're ready."

"Yes. He spoke with someone."

Jesus points to the fire, and they sit.

Philip continues, "John spoke to someone the last time he was in prison."

"Someone?"

"A Pharisee. He had been troubled by a miracle he'd witnessed in the Red Quarter in Capernaum."

"Ah, yes," Jesus says, "I know this man."

"You know him?"

"Yes, I might even call him a friend."

Philip chuckles and shakes his head. "John told me to

expect anything, to expect nothing, but I think he'd be troubled to know that you are friends with a Pharisee."

"He'll get over it."

"Well, then we received word of what you did in Cana. That was all John needed to hear. He sends his love."

"And he sends you."

"A meager offering," Philip says.

"Hardly meager. You will be the most experienced of all my followers."

"John is hardly standard procedure."

"Even better," Jesus says, chortling.

"If I may be so bold, what are your intentions here in Bashan?"

"Just passing through."

"To Caesarea Philippi?"

"Caesarea for one night, and then we'll continue north, into Syria."

"I heard you were just in Samaria, and now to Syria. You and John really are cut from the same cloth. If I didn't know any better, I'd say you each have a death wish."

"I wouldn't exactly call it a wish," Jesus says.

"But a what? A death what?"

Jesus shakes his head. "It's nothing. I'm still thinking through how to talk about it. It's why I was gone for a couple of days. A lot on my mind."

"Yes, I can imagine. In Syria, will we go to Damascus? Antioch?"

"Not to the big cities, no. To the smaller places."

Matthew stirs in his sleep.

"I'll wake him later. You should get some sleep, Philip. We've got a long road ahead of us tomorrow. I'll tend the fire."

Philip rises. "Rabbi, one last thing. If there's time, I've a friend in Caesarea who I haven't seen in quite some time."

"Your friend lives in a Roman city?"

"He's an architect. If there's time, I'd love to—"

"Of course, of course."

"Only if there's time."

"Listen," Jesus says, "if we don't make time for friends, we won't have any."

## Chapter 12

# THE THANK-YOU

*The next morning*

The disciples awake, dress, and arrange the camp for another day. They laugh and tease, cajoling each other.

In the women's tent, Ramah squints against a ray of sun peeking through the flap and realizes Mary is already up and tending to her pack. How her new friend can look so radiant so early is beyond her. Ramah says, "Did I sleep late?"

"The sun is hardly up," Mary says.

Ramah sits up, only a blanket between her and the ground. "Oof, my back."

"It gets easier—a little. You get used to it."

Mary is filling her sack. "Are you packing?" Ramah says.

"I am. I pack every morning now. I never know if we'll be somewhere for a night or a week."

"That sounds hard. I didn't think about how this would really work."

"I think everyone's struggling with that," Mary says. "In some way."

"How about you?"

Mary's thoughts appear to be elsewhere.

"Mary?"

Mary reengages. "Wasn't it exciting yesterday when the men began reciting prophecy?"

Ramah can't deny that. "And, uh, a little intimidating."

"Oh, yes. We need to catch up with them."

"Okay," Ramah says. "How? I can't read."

"I'll teach you to read and write."

"Where would we get materials?"

"Leave it to me. I know who to ask."

Of course she does, and how exciting is this prospect!

As Mary finishes packing, Ramah begins her morning prayer. "I am thankful before You, living and enduring King, for You have mercifully restored my soul within me. Great is Your faithfulness …"

• • •

Simon, Andrew, and Thomas stand over the new supply of wood near the campfire. "That's more than two days' worth," Thomas says.

"It's wet," Simon says.

Philip approaches. "No! It's damp. That stuff will smoke something terrible if you light it now, but by nightfall …"

Simon has to admit it. "You did well."

"I didn't do it," Philip says.

"No? Then who?"

"Our young smart friend."

"Thomas?" Simon says.

"No. Matthew. Who's Thomas?"

Simon points at him.

"Aah, I'm sorry, Thomas," Philip says. "I'm still learning everyone's names. That reminds me of a time with John—"

Andrew says, "Simon calls him Creepy John."

Simon glares at his brother. "I, uh—"

"Ha!" Philip says. "That's good! I like that. So, anyway, the flock was evading Roman patrols, moving up and down the Jordan."

"You were on the run?" Thomas says.

"One day, John starts addressing us by name. 'Zachariah, Tobias, Michal!' We all start looking around at each other like 'Who's he talking to?' And then we realize we don't know each other's names. We'd been out there for months, and we only knew each other's nicknames or aliases."

"How is John?" Andrew says.

"Same old John. He's proud of you, I can tell you that much. Like a father." He looks away. "You know? I think it's nap time. Wake me if there's work to do, boys."

Simon is dumbfounded. *Nap time? At dawn?*

He's about to ask Philip what he's talking about, but the man has such an air of confidence. Not arrogance. Innocence.

Philip says, "And, uh, Simon—thank Matthew if you see him."

There's nothing Simon would rather do less, yet something deep within tells him Philip is right.

Andrew grins. "John remembers me," he whispers.

• • •

Matthew sits with his back against a tree, alone with his thoughts, writing in his journal. Thaddeus approaches and says, "Ah, I thought that might be what you were doing."

"Hiding?" Matthew says, not looking up.

"No, writing. *Are* you hiding?"

"Philip says I don't have to do that anymore," Matthew says, concentrating on his work.

"The new guy?" Thaddeus says. "I like him already."

"Everybody does. He's like Simon, but not—like Simon." They both laugh.

Thaddeus sits next to Matthew. "What are you writing?"

"Just notes on what I see." He glances at the camp. "This. I'm used to writing daily now. It began as a chore, but it's become a habit."

"I think prayer is like that," Thaddeus says. "At first anyway, the way Rabbi taught me. Now I love it."

Matthew finally looks at Thaddeus. "In the short time that I have followed, people have quarreled over things Jesus said, remembered things differently, and disputed his meaning. I think it's best we have a written record to refer back to."

Simon appears. "Everything he says and does?"

"Yes," Matthew says.

"That's not a good idea."

Thaddeus looks surprised. "Why?"

"We have enemies," Simon says. "There are people trying to trap Jesus in his words. They could twist something he said to defame him. Have you thought about that?"

"They will find it easier," Matthew says, "to twist something he is *reported* to have said than if it is confirmed in writing."

"That's not how the world works! People can twist words however they want."

"But if it's clearly written—"

"Yeah, I'll bet as clear as the last time I saw you writing in your journal, spying on me for the Romans! And to think I came here to thank you …"

This gives Matthew pause, grateful for what Philip taught

him the day before. "People out there want to define all of us by our pasts. But we do things differently because of him."

Simon looks flummoxed. Has Matthew actually rendered him speechless? No. "For the record, it's a bad idea. Write *that* down." He pauses, then stalks away, calling over his shoulder, "We head out in an hour."

Matthew sits embarrassed. On the one hand, he has stood up to a bully. On the other, avoiding such confrontations—as he has done his whole life—was much easier.

Thaddeus seems to study him. "He's not wrong," Thaddeus says. "Just be careful."

## Chapter 13

# SOON

*Rural Bashan*

Simon, feeling like the leader again—or at least assuming the role—walks alongside Big James as the rest of the disciples and the women follow. James is muscling the largest, most heavily laden cart containing most of the belongings and supplies.

"Had enough?" Simon says.

"I wouldn't mind a break, if you're offering."

"It's Andrew's turn. I'll get him."

Simon heads back down the line as the entourage straggles on as individuals or pairs, stretched out along the road. He passes Thaddeus with the second cart, one he can easily manage by himself. He pats the young man on the shoulder. "All good?"

As Simon passes Philip and Matthew, he greets only Philip. Then come Mary and Ramah. "Ladies."

Thomas is ten feet behind them, and Simon playfully grabs him.

Finally, he reaches the last two in line, Andrew—munching an apple—and Jesus. "Is my brother slowing you down back here?"

"Always," Jesus says.

"Hey!" Andrew protests, and Jesus laughs heartily. "You watch Simon and me in a footrace, and we'll settle this once and for all."

"Race yourself to the front," Simon says. "James is asking for relief on that cart."

"Already? I thought we called him Big for a reason."

"Yeah, and that's why his shift is the longest. Go on, you're up."

"I'll be up next after you, Andrew," Jesus says.

"No, no," Simon says, "You don't need—"

"I want to."

"You shouldn't," Andrew says.

"Let me tell you something," Jesus says. "Some days I miss manual labor. Fewer questions, less speculation, honest sweat."

Simon grabs his brother's shoulders from behind. "Time to get honest, Andrew."

Andrew jogs ahead.

Finally alone with Jesus, Simon has something on his mind. But the Rabbi speaks first. "You know, it's funny, I would've thought that the keeper of the shifts would have been Matthew's job, not yours."

*Matthew! Of all people.* "Why is that?"

"He thinks in divisions, calculation, order."

"Yeah," Simon mutters. "I've noticed. Speaking of Matthew, I wanted to tell you—he's writing down everything you do."

"Of course he is," Jesus says with a smile.

"And that's fine with you?"

"It is."

"All right, good to know."

"Simon, you strike me as someone who acts on instinct, feeling."

"Yeah, but I do think. I think all the time. That's what I was hoping to talk to you about."

"You were?"

"Yeah, I've been thinking. The group is growing every day. And with greater numbers come more opinions and perspectives."

"Sure."

"And we're all unified behind you."

Jesus raises a brow. "You're all unified?"

"Well, we all agree on you. But sometimes you're away, and during those times, we don't have your authority to defer to."

"You have my instructions."

"Yeah, we have a goal or an instruction or someplace to go, but how we get there, how we achieve it—sometimes there's a lot of noise."

"So what are you suggesting?"

"Well, I'm suggesting we formalize a structure."

"For what?"

"For how decisions are made, how plans are formed, and what the process is for raising objections to those plans—when and how they are vocalized, and to whom. Such as how you sent Little James and John ahead to Syria to prepare. We can schedule that in advance. Or, for instance, maybe all contrary ideas are routed through Big James, filtered, and then brought to me for consideration. Just thinking out loud here."

Jesus sighs. "Simon, I love that you are trying to make things better for the whole group. You could stand to be a little nicer sometimes, but you're a leader. You always have been and always will be. I cherish that in you, and I will need it. I will need it—in time. Every one of these people I have called for a reason. Each of them brings something unique and important to the whole. I want every voice heard and none silenced. Everyone can learn from each other."

Simon's mind races, wincing from the *nicer* counsel but thrilling at the *leader* label. "Yes," he says, "but some people are troubled with tiny things, and they slow us down."

Jesus turns to Simon and stops, making Simon stop too. "I won't ask who you mean by that. But I will say that if someone is thinking about things *you* feel slow everyone down, maybe *you* need to slow down." Simon hangs his head, and they walk on. "One day, Simon, there will need to be more structure. And I see you playing a big part in it."

"With all humility, Rabbi, why not now? Why not more structure today?"

"Because I am still here."

"Yes, of course you're still here." But this gives him pause. "Are you saying one day you won't be?"

"That's a conversation for another time."

"But we will talk about it?"

"I think so," Jesus says.

"Soon?"

"Ah, there's that word, *soon.* It's the most imprecise word in the world. What is soon? A few hours? A few days? Years? A hundred years? A thousand years? Ask my Father in heaven how long a thousand years is, then talk to me about soon."

Jesus begins jogging.

"Where are you going?" Simon calls.

"To relieve Andrew of the cart."

"But it's not your time!"

Jesus chortles and turns to face him again, arms spread. "That's what I tried to tell my mother at Cana. How much good did it do?"

• • •

Matthew walks alone, Philip having gone ahead to join Jesus as he spells Thaddeus on his cart. Matthew hears footsteps as the women catch up and flank him. *How nice,* he thinks, but he also finds himself wary. "Mary, Ramah," he says. "Is something wrong?"

"Nothing wrong," Mary says. "I wanted to ask a favor."

"Of course."

"Can I borrow a tablet?"

This could be a trick, a way for Simon to see what he's been writing. "Did Simon put you up to this?"

"No! I'm going to teach Ramah how to read. We want to study Torah."

"That's what I want to do," Matthew says.

"Well," Mary continues, "they don't allow women in the bet midrash to study. How can I get to the scrolls?"

"I could copy them for you."

"Matthew, they're really long."

"Maybe," he says, "we could ask Philip what is the most important part."

"I'm pretty sure it's all important," Mary says.

"We don't even know where to start," Ramah says.

"I'll ask Philip," Matthew says.

Mary says, "Why Philip?"

"He's kind to me. Thaddeus too."

Mary looks crestfallen. "I'm sorry they're the exception, Matthew."

She looks on him with such compassion he wishes he could embrace her. Instead, he hurries on. "I'll talk to Philip."

• • •

Thomas rushes to catch up to the women. He misses time with Ramah, finding himself nearly envious of her connection to

Mary. He clears his throat to get Ramah's attention. "Everything good up here?"

"We're going to study Torah," Ramah tells him.

"Who? You and Mary?"

"And Matthew," Ramah says, making Thomas laugh.

"Matthew doesn't know anything about Torah," he says.

"How do you know what Matthew knows?" Ramah says.

"That's the point," Mary says. "Why he wants to learn."

Thomas says to Ramah, "You don't read."

"I wasn't sent to Hebrew school like you, so that's exactly what I'll learn from Mary first. It's not like we're trying to be teachers or anything. We just want to learn more."

Thomas wishes he could argue, but he doesn't know what to say. He feels conspicuous under her gaze. And she presses him. "Have you taken your shift with the cart yet?"

*That's embarrassing. And off the subject.* He wants to be her guide, her source of knowledge. "Anything you need to know you can always ask me. Happy to answer any questions. You know that, right?"

"Of course."

"Good. My turn with the cart." He runs ahead.

• • •

Matthew catches Philip and poses the question.

"A passage to memorize," Philip repeats.

"Anything that would get me started. To make up for lost time."

"No, Matthew. You didn't lose any time. It just got rearranged. You're gaining it all back now."

"But in the meantime, I want to understand the same things you do—and everyone else."

"Ah. It doesn't happen overnight."

From the front, walking next to Jesus, who is pushing the cart, Big James calls over his shoulder to the others, "There it is!"

Matthew sees the city on the horizon, and Philip says, "Caesarea Philippi, my namesake!"

Stunned, Matthew says, "Really?"

Philip smiles. "No. It's named for Philip the Tetrarch, brother of Herod Antipas—a family that does not take kindly to my former rabbi."

"Why?"

"Well, John criticizes them for things like killing their own sons and marrying their own nieces, things like this."

Matthew is learning to weigh whether his new friend is serious or kidding. This sounds serious. "I suppose he should."

"Welcome to the empire," Philip says with a wry tone. "Of course, you know more about that than any of us. No offense." He playfully tugs the expensive cloth of Matthew's raiment. Matthew nods, finally understanding some subtlety. And strangely, he is not offended.

Philip lays a hand on his shoulder. "I'm going to go up ahead. A passage to memorize—I'll work on this."

Chapter 14

# "COME AND SEE"

*Caesarea Philippi*

Philip has found Jesus even more fascinating than he expected. John the Baptizer had prophesied the appearance of the Messiah for years before finally identifying him one day. But still, Philip had not known quite what to expect. The Scriptures seemed to indicate he would be a liberator, a conqueror, a hero to Israel—setting things right between them and Rome.

In the brief time Philip has been with him, Jesus proves to be so much more—a teacher, an example, a mentor, a counselor, a friend. Philip has never met anyone so insightful and compassionate. It is as if Jesus can peer into anyone's soul and understand that person's deepest need—and potential.

The entourage enters the city and the triumvirate of John, Big James, and Simon compete to see who can arrange the most appropriate lodgings—not to mention a robust repast after a whole day on the road. Jesus asks John to take a supper he can eat on the road and go check on things in Syria. He then pulls

Philip aside. "After dinner would be the perfect time for you to look up your friend."

"Tonight?"

"Tonight. We will not be here long. In fact, we leave here tomorrow. So, as soon as you've eaten, go."

Refreshed by dinner and warmed by the conversation around the table—always most civil with Jesus present—Philip steals away to reconnect with his old friend.

Nathanael's humble apartment is less than half a mile's walk, but Philip's weary knees remind him of the day's journey. The very thought of the reunion, however, makes his fatigue fade. Nathanael was always the one with the most potential among his old friends—the one who would make it, succeed, make something of himself. And now he is an architect—imagine.

It is just like Nathanael to remain in tiny lodgings. The young man cares for his work above all—and his devotion to God. Philip can't wait to tell him about Jesus. But when he gets to the address he'd been to many times before while following the Baptizer, he gets no answer to his knock. Through gaps in the door, he sees candles and lamps burning, so Nathanael has to be home. He's much too meticulous and careful to leave without dousing those.

Philip knocks louder and calls for his friend. He takes to banging with his fist. It's much too early for bed, and he also espies Nathanael's desk and his bowl of rolled parchments. Philip makes his way around to the back and calls through the window. Strange. He climbs in, worried now.

Rushing to Nathanael's bed, Philip finds him sprawled atop his blankets, still dressed in the clothes that set him apart from laborers. If Philip didn't know better, he'd have wondered if his old friend were drunk.

He tries to make enough noise to rouse Nathanael and not

shock him, but the man is not moving. Philip gently places his hands on Nathanael's shoulders. "Hey!" he says as Nathanael groggily tries to sit up and focus. "Hey! Are you sick? What's going on?"

"Philip?"

"Yeah! Why are you in bed? What happened, my friend? Are you okay?"

"Sure," Nathanael says, but he looks terrible.

Philip holds his friend's face and raises one of his eyelids. Bloodshot. Maybe he *has* been drinking. "Oy, we need to get you some water."

Philip pours from a pitcher, and when he returns the two sit with their backs against Nathanael's cot. He waits, knowing Nathanael will open up when he's ready. Finally the whole story spills from him—the collapse of his designed building, his ruined reputation.

Philip shakes his head. "I am truly sorry, my friend."

Nathanael shrugs. "No one was killed. It could have been worse—I could be in prison."

"I'm still proud of you," Philip says, smiling, and Nathanael shoots him a look as if dubious. "I've lived through you at times, you know that?" Philip adds.

"Through *me*?"

"Yes."

"I'm living through you, man," Nathanael says.

"I mean it."

"What part?" Nathanael demands. "Going to classes endlessly? Dealing with bureaucrats day in and day out?"

"I skipped that part. I mean the part about building something with your own hands. I had a calling. I don't regret it. But while you were in the city being validated by top professionals, I was in the wilderness. With a lot of yelling. I don't deny occasionally being jealous that you had actual physical evidence to show for your efforts."

Nathanael looks away. "A pile of rubble."

Philip studies him. "You don't know what your impact was, or will be."

"I have a good idea what it'll be! A cold day in Gehenna before they hire another Jew."

Respecting his friend's genuine angst, Philip falls silent, praying for the right words. Finally, he says, "I thought I knew where God was putting me too."

"So, what *are* you doing here?" Nathanael says, smiling at last. "I thought you were out making enemies all over the place."

"I'm about to make a lot more enemies. The Baptizer sent me to someone new."

"You sure know how to pick 'em."

"He's not just anyone, Nathanael."

"That's what you said about John."

"And I was right. But this is—more."

"Hmm."

"*This* is who the Baptizer has been preparing us for."

"Mm." Nathaniel nods, clearly not buying it.

"Nathanael," Philip says, serious as a centurion. His friend looks at him, and Philip narrows his eyes. "He's the One."

"The one?"

"The One Moses foretold of and the prophets said would come."

"*The* One?"

"The One. Jesus of Nazareth, son of Joseph."

"Nazareth!" Nathanael says, laughing aloud. "Can anything good come out of Nazareth?"

"Come and see."

"Oh, a little dump on a craggy hilltop."

"I'm serious."

"No paved roads, no public buildings—they barely have a synagogue!"

"You can't do this. You really can't."

"Hey," Nathanael says, "I'm just telling it like it is. Why can't I do that?"

"Because you're mean."

"The families—illiterate day laborers and peasants, by the way—sleep under the same roof as their livestock!"

"Listen to me—"

"Honestly, Philip, saying the One is a Nazarene is practically heresy."

"Just come and see."

Nathanael sighs and shakes his head. "I—"

"What? You're gonna be late for work?"

"Wow," Nathanael says. "That's dark. So dark."

*Okay,* Philip decides, *no more levity.* "Your whole life you've wanted to serve God, to meet the Son of God, the King of Israel. I promise, you will not regret it. And if you do, I'll refund your misery. But I know you. You don't mess around. You will want to join him. He's like no rabbi who ever has been or will be."

That makes Nathanael pause. "I've never seen you talk like this." He holds Philip's gaze. "I'm still hung up on the Nazareth of it all."

But Philip is not amused. "Come and see."

Chapter 15

# LIKE JACOB

*Half an hour later*

As he and Philip trudge toward the inn where this Jesus and the others are staying, Nathanael wonders what he has gotten himself into. He will be cordial, of course, but he's not about to simply fall for any wild talk from a so-called prophet. His own career may be over, but that doesn't mean he has to settle for becoming some radical wanderer.

As they move under an elevated walkway, Philip suddenly spreads his arms. "Rabbi!"

*This* is the famous wonder worker? He's not much to look at, pleasant in expression but less than handsome. And dressed plainly, like anyone from Nazareth.

"Well!" the man says. "This is a good night, Philip. You know who stands beside you there?"

"This is my friend Nathanael."

"Yes," Jesus says. "The truthteller."

Nathanael cocks his head. "I'm sorry?" He *is* a truthteller, but—

Jesus appears to bore into him with his eyes. "Man is often deceitful, and Israel began with Jacob, a bit of a deceiver, yes?"

Nathanael steals a glance at Philip. Just because this man knows Torah . . . "Yes," he says tentatively.

"But one of the great things about you is that you are a true Israelite, in whom there is no deceit."

He speaks with such quiet confidence, such authority, but how can he know this? Nathanael turns to Philip. "What did you say about me?"

Philip shakes his head.

Nathanael turns back to Jesus. "What is this? How do you know me?"

"I have known you long before Philip called you to come and see."

Nathanael looks to Philip yet again, but Jesus says, "Don't look at him. Look at me." Jesus steps closer. "When you were in your lowest moment, and you were alone, I did not turn my face from you."

Nathanael's eyes fill. He has told no one about that moment, not even Philip.

"I saw you," Jesus continues, "under the fig tree."

Nathanael can hardly breathe. Not a soul was in sight when he sat languishing in misery there. "Rabbi," he whispers.

"There it is," Jesus says.

"You *are* the Son of God. The King of Israel."

Philip laughs and raises his hands. "I knew it!"

"Well," Jesus says, "that didn't take long."

"Nathanael doesn't mess around."

Chuckling, Jesus says, "Because I said to you, 'I saw you under the fig tree,' you believe?"

*How could I not?* Nathanael nods.

Jesus places a hand on his shoulder, and Nathanael believes

he's being touched by the Messiah himself. "You are going to see many greater things than that," Jesus says. "Like Jacob, you are going to see heaven opened, and the angels of God ascending and descending upon the Son of Man." He pauses. "That's me, by the way."

"Yeah," Nathanael says, laughing. "I got that."

"Good. I know you like to be clear."

"Rabbi!"

They turn to see Andrew running from the inn. "Sorry to interrupt," he says, breathless. "But John just arrived with a message from Syria."

Simon emerges and joins them. "He said people are already gathering to meet you, many with afflictions to be healed. Your fame is spreading. The good kind!"

"You should rest, Rabbi," Andrew adds. "We should leave early."

"Thank you, boys."

The brothers run back in, and Jesus turns back to Nathanael. "So, you wanted to help build something that would cause prayer and songs, something to bring souls closer to God, yes?"

Unable to speak, Nathanael nods. There's nothing he'd rather do.

"Can you start tomorrow?"

# PART 3
# All

Chapter 16

# THE ENDLESS LINE

*The Syrian countryside*

To Matthew, Jesus seems unusually eager to get to the site where John and others have arranged for him to see and heal hundreds of people. And that's no exaggeration. Word has spread, and reports have come back that people—mostly with afflictions great and small—have been mustering all night, waiting for him.

Having heard it's a four-hour walk, Matthew worries that Jesus does not seem to be pacing himself. Customarily he walks at or near the back of the pack and lets the others set the pace. But this is not one of those occasions where he needs solitude to prepare his message. No, he's told several that today is about meeting individuals one at a time, face-to-face, encouraging them, calling them to repentance, and healing them.

The Master strides briskly, several yards ahead of the carts containing the disciples' tents and provisions. They're scheduled to remain at this site until he has ministered to everyone—and he means *everyone*. Then they will retire for the night and move on in the morning.

As Matthew and the others try to match Jesus' pace, trading off manning the carts more frequently to avoid exhaustion, John, Big James, and Simon wend their way through the line, back to front and front to back, instructing everyone on their roles for the day. Many are assigned tent construction for the campsite, others gathering kindling and getting fires going. Still others are to prepare food. Some will fashion a tentlike booth where Jesus will welcome the crowd one or two at a time. All the disciples are expected to take turns working the crowd and staying close enough to where Jesus will be so they can help with anything he needs.

When they reach their destination, Matthew is pleased to find himself assigned to crowd control with Philip. How hard can that be? Thank the people for their patience, tell them they will soon see Jesus—in essence, keep them from becoming impatient. That should leave plenty of time for Matthew to glean what he needs from Philip. And he'll get a chance to interview people after their encounters with Jesus so he can document all the goings-on in his journal.

A little later, with the booth up and Jesus beginning to minister to people, just a few paces beyond and out of sight of the line, Simon calls out, "Philip! Matthew! You're up!"

Matthew grabs his bag and follows Philip several yards to the healing booth, basically a lean-to draped with blankets to block the sun. Jesus is inside, greeting each person, and sometimes a healthy family member or two, and immediately setting them at ease. He encourages them, hears them, and heals them. All of them.

Matthew and Philip wander the line of those waiting. It's almost as if they are in line for food, but of course there is no physical food—only spiritual. People recognize that he and

Philip are part of Jesus' entourage and look to them for instructions. Matthew is wholly out of his element. As a tax collector, he carried authority that allowed him, despite his shyness, to superintend a daily line. Here he doesn't know what to say and so mostly just watches Philip—somehow a natural at this. He's moving the line, angling it this way and that for the best efficiency. His air of authority makes people comply without question. Astonishingly to Matthew, the line keeps growing, even though latecomers should be able to see they might be standing in the sun for hours.

When things seem under control and while he waits to interview those who have met Jesus, Matthew asks Philip where would be a good place for him to start memorizing Torah. "The Law of Moses? The prophecies of Isaiah? The wisdom of Solomon?"

"For you, I think the psalms of David. A good start."

Matthew pulls out a tablet and writing implement. "I'm ready."

"For example, 'To the choirmaster, a psalm of David. "If I ascend to heaven, you are there! If I make my bed in the depths, You are there."'"

Matthew scribbles quickly. "And?"

"Just that." He turns to the crowd. "Just a few more minutes. Thank you for your patience, folks. Thank you."

"But," Matthew says, "I'm not planning on ascending to heaven or making my bed in the depths."

"You asked for a passage."

"Yes, but one that could help me understand how you and everyone else knows more."

"That's what I know and which you must come to believe if you want to make any meaningful study of Torah."

"I don't understand."

But before Philip can explain, an emotional woman hurries out of the healing booth. "Excuse me!" Matthew says.

"Yes?"

"Can you tell me what happened with Jesus?"

"He healed me!" she says.

"Healed you of what?"

"Epilepsy!"

Matthew is scribbling again. "Yes, and how long have you—" But she is gone.

"Say it back to me," Philip says.

Matthew tries to remember but peeks at his notes. "If I ascend to heaven, You are there. If I make my bed in the depths, You are there."

Philip smiles and explains. "There's nowhere you can go. No heights you can climb to in your intellectual mind, no depths you can reach in your soul where God is not with you. Do you get it?"

Matthew isn't entirely sure, but maybe. "I think so," he says.

Philip continues, "No amount of learning can bring you closer to God or make you more or less precious to Him. He's always right here, right now, with you and for you."

That sounds magnificent, and Matthew longs to believe it. But he has to admit, "I don't feel it."

"The feeling doesn't always come first," Philip says. "Sometimes you have to believe first."

Matthew knows better than that. "Believing a thing does not make it true."

Philip appears to study him. "That is wisdom. But these are not just any words. They are David's, in Scripture."

"But how do you know whether David was only talking about himself and not about everyone else? He did say, 'If *I* ascend,' not 'If *people* ascend.'"

"It almost sounds like you don't want it to be true."

A man hurries away from the booth. "Excuse me!" Matthew calls out. "Can you please tell me what happened with Jesus?"

"Are you with him?" the man says.

"Yes," Philip says. "Yes, we are his students."

At that the man rushes them, embracing first Matthew, then Philip, before running off. Matthew drops his tablet, annoyed, then scoops it up.

"Are you okay?" Philip asks.

"I'm fine. So with the passage of David, I'm just trying to understand."

"The trying is the thing," Philip says. "Meditate on it for a few days and come back to me. You're always writing things down. Try writing it down several times. Something about writing it down goes a long way."

"That's what I say too!"

"Matthew, I think we've only just begun to know all you can do."

They head back to the camp as others run by, shouting that they've been healed.

"Thaddeus! Little James!" Philip hollers. "Your turn!"

Thaddeus leaps to his feet and heads out. "How's the line?" he says.

"Getting longer," Philip says. "I'll come back out soon and help you. I won't take my full break."

Big James approaches with a full cart. "Where's Nathanael?" he says. "It's my turn to replace him."

"Says he's staying through. Doesn't want to stop his shift."

Little James limps away from a board game with Thomas. "Philip, take my place. See if you can make some headway. He's scary good."

Matthew reads from his notes to anyone who will listen.

"There have been over sixty people already, with fifty waiting in line currently, not including lepers and others who are still in line."

"Did you say over fifty in the line right now?" Big James says. "How long is this going to last?"

As usual, Matthew takes his question literally. "Well, it depends on the length of each encounter—"

"Never mind. I get it."

Chapter 17

# FAME

As Little James hurries off, Mary and Ramah approach. "Matthew!" Ramah says, "Did you get some ideas from Philip?"

"Yes, from the psalms of David—the passage to study before we learn more." He quotes it for them.

Behind him, Big James and John carry huge stones to ring the main fire as the sun finally starts to arc down from its peak. Big James assesses his hand. "It's still bleeding."

"What?" John says. "Is that from the firewood from before?"

"Yes, and then when I pushed back the man that was rushing the line, I cut it more on his bag. Hand me that rag."

Philip, sitting at the game with Thomas, says, "That same man you speak of bumped into me on his way out, after Jesus healed his wife. I believe he's one of the men who arrived here last night."

Big James shakes his head. "Almost a four-hour walk this morning, and then we didn't even have a moment to settle in. I mean, it's great what Jesus is doing, obviously, but I wish it would have happened tomorrow."

Thomas says, "That's just it. What *is* happening? What are we a part of?"

"Is it wrong to say I have no idea?" John says.

"No!" Thomas says. "It makes me feel better."

Ramah steps away from Matthew and Mary. "I think that I haven't had time to think about it," she says. "All this time my parents, I just know, hate it. Other than that, I figured Thomas and I would get our answers from the rest of you."

"The word is already spreading so fast," Thomas adds. "I didn't expect that." He rises and approaches the others. "Have you thought about the fame from all this?"

"I wouldn't mind being famous," John says.

Big James laughs at his brother. "I'm not surprised."

Matthew wonders if John knows what he's saying. Matthew himself has been famous, but for all the wrong reasons. He'd just as soon remain invisible now.

"It's not as fun as you might think," Philip says.

"I cannot remember a time," John says, "when I did not think about the Messiah at least once a week. My whole life I prayed and prayed that he would come during this time, and I just hoped that I would at least get to see him. But to be close to him, like this? A nobody like me? What's not fun about that?"

Big James appears dumbstruck. "You call today fun?"

"Maybe not fun," Philip says. "But good. But with this fame come enemies. You will be hated too."

*Finally,* Matthew thinks, *wisdom from someone who's been there.* "I'm used to that," he says.

"Well," Philip says, "you were protected. And your enemies weren't powerful."

"Speaking of enemies," Big James says, "if someone had told you, growing up, that *you* would be a student of the Messiah, you would be close to him, and you would help him in his mission, what would you have thought?"

Ramah responds slowly. "I would have said, 'Sorry, I'm a girl. Ask my brother.'"

"Fair enough," Big James says. "But really, Thomas, what would you have thought?"

"I would have thought that I don't have military training. That's still a problem, actually."

"Exactly," Big James says. "When I was a child, I used to think how amazing it would be to see Messiah kill all the Romans on my street. And I wanted to help him. I trained every day with a wooden sword."

John nods and lifts his sleeve to show his elbow. "Yes, and I have this scar that proves he was pretty good."

"I used to imagine," Ramah says, "that the Romans would break into our home, and I would be hiding under the bed with a knife. And just when they came to get me, Messiah would rescue me at the last moment."

Big James looks down. "I didn't think we'd be spending our time healing—well, watching *him* heal. And they'll never stop. The people come the more they hear about it, and we're just going to be doing this the next five years, and we'll never get to the fighting part."

Philip smiles. "Eager to bring out that wooden sword of yours, are you?"

Big James does not appear amused. "Do you honestly not know what I'm talking about?"

Mary looks self-conscious. "I guess I haven't had any expectations. That's probably why it's been a little easier for me. I can remember as a little girl hearing about how someone would save us someday, but I don't remember much about it." She looks to Thomas. "Why is it you expect a warrior?"

"Zechariah," Thomas says. "'For I will gather all the nations against Jerusalem to battle, and the city will be captured. Then the Lord will go forth and fight against those nations, as when He fights on a day of battle. In that day His feet will stand on the Mount of Olives, which is in front of Jerusalem on the east.'"

"Yes, yes, yes," Philip says. "The Mount of Olives will be split in two from east to west, and half of it will move in all this craziness, but we don't even know when this is going to be, if it's even in this lifetime."

"Here's what I also don't understand," John says. "Isn't the Messiah supposed to come at a time when all is holy? At least that is what James has been telling me."

"What is that from?" Ramah asks.

"A prophetic poem from the rabbis not so long ago," Big James says. "'And there shall be no unrighteousness in them on his day, for they shall all be holy, and their King shall be the Lord Messiah.'"

It seems to Matthew that John is trying to lighten to mood when he says, "I guess that's why the Pharisees do not think he is the One, Mary. You have to help clean out the Red Quarter first."

She laughs along with the others, then grows serious. "I don't think he's waiting for us to be holy. I think he's here because we can't be holy without him."

Matthew stares at her as the others fall silent.

Philip says, "Whoa. That's good. The Baptizer will want to use that."

Jesus has been at his task for hours, and Little James lurches into view as dusk seems to announce itself. "Big James!" he calls out. "They need you to help with crowd control. People were bickering and getting physical, and I can't help much in that department."

"Bickering?" Big James says, heading toward the line. "Are you serious? I'm going to have to use my sword on them before the Romans."

Chapter 18

# THE DILEMMA

Little James can't help envying Big James's powerful stride as he hurries off to help manage the crowd. John's big brother is a full head taller than Little James and seems to manage any physical challenge without a second thought. To Little James, it seems everything in life is a trial. Because of his stature and his pronounced limp, he must choose where he walks, scope out the terrain—and in towns with stairs, it's even more crucial that he pace himself. The others move about without concerning themselves with how they get from here to there—freeing them to ponder great thoughts, to discuss and debate. He can do that only once he's planned every step.

He's also had to learn to deal with curious eyes—some full of pity, some scorn, and some judgment. What must he or his forebears have done to leave him with such an obvious curse? He has spent his brief lifetime working to put people at ease, to hold his head high, and to ignore comments people think they're making under their breath.

Yet Jesus chose him, called him, must have seen something

in him. But what? The other disciples appear to accept him, treat him as if he belongs. Since he's been a part of this group, he has felt more comfortable, more valued, than at any other time of his life.

He heads back to the game with Thomas that he had asked Philip to take over for him. "Let's see here. How are we doing?" He laughs when he sees the mess Philip has left him.

"How do I put this?" Philip says.

"What? Are you serious?" Little James says, exaggerating his frustration. "I'm worse off than I was!" It's only a game, after all, and Thomas had been winning as it was.

"Yes," Philip says, clapping him on the back, much to Thomas's glee. "Yes, you are."

"I thought you said you were good at this."

"I thought I was."

Little James takes Philip's place at the table. "I can't get out of this now."

"Sorry, James," Philip says as he moves away.

Little James picks up a game piece, but he's less interested in this hopeless cause than in what's been going on while he was gone. "So, what was everyone talking about?"

"Eh, not much," Thomas says. "Just prophecy, our growing fame, the Messiah healing disease instead of overthrowing the Romans—small topics like that."

Little James smiles. "Well, I'm not sorry I missed it. I'm ready for this day to be over."

"What about out there? Anything happen in your short shift?"

"No, it's the same as all day. One thing that is annoying me, though, is these people. They are believing in him and praising him, and don't get me wrong, that's great. But it's because he is healing them. The Samaritans."

"Yeah, that's pretty much what he said," Thomas says. "That's all they needed."

Little James sits back, frustrated. "I know. I just don't know how many of them would believe in him if he wasn't healing them."

Thomas stares at him, and Little James has an idea what's coming. "So," Thomas says, "I have to ask—"

"I think I can guess."

Thomas smiles to assure him of his sincerity. "I have two questions. Forgive me, but I speak plainly." He hesitates. "What *is* your malady? I don't mean to offend."

"It's fine. It's a form of paralysis. It's caused problems since birth."

Many of the rest of the group have been adding to the fire and moving things into position. Mary Magdalene calls from nearby, "It's almost time for evening meal. Are you hungry?"

Little James and Thomas nod and continue their conversation. "So then why," Thomas says, "I mean … why hasn't he healed you? How do you watch all these healings today? Does it bother you?"

Little James studies the darkening sky. "Whew! Fair questions." When he was close enough to Jesus' healing booth to see what was going on, he couldn't help but wonder the same things. But he notices that every time Jesus lays hands on someone and prays for the person, he shudders, as if it costs him something, some part of himself. The Master looks spent, exhausted. Little James wonders how long Jesus can continue. It has been constant since they arrived.

But Little James owes Thomas an answer. "Um, I'm still trying to figure out how I feel about all of this. I mean, I suppose one big thing is that I haven't asked."

"Why not?"

Talk about a good question. “I don’t know,” Little James says finally.

“If I had your—struggle—and I was watching what was happening today, I’d demand it.”

“I don’t know if I should. It just doesn’t feel right. I suppose I’ve just been grateful that he called me to follow him in spite of it, but it’s never come up, not even once. I’m just afraid that if I mention it to him, it will make him change his mind about me or something.”

Thomas laughs aloud. “I’m pretty sure he knows your situation. It’s not like if you point it out, he’d be surprised.”

“That’s true!” Little James says.

A sudden clamor by the fire distracts them, and Little James is warmed to see Jesus’ mother arrive. He and Thomas join the group, welcoming her. Mary Magdalene tells her they were expecting her the next day. Mother Mary explains that friends were traveling to the area, so she came with them. “Oh, Philip! Shalom! What are you doing here?”

“I’m with your son now.”

“Is my nephew all right? I haven’t spoken to John in a while.”

“He’s fine. But he said it was time, so here I am, trying to make myself useful.”

Thaddeus introduces Matthew to Mother Mary and explains that “he wasn’t with us at the wedding in Cana.”

She welcomes him. “Oh, look,” she says, “that’s fine clothing.”

Matthew looks embarrassed. “Thank you.”

“What do you do?”

“I don’t—I was …”

“He’s a new student,” the younger Mary says. “Jesus called him.”

“Ah, lovely,” Mother Mary says. “Well, I’m sure you’re

someone special." She turns to the rest. "So was today a very long day? I saw a lot of people in line. Simon told me to come back here. Do we know when Jesus will be finished?"

"We walked here from Philippi this morning," Ramah says. "And he hasn't stopped since then."

His mother looks concerned, but she says, "He's always been a worker. He gets that from his father. Well, from both his fathers, I suppose. Speaking of work, I see the food. You all look exhausted, and I'm here to help. We'll have it ready very, very soon."

In spite of everything, Little James considers moments like this the reason he would rather be here than anywhere else in the world.

Chapter 19

# AROUND THE FIRE

Mary Magdalene nods to Ramah, and they follow Mother Mary to prepare a hearty meal for everyone. Even though there's only a rim of light remaining on the horizon, the heat of the day has barely dissipated, and faces in the firelight glisten and evidence exhaustion.

By ones and twos, the disciples head back to the healing line to trade shifts, some taking their dinners with them, others appearing greatly relieved to receive theirs upon their return. Thomas, pushing a cart, returns from his shift. Philip and Matthew finish draping the tent where Jesus will sleep—if he ever finishes his day. Mother Mary sends someone with a plate for him saying she's worried he hasn't eaten all day. It comes back untouched.

By the time the starlit sky is black, all seem to have had their fill, and Mother Mary appears to be in her element. She bustles about, collecting dishes and being sure no one remains hungry.

Eventually all wind up around the fire, the three women finally done with their chores and sitting together, Mother Mary in the middle. Mary Magdalene steals glances at the older woman, who seems to live for the comfort of others. And yet concern for her son lines her radiant face.

Eventually Simon, Andrew, and Big James tramp back, clearly dragging. Mother Mary rises quickly to fill three more plates, and when she hands Simon a cup of water, he takes a sip and pours the rest over his head.

"Who remains with Jesus?" Mother Mary says.

"Thaddeus and Little James," Simon says.

She looks toward where she'd seen the line earlier in the day and seems to consider checking on Jesus herself. But she rejoins the group as the three stragglers finish their meals and collapse by the fire.

Mary Magdalene finds herself amused at Simon, who rests on one elbow and mutters, "Andrew, I need a mental break. Do one of your meaningless question games."

"They're not meaningless," Andrew says. "They're interesting. And I've got one I've been thinking about lately. What would you do for unlimited money? Or what would you give up to have all the money you could ever want for the rest of your life?"

"You mean," Big James says, "would I do something painful?"

"Yes!" Andrew says. "Or crazy? Would you run through the marketplace with no clothes on, screaming?"

Mary winces, and Mother Mary looks shocked. Ramah smiles broadly.

Thomas says, "Of course not. I'd be killed by a soldier."

"Plus it would be immodest," Big James adds. "It would be a sin."

"Fine," Simon says. "Something that wasn't a sin. Would

you give up your left hand if you would be rich the rest of your life?"

"Maybe not a full hand," John says, "but a couple of fingers, sure."

At chuckles all around, Andrew says, "What about love? Would you give up ever getting married?"

"I don't know," John says. "Simon? Is marriage worth it?"

"Absolutely. But you'll never be so lucky to find someone like Eden, so—take the money."

Mary Magdalene is struck at the quiet reverence of the others when Mother Mary speaks. "I've never had much money my whole life," she says. "And I've been happy."

"I don't expect we'll have much money for as long as we're following him," Thomas says.

"But I can tell from your clothes," she says, "that you have had some money before, yes?" He looks down, smiling. "Are you happier now or then?"

John interrupts. "Ask Matthew."

Andrew stares him down. "John ..."

"What?" John says. "That was a bad question? You brought up money. Matthew's had it; we have not."

Mary Magdalene is horrified for poor Matthew, who looks miserable. "I feel better now," he says softly. "I don't know if that means happy."

Big James says, "It's not polite to talk about personal money."

"It was just a question," Andrew says. "I think about it sometimes, and then I feel guilty."

"For what?" Ramah says.

"For thinking about things I shouldn't. For wanting things I shouldn't care so much about." He pauses. "Sometimes I feel like I'm living someone else's life. Like when I look at myself from the outside, it doesn't always feel like me. It feels like someone who's trying to live up to the heroes of our history. Like I have to do something great. But I know I'm not great. Know it even more now, being with him."

"I understand," Ramah says. "I feel like I need to not make any more mistakes."

Mother Mary leans toward her. "How do you think I felt?"

"You must feel that every day," Andrew says. "No?"

"Not anymore," she says. "He always reassured me. And God always made me feel like I shouldn't be burdened."

Mary Magdalene has long wanted to ask. "So how did you feel when it happened? His birth. Even before that. How did you know—when did you know—who he was?"

"Oh, I don't know," the older woman says, smiling. "We're all tired. Do you really want to hear all that?"

In unison, everyone says, "Yes!"

Mary Magdalene and the others wait as Mother Mary laughs and pauses. "Well, nothing about it was easy, I can tell you that. It didn't happen in my hometown, my mother wasn't there, we had no midwife. I don't know if I'm ready to give all the details, maybe some other time. But I do remember this: When Joseph handed him to me, it was like nothing I expected. It was like everything I'd heard about having a baby, but I thought this would be completely different."

"What do you mean?" Simon says.

She looks directly at him. "I had to clean him off. He was covered in, um, I will be polite; he needed to be cleaned. And he was cold, and he was crying. And—he needed my help. *My* help—a teenager from Nazareth. It actually made me think for just one moment, *Is this really the Son of God?* And Joseph later told me he briefly wondered the same thing. But we knew he was. I don't know what I expected. But he was crying and he needed me. And I wondered how long that would last."

She pauses, her glowing eyes alive with the memories. "He doesn't need me anymore," she says. "Not since we taught him how to walk and eat. He hasn't needed me for a long time, I suppose. And after Joseph passed—may he rest in peace—he grew up even quicker. And I wish I could say that made me happy. Of course, as a Jew I'm excited to see everything he does for our people, and I'm proud of him. But, as a mom, it makes me a little sad sometimes."

She pauses again and looks down. Finally she says, "So it's good to be with all of you for a bit. I can find ways to help."

"We'll take it," Ramah says, placing a hand on Mother Mary's knee, and others nod.

"Simon," Mother Mary says suddenly, "when you were just with him, did it seem it would go for very long?"

"It's tough to tell. The line was dying down, but he won't send anyone away, so we'll see."

"I'll go check on them," Mother Mary says. But before she leaves, she gathers more plates.

When she finally moves toward the dwindling line, those remaining with Mary Magdalene at the fire have fallen silent. Finally Thomas whispers, "I didn't know he lost his father. I lost mine several years ago. I'll have to ask Jesus about that. Has anyone else lost a parent?"

Mary raises her hand. "Mm-hm."

"I'm sorry. Was it recent?"

She shakes her head. "It was when I was a little girl."

"That's painful," Simon says. "Sorry."

"Thank you. It was. I didn't fully understand it right away. But eventually it made me really angry. And I left when I was young."

"Left home?" John says.

"Left everything. Everything. I tried to stop acting like a

Jew. I tried to stop being myself. And then later, as some of the people from our town—including some of you—knew about, worse things happened. Most of it is a blur, but I forgot so much of everything I learned as a little girl."

"But now you can catch up," Big James says, and she appreciates the kindness in his voice.

"Yes. I hope. With Matthew and Ramah. You all are so far ahead, and you're so good at all of this."

"We're not as good as you think," Big James says.

"Most of us are not, James," John says, "but you were the one with your nose in the writings. Still are."

"Ah, a little," Big James says. "Not as good as others."

"Oh, come on, you could recite half of Torah if you had to."

"Maybe. Yeah, maybe."

Thaddeus returns and joins the circle. "Still going," he says with a sigh. "I couldn't do any more, but they said they've got it."

Mary shakes her head. "I really want to be a good student."

Andrew says, "I don't think any of us went to bet midrash to study after school. That's what's so surprising about all this. Thomas, did you?"

"No, I was in the family business the day after I graduated. Thirteen years old and I was preparing and serving food at weddings. I was not a student at all, believe me."

Thaddeus says, "I wasn't even good at praying until recently. I would get bored with it. You know, the same thing over and over. I learned to love it as I got older."

"I wasn't great at any of it when I was a student," John says.

"I wasn't either," Thomas says. "I didn't like all the rules."

"I never struggled with it," Ramah says. "I do what I'm told."

Andrew says, "Yes, I'm the same. I've always been a rule follower."

"I've always loved the history, the stories," Big James says, "so I've always loved the rules too."

Andrew, a twinkle in his eye, says, "Simon?"

"I've had my moments."

This makes the others laugh. Thomas says, "One time when my parents were asleep, I had meat with cheese, just to see what I was missing. Have you ever done that?"

"No," Andrew says. "I'd feel too guilty."

"You feel guilty about everything," Simon says. "Right after you were born, you said sorry to Ima for causing her pain."

"Forget the guilt," Thomas says. "I was sick for days. I haven't violated a single food rule since."

"I tried pork once," Thaddeus says. "We were traveling, and we were in a Gentile marketplace, and I just grabbed a piece. Aah, it was marvelous!"

"One time on the boats," Big James says, "we were approaching a Shabbat sunset. Abba and John had finished their tasks, and I still had to put my fish in the barrels because I had so many."

"No," John says, "it was because you were going too slow, because you're too careful."

"No, it was because I had so many."

"Okay," John says, but shakes his head at the others.

"So," Big James continues, "you have to put them away, obviously, before the sun sets, or they'll rot the next day, and you can't clean them during Shabbat. So I started yelling to the others, 'Hey! Come on! Help me!' No! They laughed at me and walked home. And I had to work so hard and so fast, I ended up spilling some of the fish back in the water. But I finished just in time. And I was breathing so hard, I vomited on the shore."

"He had to wait two whole days to clean it up," John says. He looks to Mary and Ramah. "Oh, uh, sorry." They giggle.

"I've grown to love being Jewish," Thomas says. "And I've grown to love following the Law. But it can be exhausting."

"Following the Law?" John says, "or being Jewish?"

"Both," Andrew says.

"It always has been," Big James says. "Even before the occupation."

"Yes," Mary says. "But aren't we used to it by now? Hasn't it made us stronger?"

After a pause, Thomas says, "I don't get it, if I'm honest. I don't know why God has allowed the occupation. I'll have to ask Jesus more about that. Why this has been allowed for so long? It's hard to feel like the chosen people."

"I've been there," Simon says.

Ramah says, "But it's all worth it now, yes? The wait is over."

This seems to silence everybody, but Mary can see something in Simon's expression. He's staring at Matthew. *Please, no,* she thinks. But of course he will not be dissuaded.

"What about you?" Simon says to Matthew.

He looks up, appearing pained. "What do you mean?"

"Has it been difficult for you, all this time? The occupation, following Jewish Law?"

Mary knows what Simon is driving at, and she knows it cannot be lost on Matthew.

"My life has not been easy," he says.

Sarcasm dripping, Simon says, "Oh, it hasn't? What was more painful for you—escaping Roman persecution by working for them or escaping your guilt with all the money? And now you're catching up on Torah and wanting to follow the Law. Why now, all of a sudden? Why not all the other times you had the chance?"

"Simon," John scolds.

Mary wishes this would stop. A fun, healthy, robust conversation has come to this.

"No, no, John," Simon says. "I want to know. Mary had horrible trauma. She didn't choose what happened to her. What's your excuse, Matthew?"

"What do you want me to say? I don't know what you want from me."

"An apology," Andrew says, and Mary wonders, *him too?*

"What?" Matthew says.

Mother Mary and Little James return, making the younger Mary's heart sink. Surely Jesus' mother needn't hear this bickering.

Chapter 20

# THE ATTACK

Mary Magdalene feels helpless. It is not her place to tell the men to lay off Matthew. But how she wants to, especially with the older Mary taking all this in! Don't they all have pasts, things they shouldn't have done, things they bitterly regret? Can't they focus on everything that is new because they've been chosen to follow Jesus?

But they don't let up. Andrew continues the attack. "Simon's not wrong," he says. "He could be more delicate about it, but you did choose to work for the Romans, and you made my life even harder than it already was. And you haven't apologized."

It appears to Mary that Matthew is eager to apologize. But Simon must have noticed that too, for he immediately cuts him off. "No, don't say it," he says, standing. "I don't want you to apologize. It doesn't matter. What will hearing him say he's sorry do? I won't forgive it anyway."

John turns on Simon. "What keeps putting you in authority? Who are *you* to forgive or not to forgive?"

"What, you're on his side?"

"No, of course not! But you've had your problems too! What about apologizing for what you almost did to my family with the Romans?"

"I didn't go through with it! I was trying to save my family's life, and I love you, John, but that's not something you had to worry about with Zeb and Salome looking out for you. But you, Matthew, you put me in a desperate position where I did things I would never have done otherwise, and I've repented for them. And John and James, I *am* sorry, but I didn't go through with it!"

Now even Thomas weighs in. "What *is* your excuse, Matthew? I was a successful businessman, and yet I was always behind."

"He wasn't your tax collector," John says.

"Quit defending him!" Thomas says. "I want an answer!"

Now Big James stands. "Hey! You're new!"

Simon stares down at Matthew. "Do you even know what it's like to be Jewish? To suffer for centuries and centuries because of it, but to still commit to it? To protect our heritage, even though it never stops being painful? Because the *one* comfort we have is to know that we're doing it together, that we're all suffering together. But if we just wait a little longer, if we hold tight just a little more, we'll have rescue because we're chosen. All of us. And you betrayed that, and you spit on it! I can't forgive it! I'll never forgive it!"

Big James faces him. "All right! You've said what you needed to say. Sit down, Simon."

Now Andrew rises. "You sit down first!"

With the two sets of brothers facing each other and the rest appearing to watch breathlessly, a noise from the trees silences them all. Someone approaches. It's Jesus. Even from a distance, Mary can tell he's drained, spent. It's as if he can barely put one foot in front of the other. He's staring at the ground, shoulders slumped as he staggers toward the camp.

She wonders if the argument, the vitriol, now sounds as meaningless to the combatants as it does to her. The men look chagrined, ashamed, and they clearly don't know where to look. As Jesus slowly reaches them and passes, Mary winces at the sweat pouring from him, the fatigue in his face. There's blood on his hands and face. He appears to struggle for breath. He slightly lifts one hand in greeting and wearily sighs. "Good night."

He slogs to his tent and holds one of the poles for support, breathing shakily. Bending to reach for his sandals, he groans. His mother watches, deeply pained. She hurries to him, and as the younger Mary looks on, she helps him shed his tunic. "Oh, Ima," he whispers. "Thank you."

She takes off his sandals and sponges his feet. Mary Magdalene notices Big James and John sit back down and the others look away.

"You've got blood on your hands," his mother says, cleaning them as well. She wipes his face, cleaning blood from his forehead.

"I'm a mess," Jesus says. "Good now?"

"Good," she says, and he embraces and kisses her. "What would I do without you, Ima?"

"Now get some sleep," she says.

"Okay. I'm so tired."

She helps him down as he crawls onto his mat, shuddering. While his mother sets his sandals aside and hangs his tunic, he begins his bedtime prayer. "Blessed are You, Lord our God, King of the Universe, who brings sleep to my eyes and slumber to my eyelids. May it be Your will, Lord my God, and God of my ancestors, that I lie down in peace, and that I arise in peace."

With the fire crackling, crickets chirping, and the wind

picking up, young Mary is overcome. She and Ramah rise with the others, and all head for their beds. If Jesus' mother hadn't felt his need for her for years, she had to feel it this night.

# PART 4
# Opportunity

Chapter 21

# PARALYZED

*Hebron, Palestine, 14 BC*

Six-year-old Jesse is up early, earlier than the friends with whom he loves to romp. Full of energy after breakfast, he begs to go out and play before milking the sheep. His mother relents but tells him, "Be back soon. Father is counting on you."

Jesse races through a meadow outside the city to the tree he loves most to climb. Today he's determined to go higher than he ever has, to see over the walls and espy his own house. Later he'll bring his friends back and see who can go even higher.

He scrambles up the familiar branches and looks to see how much farther he might go. Plotting each grab and foothold, he shimmies ten more feet to where he can reach and pull himself higher. He grabs a thick twig close to where it juts from a long branch and envisions settling on that and seeing as far as the horizon.

But just as he supports his weight with both hands, the twig snaps and gives way, and he hurtles down. Reaching for anything to break his fall, Jesse is merely flipped, cartwheeling in the air. He has only enough time to pray he lands on anything but his head—which would surely kill him. He somehow lands feet-first, and everything goes black.

• • •

An hour later, Jesse's father angrily calls for him, wandering the neighborhood. None of his friends have seen him. One points far to the north, where the top of Jesse's favorite tree looms. "Wait here," the man tells the boys.

As more of the tree comes into view over the rise, Jesse's father sees nothing and calls for him again. Finally, he finds the boy in a heap at the base of the tree. Dead? He races to him and gently, urgently positions him on his back. Jesse's little chest is heaving. His father tries to urge him back to consciousness, to no avail. He gathers Jesse in his arms and runs back to the village, the boy's head and limbs flopping.

By the time they reach a healer's home, the boy has roused, moaning.

"Where does it hurt?" his father says.

"Head. Shoulders. Back."

"How about your legs?"

"Fine, I think."

Jesse's father sets him down to walk into the healer's place, but the boy cannot stand on his own. The healer rushes out and helps carry Jesse inside and onto a table. He assures the father that the wounds above the waist are superficial and should heal in time, despite some pain. Nothing broken. But as he probes Jesse's feet and legs with a pointed instrument, he asks what the boy feels. Nothing from his toes to his hips, despite no evidence of broken bones here either. "Only time will tell," the healer says.

• • •

Time proves cruel. Jesse puts on a brave face, but it pains him to have to drag himself anywhere or be carried. His father sits him under the sheep where he can still help with milking, but he knows his father could more easily do this himself. Most days Jesse watches his old friends run and play. Often they wave to him and occasionally sit with him, but he knows they will soon tire of this.

His mother kindly spends a lot of time with him, but Jesse feels guilty, responsible for the pain in her eyes. It seems to excite her when she tells him she is with child and presses his hand against her belly to feel the movement of a new brother or sister. Jesse eagerly awaits a sibling, though he worries that having a healthy child around will make him feel even more alone.

When the day finally arrives that a midwife appears and his mother gives birth, Jesse's father tries to reassure him that her cries of distress are normal and will soon be forgotten in her joy over another son. But at an almost inhuman shriek, the father rushes in to help the midwife, only to find that his wife has died. Now it is left to Jesse and his father to raise baby Simon.

Jesse is immediately enamored of the little one and feels more needed than ever. As his father takes on the roles of both parents, awkwardly learning to cook and clean, Jesse must hold and feed the baby. His deep grief is softened by little Simon's coos and smiles, and it seems to Jesse that they're bonding when the baby locks eyes with him.

• • •

By the time Simon turns six—the age Jesse was when he was paralyzed—Jesse is twelve. The boys are thick as thieves, sharing a bedroom, even developing a ritual good-night handshake, and regaling each other with whispered stories and jokes. Their father carries Jesse to Hebrew school every day as Simon tags along. He can't wait to be big and strong enough to take Jesse himself. He feels fiercely loyal and protective of his big brother.

When their father remarries, Simon is pleased with his choice of a bride. Simon and Jesse happily look on at the wedding ceremony. Simon stands next to Jesse, who sits on a mat, his lifeless legs outstretched. When Simon is pressed into the ritual marriage dance with the other boys, he stops them midway through and beckons them to Jesse's mat. He takes one of his brother's hands, and another boy takes the other, and they form a circle around him, pretend to dance as Jesse sits there, including him in the activity in the only way possible.

At home, their stepmother proves to be just the tonic for Simon's father—and for him and his brother. Besides being a good cook and truly caring for her husband, she seems to genuinely like the boys. Simon and Jesse grow even closer, spending hours together every day and talking into the night till they fall asleep. One of their most common topics of conversation is the occupation of the city and how oppressive the Romans are to them and their fellow Jews. Simon dreams—and talks—about one day doing something about that.

When Simon turns fourteen and has become as big as his brother, he pushes twenty-year-old Jesse around Hebron in a cart. They go everywhere together. One day as they wend their way through the narrow streets of the city, they come upon Roman soldiers hassling citizens, one of whom tries to break free and run. A centurion throws the man to the ground and beats him unmercifully. As the citizen lies there, unable to defend himself, the centurion kicks him.

Simon is outraged but feels helpless. He narrows his eyes and vows to do something—some day. He parks Jesse's cart near a wall and walks across the way to talk with friends he knows as secret rebels. They urge him to join their cause and offer him a scroll of instructions and plans. He hesitates and looks back to Jesse, who shakes his head. Simon takes the scroll.

That night, before they fall asleep, they talk about it.

"I hate them too," Jesse says, "and I'm angry that I will never be able to fight them. But you're much too young to become a Zealot, Simon. Promise me you won't."

"They train people my age," Simon says. "I can't just stand by and allow our people—not to mention our own family—to suffer at the hands of Rome." He reaches across the small table between their beds, and the brothers share their ritual handshake.

• • •

Jesse labors to fall asleep, troubled by the anger and resolve in his brother's eyes. Everybody hates the Romans, but to openly oppose them, as the Zealots do, means risking one's life. Happy as Jesse has been with his stepmother, he still misses his birth mother and cannot fathom losing another family member. Plus he needs Simon, not just because of the myriad ways he helps him get through everyday life, but also because they truly love each other. Simon has been his constant companion his whole life, his best friend.

In the morning, Jesse awakens slowly, not surprised that Simon has already risen. It's not uncommon for his brother to help their stepmother prepare breakfast before returning to rouse Jesse. But what's this? A small scroll in Simon's bed. Jesse pulls himself to where he can reach it and settles back onto his cot to open it.

His eyes fill as he reads:

*My dear brother, by the time you read this, I will be halfway to the mountains to join the Zealots of the Fourth Philosophy, in the spirit of our great King David who sang: "Zeal for your house has consumed me."*

*And from Zephaniah, "Behold, at that time I will deal with all your oppressors. And I will save the lame and gather the outcast, and I will change their shame into praise and renown in all the earth."*

*Jesse, when you stand on two feet, I will know the Messiah has come. I will fight for the freedom of Zion in order to see that day.*

*With deepest affection, your loving brother, Simon*

## Chapter 22

# DESPAIR

From the day his beloved brother disappears to join the Zealots, Jesse spirals into a pit of misery he cannot escape. He realizes more than ever how dependent upon Simon he has become. Not only has Simon been his mode of transportation, but they are more than siblings. They are best friends, confidants, and until now—Jesse believed—inseparable. Their nightly ritual handshake means nothing now, if Simon could abandon him.

Jesse knows enough about the Fourth Philosophy to know that acolytes are forbidden to maintain contact with their families. They are to give themselves completely to the Order for rigorous training, which only a select few endure to become official members. Jesse prays that Simon will be among the majority of recruits who voluntarily muster out and return to their former lives. But he knows better. Simon, even as young as he is, is nothing if not a man of resolve. He had exercised and built muscle just to be able to serve Jesse, all while fuming over the Roman occupation and committing himself to rebelling at his first opportunity.

To keep his aging father and stepmother from having to cart him everywhere, Jesse is forced to rely even more on his overdeveloped hands, forearms, and elbows, thickly calloused from dragging himself everywhere. He's always been frustrated by his physical malady, of course, but his brother had kept him occupied and engaged.

But now Jesse allows bitterness to creep in. He's asking *Why me?* and resenting having to ask others for help. The friends he and Simon ran with soon tire of including him in their activities because he's a burden. And when they do lug him to where he can watch their activities, that's all he can do—watch.

Though he knows his predicament is not the fault of his father and stepmother, Jesse can't help taking out his anger on them. Deep in his heart, he knows that even a secret message from Simon, spirited out of the Fourth Philosophy's enclave in the hidden caves, would assure him he's still loved and that his brother still cares.

But nothing comes.

Jesse sees the pain all over his parents, who try to cheer him. Every day he feels worse, useless, hopeless. He cannot fathom a future beyond despair, and he resists when they take him to the synagogue every Shabbat.

Finally, his father prevails upon his own bachelor brother, Jesse's Uncle Ram, to travel all the way from where he has settled in Egypt and become a live-in attendant to Jesse.

Late one night, Jesse hears his uncle trying to persuade his father to take Jesse to the Pool of Bethesda in Jerusalem, where miraculous healings have been rumored. Every so often, it's believed that an angel disturbs the water, and the first person in is healed.

"It's near the Sheep Gate, surrounded by five covered porticoes—"

"I know where it is, Ram," his father says, sounding disgusted. "And I know what it is—nothing but a shrine for a healing cult. We Hebrews are forbidden—"

"You've tried everything else!" Ram insists. "What could be the harm? Do you expect me to invest the rest of my life—"

"I thought you were willing! And I'm paying you ..."

"Not enough."

Jesse can't confide in Uncle Ram the way he could with Simon, and his uncle doesn't seem to want to hear Jesse's complaints. But this whole idea about the Pool of Bethesda intrigues him, actually gives him hope.

And so he hatches a plan.

• • •

Meanwhile, in the hills fewer than thirty miles from Hebron, Simon has already become a favored trainee. With long, full days of training, he is layering muscle upon muscle and learning both offensive and defensive hand-to-hand combat techniques that quickly turn him into a human weapon. In just a few years, he becomes deft with weapons until he is finally presented with his own custom-made dagger and welcomed into the Order as the youngest-ever official member of the Zealots.

But he too has been suffering. On the one hand, he has never felt more like a man, stone-faced and committed. He detects fear in the eyes of other recruits when they're assigned to spar with him, and he senses that even the mature members are wary of his fierce aggression. And yet he cannot stanch his own tears in the night as he misses his family—and mostly his brother. Has he done the right thing, trusting others to manage Jesse?

No one must see his emotion or they would suspect his determination and commitment.

• • •

Back home, Jesse has deteriorated into a miserable, bitter man. He barely speaks to anyone in the family and must be forced from his bed every morning. He allows himself to be moved only to the river for his morning ablutions and to the table for meals. He has given up fighting the weekly trip to the synagogue, but he doesn't even pretend interest. He resists any attempts to get him out into society.

Late one night, Jesse quietly wakes his uncle. "What would you do for me if I were to promise you my entire inheritance upon my father's death?"

"What are you talking about?"

"You know what I'm talking about. As firstborn, I am to receive—"

"I know, and with your brother having turned his back on the family …"

"I am entitled to his share too."

"That could amount to a lot of money, Jesse."

"And it can all be yours."

"Don't ask me to do anything illegal, or to have any part in harming your father."

"Don't be ridiculous. I just need you to get me to the Pool of Bethesda. And for that I would guarantee in writing that you get my inheritance when Father passes."

"He would never forgive me. But he might be relieved that you're gone—you give him nothing but grief."

"Will you do it?"

"Of course, but I need you to understand, it would not be just for the money. I truly believe it's worth a try. But I dare not enter the edifice. The only Jews allowed in there are Pharisees who watch for this very thing."

"Get me to the entrance and I can make my way to the edge of the pool."

"But how will you get into the pool when the waters are disturbed?"

"Leave that to me. I'll find a way."

## Chapter 23

# THE ASSIGNMENT

*The Pool at Bethesda, Jerusalem*

Uncle Ram carts Jesse to the entrance and lays him on his stomach, loading his back with as many foodstuffs as he can carry and covering him with a thick mat of blankets. He bids Jesse farewell and Godspeed and tells him he'll try to keep in touch. Jesse knows he will not likely ever see his uncle again, and neither will his own father—betrayed by Ram when he acceded to Jesse's plea to be delivered to the pool.

Of course, Jesse's father will never know of the arrangement the two have made, but he threatened to disinherit Jesse if he left. Uncle Ram may have made this trek for no reward when his brother passes. Jesse can't imagine ever seeing his brother, Simon the Zealot, again either, as the Fourth Philosophy Order is as opposed to the dark magic origins of the pool as the Jews are.

Jesse is full of hope, excited to carefully, painstakingly pull himself poolside without spilling his cargo. When the blankets shift, he tries to wriggle them back into position. A small band of seemingly helpful people—most of them women—approach and help him, welcoming him. "We haven't seen you here before," one says. "Is anyone with you?"

"No. But I will be here only as long as it takes to be healed."

"Well, if your food runs out, call for us. We try to bring a little something for everyone every day."

"Bless you," he says, hoping to never need their help.

But as he deftly pulls himself along on his elbows and finds a spot near the water's edge, the stench of the place overwhelms him. Many of the men and women—the blind, the deaf, the mute, the lame, the crippled—look and smell as if they have been here for ages. One would think that their frequent plunges into the water would keep them somewhat bathed. But of course there's no reason to be in the water unless you are first.

Jesse stakes out his spot and begins arranging the fruits and vegetables and loaves he hopes he won't need for long. Then he practices surging off his mat of blankets and onto the stone floor, feeling young and strong enough to beat anyone to the water when it stirs. But after his third practice run, he returns to find people absconding with his food. "Hey!" he shouts. "That's mine! Leave it!"

They ignore him and deliver the food to their loved ones, also waiting for the stirring of the water. What can a virtually legless man do?

Jesse lies on his stomach, facing the water, ready to pounce at the first movement in the pool. A man lying nearby tells him, "Nothing happens after sundown. Get your rest and be ready at dawn."

Jesse thanks him but cannot sleep. He worries about more theft, but mostly he is eager to show the rest of these unfortunates his speed. He is through with the practice runs, but occasionally pulls himself up and tries a first maneuver on his elbows. He's confident, ready, but already exhausted, especially with no sleep.

The next morning, Jesse eats the last bit of food the robbers have left him and stares, trying not to even blink, at the water. The sun reflecting off the pool makes him squint, but he's ready. "How often does the water stir?" he asks his neighbor.

"We never know. That's up to the angel. It's happened as many as three times in a day, but then we might go four days with nothing."

A small group of Pharisees keep their distance but are clearly on watch.

"Looking for Jews who shouldn't be here," the man says. "Ignore them."

"Don't worry."

Jesse's eyes grow heavy, and he fights with everything in him to keep from dozing as the morning hours wane. He had no idea how uncomfortable lying on a stone floor all day would be, even with his thick mat of blankets.

Suddenly a cacophony erupts, and with groans and shouts, every lame and sick person scrambles madly toward the water as a bubbling rises in the center. Jesse is off like a slingshot, despairing to find he is among the last to even get near the edge. Dozens have run, dived, or been thrown into the water by loved ones. Many stampeded right over him. He can't tell who is first in, but they apparently are not healed, as surely they would be celebrating.

But it'll happen for him, he knows that. Next time, he will be ready. He sets up as close to the water as he can, as optimistic as ever. He might even return to the synagogue, the Torah, to God, if he's successful.

• • •

Decades later, Jesse is emaciated, grimy head to toe, and his reflection in the pool is of a man whose unkempt hair and untamed beard are speckled with gray and white. He's tried to get into the water hundreds of times, not even once being among the first dozen. And now he's too old, weak, and frail to even keep trying. He's not once been visited by anyone.

He subsists on the fruits, vegetables, and stale bread brought by the charity workers. The Pharisees long ago quit even giving him a second glance. His mat is a ragged, stinking mess, and he spends most of his days on his back, often napping more than he sleeps each night. More than once he tries to drown himself in the middle of the night, holding his head under the water.

• • •

*The Jericho Enclave catacombs of the Fourth Philosophy*

By now, Simon has earned seniority as a Zealot, favored by his rabbi and the leadership. The day finally comes when he is considered for an assignment unlike anything he has had before. He's considered for a role in distracting and then assassinating a Roman magistrate on the streets of Jerusalem.

Simon and the other conspirators are taken to a secluded village near the Dead Sea where they rehearse the entire episode until every man knows his part. Simon is to carry a basket of fruit, run into a passerby, and drop his basket while a man haggling with a merchant starts shouting and another sets afire a wagon of hay. When the magistrate and his bodyguards startle at the conflagration, Simon is to attack from behind, thrusting his dagger to the neck of the Roman and whispering in his ear, "No Lord but God," before slicing his throat.

When Simon and the others return to the enclave, he receives word that he has been summoned by Menachem, the leader of the Order. Simon's rabbi confides in him, "I told him you were up to the task, as inventive as you are dedicated, and that you have never failed me."

Simon bows, jaw set.

"Make me proud. If Menachem signs off on this, it's a go."

• • •

*Campsite outside Jerusalem*

Jesus' disciples gather materials for a little building project. As Mary Magdalene weaves flowers with Mother Mary, she says, "I've never been to Jerusalem."

"Really?" the older Mary says. "How is that possible?"

"My father never took me and my mother to the feasts."

John, stacking branches nearby, says, "This is your first Feast of the Tabernacles?"

"No," Mary says. "This is just my first time in Jerusalem."

Behind the women, Thaddeus, Philip, and Matthew work on a rudimentary wood structure. Thaddeus tells Matthew, "A tabernacle is a temporary dwelling."

"A tent," Philip adds.

Matthew looks offended. "I know what a tabernacle is," he says. And then he clearly attempts a joke, grinning. "So, what, do we have to build one to eat?"

No one responds.

"I was being facetious," he says.

Philip stops his task to face him. "God says to live in a booth for seven days during this feast to commemorate how the Children of Israel lived in temporary shelters for forty years in the desert."

Matthew looks at the largely roofless construction. "We still are."

Big James weighs in. "One of three pilgrimage holidays where every able-bodied Israelite male would travel to Jerusalem and present himself before Adonai. You really don't know about any of this stuff?"

"I've already admitted I don't know all of it. I didn't pay much attention. I do recall my father used to leave three times a year."

Mary has a question. "Why is it only the men are required to go?"

"It can be a perilous journey," Simon says. "Difficult for children and the sick, people who need caretakers, but no one is prohibited. I've taken Eden many times."

Andrew, working next to Thomas, pricks his finger on a thorn and shouts, "Ow! Sharp!" He shoves his finger into his mouth.

"All right," Simon says, "I need some bodies to go into town with me. Nathanael gave me a list of supplies for this masterpiece of his."

Andrew, finger still in his mouth, raises his other hand. "Mmm! Pick me."

Simon squints at him.

"Pick me, Simon!" Andrew says, like a little boy.

Simon nods. "As long as you stop doing that."

• • •

*The Enclave catacombs*

Simon the Zealot finds Menachem, leader of the Fourth Philosophy, in his massive office and stands in the doorway, waiting to be recognized.

Menachem looks up from his work. "Enter."

As Simon approaches, Menachem points to the floor. "Please."

As Simon removes his skull cap and kneels, the leader steps from behind the desk and joins him, sitting cross-legged on the floor. Simon fights to control his pulse and breathing. He has never been alone with Menachem and knows this meeting alone is monumental to his future.

Menachem seems to study him, his eyes barely visible in the candlelight, set deep under his forehead and framed by long, black hair and a beard to his chest. Finally, the older man speaks. "Whom do you serve?"

"El Shaddai. God of power and might. God of war."

"What is your name?"

"Simon, son of Zebulon, son of Akiva of Ashkelona." How he wishes he could add, "Brother of Jesse," but his beloved sibling has become a wisp of memory.

"For what were you born?"

Simon has never tired of answering this question. Face set as stone, he says, "To cleanse Israel of her enemies. To expel all non-Jews from Jerusalem, as the Scriptures demand."

"Which Scriptures?"

"From the scroll of Moses, Shemot: 'Whoever sacrifices to any god, other than the Lord alone, shall be devoted to destruction.'"

An ominous pause nearly makes Simon wonder if he has failed to recite the quote verbatim, but he knows better.

"You will travel to Jerusalem for the Feast of Tabernacles."

This is not news. He has done this annually since joining the Zealots. "With the Order?"

Menachem shakes his head. "Two days prior. You will leave first thing in the morning. In Jerusalem, you will assassinate an enemy of God."

This is what he has been training for. "The Roman magistrate, Rufus."

"You will be met by your brother in the city."

His brother? Simon has not mentioned Jesse's name in all the years he has been here. He looks up. "M-my brother?"

"A Jerusalem Zealot and his team. They have been tracking Rufus. Once you have been briefed on the Roman's movements, you will lead the team."

"Yes, Master."

"Carry out your orders, Simon of Zebulon, or never return."

• • •

*Jerusalem market*

Shmuel searches an alleyway for something, anything to stand on to speak. As he emerges with an apple box, his Pharisee superior says, "It doesn't matter. Any kind of crate or pallet. A stone would work."

"A stone, Yanni?" Shmuel says, incredulous. "This is a public teaching!"

"I picked this market specifically because it serves so many poor. They're hungry for the words of a teacher. And they're probably afraid of you."

"Afraid? Of what?"

"It's the Holy City. You're a Pharisee. Just relax. Let us pray. 'Blessed are You, Lord our God, King of the Universe, Who bestows good things upon the unworthy'—"

"The *Birkat Hagomel*? But that's the blessing for life-threatening situations."

"You'll be fine. This is the first step to gaining a following. And once you have, your message will have even greater weight in the Temple—for both of us. Good luck." And Yanni turns to go.

"You're leaving?"

"These people are hungry for the Word. I'm hungry for breakfast. Would you prefer we pray the *Ha'tov ve'hametiv*?"

Shmuel nods, and they say in unison, "'Blessed are You, Lord our God, King of the Universe, Who is good and does good…'"

Alone, Shmuel realizes that no one—shoppers, vendors, or travelers—even notices him, robes and all. He's not in Capernaum anymore. What will he have to do to gain the ears of all the visitors here?

## Chapter 24

# THE PHARISEE

*The Pool of Bethesda*

Jesse perches closer to the edge than he ever has, determined to be the first to notice the stirring of the water. As soon as the bubbling begins, he drags himself forward, only to be trampled, yet again, in the stampede. In the end, he pulls himself farther away.

"You okay, Jesse?" his neighbor says.

"Uh-huh."

"You're moving from the edge?"

"There's no point. It was a dumb idea."

"You're not going to try anymore? You know, Jesse, if you don't have any hope, then why are you still here?"

He hangs his head. He's been asking himself the same thing. But where would he go, and how would he get there? His wracked body is at least accustomed to the unforgiving stone, and the reek of his mat no longer repulses him—as it does everyone else. The charity workers toss him just enough sustenance to live on, and he has proved incapable of killing himself. How much longer can he survive? His fondest wish is to die in his sleep. Perhaps God will be merciful to him that way, even if he never repents of turning his back on Him.

• • •

*Agora Gate checkpoint, City of Jerusalem*

Four nearly naked, bloated bodies hang lifeless on hideous crosses in the sun, their dried blood evidencing whippings with cats-o'-nine tails that leave them unrecognizable. The putrid odor of death draws flies and maggots. Nearby, a screaming man is stretched and nailed onto a cross that will be hoisted and dropped into a hole, ripping more of his flesh as he hangs to eventually die. Steeled as Simon the Zealot has been trained to be, even he steals a glance at this anything-but-subtle message: Don't mess with Rome!

As he nears the city wall, Simon reaches a centurion interviewing every entrant. "What brings you to Jerusalem?"

"Uh, the festival, the pilgrimage."

"You're a few days early."

"I have family here."

"In what district?"

"Near the Antonia Fortress."

The soldier scans him head to toe. "Are you carrying weapons?"

"No."

The man frisks Simon anyway. Fortunately, anything he needs for his assignment will be waiting for him inside. "You're free to go."

The condemned man whose cross is being lifted over the hole shrieks, "No! No!"

"What was his crime?" Simon says.

"Murder."

The assassination should be easy. Escaping the city will not be. Simon's risk has been made plain.

As he steps around the guard to enter the gate, a Roman in civilian garb who has been watching Simon from a fruit stand approaches the guard. "Yes, Atticus?" the guard says.

Simon has been trained to recognize such men—*Cohortes Urbanae,* a force of elite police established by Caesar Augustus to act as marshals or soldier investigators. Simon slips out of sight and stops to listen.

"What is your name, soldier?"

"Linus Cilnius, sir," the man says, sounding stricken, petrified.

"Linus," Atticus says, "I want you to take your next assignment very seriously."

"My next assignment, sir?"

"The Antonia Fortress is not a residential area. It is a public forum. That man does not have family there. Do you understand?"

Linus lowers his head.

Atticus addresses another officer. "Axius, send Linus Cilnius home and take over this checkpoint."

• • •

*Inside the city*

Nathanael finds it interesting, if nothing else, to have been pressed into service designing a rudimentary tabernacle booth for the disciples outside Jerusalem and to see it actually constructed by his new friends—laymen laborers all—in a matter of hours. He is amused now to have been assigned to buy foodstuffs along with the former wedding caterer Thomas—whom he finds quirky.

Their burlap sacks are full of vegetables and fruit. Thomas

pulls a pomegranate from his bag and holds it before his face as they walk. "Oh, I am so hungry. It's all I can do to not bite into this."

"I was hungry too," Nathanael tells him, "but the vendor had a stain on his tunic that looked like baby spit-up. It nauseated me."

"I know. I heard you tell him that."

"Be patient," Nathanael says. "You shouldn't eat right now. Your hands are filthy."

Thomas glares. "You really don't hold back, do you?"

"I'm just being helpful. You want to impress Ramah, right?"

"What?"

Nathanael is amused by this feigned surprise—as if no one knows of Thomas's interest in her. "You heard me," he says.

As they emerge from an arched walkway, they come upon a Pharisee addressing a small crowd. "Your prophets have seen for you false and deceptive visions," he announces. "They have not exposed your iniquity to restore your fortunes but have seen for you oracles that are false and misleading. I say to you, brothers and sisters, fellow children of Adonai, we must always be on guard against the false prophets among us—"

"Psst!"

Across the way, Nathanael sees Matthew, out of view of the speaker but beckoning him and Thomas.

"—who use God's words not to praise Him, not to glorify Him, but in the pursuit of their own power."

"What are you doing?" Thomas calls out, and Matthew recoils, appearing horrified at the thought of being exposed.

The speaker continues: "Often we think of false prophets—"

Thomas turns to Nathanael. "Matthew is so irritating."

"Makes sense," Nathanael says. "You're kind of the same person. All numbers and logic. Except he can't tell jokes."

"Guys!" Matthew whispers.

"We should see what he wants," Nathanael says and heads toward him, Thomas following.

"That Pharisee knows us," Matthew says. "He does not approve."

"What do you mean?" Thomas says.

"He is Shmuel, and he used to live in Capernaum. He once yelled at our master."

"That guy?" Nathanael says.

"Shh! He called for his arrest at the house of Big James and John's father. We should go."

"Where?" Nathanael says. "The meeting place is a block away."

"What are the odds?" Thomas says.

Both Matthew and Thomas begin counting on their fingers.

Nathanael shakes his head. "You guys are both actually calculating the odds. Look, Matthew, just stay out of sight. This Pharisee doesn't know our faces, only yours. If we see the others he might recognize, we'll head them off, hm?"

Matthew nods and hurries off while Nathanael lingers with Thomas to listen to Shmuel.

"Tomorrow night begins the Feast of Tabernacles," Shmuel says. "Over one million Jews are flooding into our city at this very moment from every corner of Israel. To observe the Feast, yes, but some may bring with them an agenda. Some false teachers may seize upon the large crowds to spread their heresies …"

"You see what I mean, though," Nathanael says to Thomas. "About Matthew and you?"

"Please don't speak," Thomas says.

## Chapter 25

# BETTER

*Jerusalem, evening*

In the Lower City, about as far removed as he could be from the Antonia Fortress, Simon the Zealot approaches a home. He stifles a smile, amused that the same *Cohortes Urbana* he had overheard dressing down that guard trails him now. The man—whom the guard had referred to as Atticus—must think he's surreptitious enough to remain invisible. And he might be, to everyone but a member of the Fourth Philosophy.

Simon ducks into the covered entryway and knocks, welcomed into a secret passageway to a tunnel beneath the street. In seconds, he has eluded his tail and is on his way to another entrance, several doors from the home he entered. There he is greeted quietly by a man who looks much too young to be a Zealot, let alone involved in an assassination plot.

"Ithran," Simon greets him, following him to a back room where his associate, Honi, leans over a map of the city.

"We've tracked Rufus for two months," Honi says.

"At the end of every Shabbat," Ithran says, "he goes to The Valerian, his favorite restaurant in the Upper City."

"No other patterns?" Simon says. "No other places consistently?"

"To the Praetorium every day, of course," Honi says, "but it's heavily guarded. The restaurant is utterly exposed."

"He always has a guard," Ithran adds. "And when he is with his wife, two guards."

"This Yom Rishon tradition is a problem," Simon says. "If the streets are empty for Shabbat, it will be harder to create a diversion—a challenge to get into position."

Honi says, "The Roman is smart to choose Shabbat."

"Of course," Simon says. "Never underestimate the enemy."

"We have an ally with a shop on the square," Ithran says. "We could store the weapons there and be ready as soon as Shabbat ends."

"Excellent. And I need a cart with dry straw."

Heading out, Simon espies the Roman watching from a catwalk above.

• • •

*Jerusalem campsite*

Jesus' disciples spend the day finishing construction of the Nathanael-sketched sukkah for the Festival of Tabernacles. Simon nails beams along the top as Thomas hoists fabric coverings and Nathanael supervises. Mary Magdalene and Ramah weave fronds and flowers, while others help Mother Mary prepare the food for the Shabbat dinner that evening.

• • •

*The Upper City*

Meanwhile, Simon and the other two Zealots, dressed as laborers, acquire and arrange everything they need for the diversion that will give Simon the opportunity to attack his prey. They hide weapons and roll a cart of straw into a hidden alley, where they swab it with a sticky, flammable liquid. Everything will have to go perfectly, but Simon the Zealot has trained his whole adult life for this, and he is willing to die for the cause. With the mysterious *Cohortes Urbana* shadowing him, he's still willing to commit the assassination—even if it means he's immediately killed. He will not return to the Fourth Philosophy catacombs unless and until the deed is done.

• • •

*The campsite*

Just before sunset, the rudimentary sukkah is beautifully adorned, hanging candles lit, the table laden with bread and wine and meat. Nathanael puts the finishing touch on an embellishment just over his head and proclaims, "Done!"

Everyone, including Jesus, smiles and applauds. "Woman of Valor!" he calls out.

And everyone responds, "Who can find?"

They take their places around the table and finish the Shabbat recitations.

Matthew is preoccupied with the shelter itself. "With all due respect, Nathanael," he says, "I know you are a skilled architect, but this thatched roof won't keep the rain out."

"That's the point," Nathanael says from a few seats away. "The vegetation provides shade from the sun during the day."

Mother Mary adds, "And if a few raindrops get through, it

is a reminder of our dependence on God, of His provision, and of how our people were so vulnerable in the wilderness, yet He brought us through."

The younger Mary speaks up. "There was a time in my life—in my old life—where I had to sleep outside. This *is* a good reminder of how I was delivered from that."

Jesus says, "This time of dwelling in booths is also a leveler of people. Wealthy or poor, everyone sleeps outside—as equals."

"But let's be honest," Andrew says, gesturing at the loveliness of their location. "Not all booths are created equal."

Everyone laughs.

Jesus says, "Yes, Nathanael, the beauty of this booth is itself an act of worship."

"Rabbi," Big James says, "I have a question."

"Yes?"

"In the prophet Zechariah, it is written, 'Then everyone who has survived, of all the nations that have attacked Jerusalem, shall go up year after year to worship the King, the Lord of hosts, and to celebrate the Feast of Tabernacles.'"

"Wait," Thomas says. "What?"

"Zechariah says that?" Simon says.

"They read that passage at the Feast every year," Andrew says. "You just don't pay attention."

"Well," Simon says, "there's a lot of readings. They sort of run together."

Jesus says, "What exactly is your question, Big James?"

"One day our enemies will celebrate this feast? With us? Babylonians? Assyrians?"

"The Romans!" John adds.

"Jews and Gentiles at this table? What would have to happen for that to be possible?"

"Something will have to change," Jesus says.

"But the booths won't mean anything to them," John says.

"We're the ones who dwelt in temporary shelters," Big James says, "while we wandered the wilderness. Not them."

Jesus gazes at him knowingly. "Everyone has wandered through the wilderness at some point."

Big James nods.

Matthew says, "If all the nations came to celebrate in Jerusalem, there will not be enough room—not by … I will not bore you with the calculations."

Philip smiles at him and nods.

"I think it will not be Jerusalem as we know it now," Jesus says.

Thomas says, "Certainly not."

"But if Zechariah prophesied it," Ramah says, "it will be fulfilled, right?"

"It just sounds impossible," Thomas says.

Mother Mary says quietly, "I know a thing or two about prophecies that sound impossible."

That silences everyone. Finally, Jesus says, "Anyone have other questions?" And he and his mother share a look.

• • •

Later that evening, Jesus sits alone at the campfire when Simon and John approach. "Hello, friends," he says. "Have a seat, please."

They sit and look at each other. Simon says, "You go, John."

"Rabbi," John says, "we may have a problem."

"I'm listening."

"Shmuel is here," Simon blurts.

"*Our* Shmuel?"

"He was on a street corner today," John says, "raising the alarm about—false prophecy."

"He means you, Rabbi," Simon says.

"You sure?"

"Yes, well, he's been—"

"I'm joking, Simon," Jesus says with a twinkle. "I know he means me. So Shmuel is in Jerusalem talking about me." He pauses. "That's even better."

John cocks his head. "Better?"

"I think I'm going to see someone inside the city tomorrow. You may come if you'd like. I enjoy the company. And bring Matthew. It will be good for him."

Chapter 26

# THE RENDEZVOUS

*Solomon's Porch*

Simon the Zealot and comrades from the Jerusalem Order gather at the Temple. A Levite priest reads from the scroll of Zephaniah:

"'He will quiet you by His love; He will exult over you with loud singing. I will gather those of you who mourn for the festival, so that you will no longer suffer reproach. Behold, at that time I will deal with all your oppressors …'"

Simon always warms at the promise of this familiar passage.

"'And I will save the lame and gather the outcast …'"

*The lame.* That jumps out at Simon as never before. Is it possible his crippled brother is still at the cursed Pool of Bethesda?

"'… and I will change their shame into praise and renown in all the earth.'"

Simon is suddenly compelled to leave, to find out for himself if Jesse is still in Jerusalem. He moves to a ledge of the Temple

Mount that overlooks the southeastern checkpoint at the Agora Gate, where criminals hang on crosses. Will that be him after this evening? It very well could be. He must see Jesse one last time, just in case, regardless of where that takes him.

• • •

*The Agora Gate Road*

Simon the disciple strides toward the city with Jesus, John, and Matthew. "So, Rabbi, this person you need to see—do we get to meet him in the Temple?"

"No, actually, the opposite. The Bethesda Pool."

"Really?" John says.

Jesus says, "Here we go again."

"It gets stranger and stranger with you, doesn't it? I love it."

"Why is it strange?" Matthew says.

"Because," John says, "the history of the pool is pagan. I don't know much about the details. James usually knows that stuff, but, uh—"

Simon jumps in. "The pools used to be a shrine to the Phoenician god, um—?"

"Eshmun," Jesus says.

"Right, right, and then the Greeks and the Romans turned it into a place of worship for a healing cult of Asclepius."

"Very good, Simon," Jesus says.

John looks perplexed. "How do you know this stuff?"

"James isn't the only one who reads, John. You should try it."

Jesus laughs.

"I do know about the pools, though," John says. "Every day the water steams and bubbles, and some people believe it's stirred up by an angel, who heals the first person who gets to the stirred water."

"I've read about this," Matthew says. "That there are places on earth where hot vapor steams up from the ground intermittently, or makes water boil, and no one knows how."

"Ah," Simon says, looking at Jesus. "I wouldn't say no one. Is that why we're going? You gonna tell us?"

"Someday," Jesus says, "someone will figure it out, and they'll tell everyone. But for now, we have a checkpoint to pass. Everyone behave yourselves."

To Simon, Jesus appears to agonize over the dead men hanging on the crosses in the sun.

• • •

*A Jerusalem market*

The *Cohortes Urbana* has an appointment, and to his dismay, his contact looks rich and resplendent. "Could you look any more Roman?" he chides the man. "I'd have asked you to meet me in the town square if I'd known you'd show up looking like a senator."

"I don't get paid to blend in," the man snarls. "I'm Petronius, and I assume you are the *Cohortes Urbana*?"

"Atticus Aemilius."

Petronius seems to study him. "Your reputation precedes you."

"And that is why I meet in alleys."

"You're a long way from home."

"I go where the work is."

"And what work is here for you, Atticus?"

"Your magistrate. Surprised? Something on Rufus's calendar puts him on a narrow road in the Upper City just off the square."

"The Valerian. It's a restaurant. Rufus eats there every Saturday after Sabbath."

"Oh, lovely. But you've got a skilled assassin who wants to cancel Rufus's reservation."

"What?"

"Did no one ever teach you to mix up the routine?"

"He's inflexible about it!"

Atticus can't believe it. That's the rationale? "Good," he says sarcastically. "That's good, don't deviate. Do everything exactly as you'd planned."

"No, I can't risk his life! Go arrest the assassin."

"Do you know who the Zealots are?" Atticus says.

"They're extremists. They reject rabbinical—"

"They're martyrs with a persecution complex. Arrest him and we'll be only adding fuel. Torture him and he gets a seat closer to his god. No, I want to kill him, Petronius. In the act. And then I want to watch his rat pals scurry their way back to their nest with a story they can't glorify, can't teach to the next class of recruits. And do you know why?"

"Why?"

"Because we were just better than they were. That's why. Rome won."

"You should be a general," Petronius says.

"Now, what fun would that be?"

"Well, you're going to have to lay out your plan to the magistrate and his wife."

"She'll go for it before he does."

"Ten denarii says she doesn't."

"I don't need the money," Atticus says, and walks away.

From childhood, Atticus has been obsessed with justice. Nothing fulfilled him more than defending his younger brother and sister from bullies. Joining the Roman Legion as a young adult fulfilled a lifelong dream, but it didn't satisfy. Ambitious, he wanted to do more than simply defend Rome. He wanted to become known for his vigilance, his acumen, his expertise. Atticus learned to be the first to volunteer, and for the most dangerous missions possible. He quickly rose through the ranks, and when Caesar Augustus decided to create a police force to combat roving gangs employed by various political parties, Atticus was among the first chosen. Besides higher pay, he soon enjoyed power, prestige, and the attention of the emperor himself.

Now in the prime of life and his career, Atticus had become the darling of the government, entrusted with the choicest of assignments and free to set his own schedule and agenda. He immersed himself in the clandestine minutiae of the secret orders, primarily the Zealots, and kept tabs on their every strategy.

That gave him entree also to the rest of the Jewish population and its bizarre code of ancient rules. Justice and self-advancement may have seemed incongruous to many, but such had become Atticus's life. Now, if he could pull off the ultimate ruse and thwart the Zealots' assassination plot, he could kill two birds with one stone.

## Chapter 27

# THE REUNION

*The Pool of Bethesda*

Jesse has resigned himself to his fate. He cannot fathom, nor does he wish to, how many years he has lain here, hoping against hope that he would somehow miraculously find his way into the water before anyone else. But even those with loved ones assisting them have been unable to accomplish that. It's the blind, the deaf, the mute, the ones with withered arms or hands who still have functioning legs and can fight their way past everyone else for any hope of healing.

Oddly, though Jesse forced himself to believe in the magic, he has to confess he has never seen anything miraculous. Oh, sure, there are those who plunge in first and come bounding out, shouting for joy and claiming success. But a few days later they are back, in the same condition. Still, no one surrenders hope.

Except Jesse.

But this has become his life. The occasional chat with his invalid neighbor. A few scraps to eat, thanks to the charitable volunteers. He long ago grew accustomed to the stench—human feces, oozing sores, body odor, trenchant bad breath, even rotting food. Jesse knows the odor remains pervasive, however, because visitors cover their noses and mouths and find reasons to stay only as long as they have to.

Today is no different. But for some reason, Jesse feels a tingle of excitement in anticipation of the stirring of the water. That has never left him, despite his having given up ever benefiting from it. He lies nearly catatonic when the water erupts. He is curious enough to see who wins the race—this day it turns out to be a woman, flung into the water by two young men. Her sons? She appears unable to leave the pool on her own, so who can say what has been gained, if anything?

Jesse pulls himself to where he can sit in the sun with his back to a wood pillar. He is as filthy as ever, his feet and legs caked with grime, his clothes in tatters, his scraggily hair and beard infused with gray. Wearily, Jesse closes his eyes, longing to doze even for just a few minutes. Sleep at night is rare and anything but restful.

A shadow blocks the warmth of the sun, and he opens his eyes to a well-dressed young man with a trim beard, generously muscled, and on one knee. "Jesse?"

Who knows him by name?

"I'm your brother, Simon. Do you remember me?"

"Simon?" It cannot be.

His neighbor perks up. "You have a brother?"

"Uncle Ram, at Abba's funeral, told me I could find you here."

This man knows his uncle's name, but Abba can't be gone, surely. Jesse laughs. "You must be thirty years old! You're not Simon."

"I'm almost forty, Jesse."

Is it really him? Jesse sees the resemblance. What if it's true?

He sits, staring. "I've been here twenty-five years …" Something dawns on him. "You make the pilgrimage every holiday?"

"Yes."

"And you knew I was here."

"Our order forbids coming to the pool."

"I'm your brother!"

"This place is a pagan cult."

"Since when do cults bother you?"

Simon turns, appearing to take in the ghastly scene. "I was embarrassed—for you. Do you really believe in this?"

Incensed, Jesse lashes out. "You try living for thirty-eight years without legs that work, and then tell me you wouldn't try anything and everything! Why wouldn't you at least come by once and carry me into the water? You could have tried."

"It is not in our God's nature to pit sick people against each other in a twisted game. I won't play it with you!"

"Is it in our God's nature that His children would slit each other's throats? Have you no regard for the commandment that we shall not take another's life?"

"You and I, Jesse, we both know the Scriptures: There's 'a time to kill and a time to heal; a time to break down and a time to build up.' The land must be purged."

"Then what about our family, hm? Are we to be purged too? You left me. You left all of us!"

"I left you to save you."

"Do I look saved to you?"

That appears to stop Simon. "I can't believe it," he says finally. "You are worse than you used to be."

"My legs are the same as when you left."

"I'm not talking about your legs. I'm talking about you. This godforsaken place has turned my strong brother into someone hopeless."

"And what should I hope in after all these years—you and your murderous kind?"

"Jesse, it's killed me to watch you suffer in your life, and I am sorry. I truly am. But that's not the only kind of pain, and you're not the only one who feels it. But you know what? I am at least doing something about mine. I'm not sitting in a bed waiting to die."

So, there it is. Jesse sighs and looks away. "Have you said all you need to say?"

"I have to be in the Upper City."

"Oh, that's nearby. Less than a mile away. Might as well be a thousand miles to me." Trouble is, Jesse knows what Simon and the Zealots do on such assignments. And so he talks himself into speaking his mind. "Whoever it is, don't do it. It's not worth it. If they catch you, they'll kill you!"

"I am not afraid of death." Simon pauses. "I just wanted to say goodbye. Because I didn't do it right the first time." He stands and brushes himself off. "I do love you. And I love God. Goodbye, Jesse."

As Simon turns to talk away, Jesse digs out a nearly shredded piece of parchment and reads: "… by the time you read this, I will be halfway to the mountains to join the Zealots of the Fourth Philosophy, in the spirit of our great King David who sang: 'Zeal for your house has consumed me.'"

"My note," Simon says, his back still turned. "I was a better writer then."

"'And from Zephaniah, "Behold, at that time I will deal with all your oppressors. And I will save the lame and gather the outcast, and I will change their shame into praise and renown in all the earth."'

"'Jesse, when you stand on two feet, I will know the Messiah has come. I will fight for the freedom of Zion in order to see that day.'"

Simon finally turns to face Jesse again. "I stand by it. Farewell, Jesse."

Jesse sobs as his beloved brother walks away.

## Chapter 28

# "LOOK AT ME"

*A square in the Upper City*

All lies in place for the ambush. Simon the Zealot stealthily moves into place where his compatriot, Ithran, hides with the cart of flammable straw. Simon is determined to push from his mind—at least during the assassination—every vestige of his sobering visit to his brother. Jesse looked so bad, smelled so bad, sounded so defeated.

Simon knows he has failed to fully focus on the task at hand when Ithran says, "We don't have much time. Hey. Hey! What's the matter?"

"Nothing. Just focused." How long has it been since he has so blatantly lied?

He quickly changes clothes as Ithran continues, "Our men are in position. When you see Rufus and his escorts pass the side street entrance ...Hey, focus! ... side street entrance, you'll have thirty seconds to get into position."

Simon puts on a hat and accepts a dagger from Ithran, which he tucks at his waist under his cloak. Will he become a murderer, as Jesse has charged? No, this will be just. He will be doing what God wants him to do—rid this so-called Holy City of at least one infidel. He grabs the basket of fruit he plans to drop when he bumps into another comrade to cause the first distraction.

• • •

Simon of Capernaum follows Jesus, John, and Matthew to the Pool of Bethesda, where he is immediately assailed by the foul odors. The pool itself reminds him of the smaller baths he and his fellow Jews use for purification rites. "This is what all the fuss is about? An oversized mikvah?"

They stand at the top of the entrance steps as Jesus appears to take in the whole scene.

John says, "I have a feeling we haven't seen it all yet."

Jesus slowly descends two steps and stops. "That's him," he says.

"Who?" Simon says. There are so many damaged bodies—broken, lame, deformed, dying—so many desperate people in tangled heaps on the stone floor, all appearing to peer at the water.

Jesus points to a ravaged man lying on his side on a disgusting excuse for a mat, his hands serving as a substitute pillow to cradle his face. "The one who's been here the longest . . ." Simon is struck by the sadness, the compassion in Jesus' tone. ". . . but who doesn't belong. The sad one."

Simon feels the eyes of John and Matthew as he whispers, "Why do I get the feeling this isn't just a meeting?" He pauses at the sight of a cadre of five Pharisees huddled near a wall. "Do we need to be on the lookout?"

"No," Jesus says. "Just stay with me and watch." He moves down the stairs, gingerly stepping between the afflicted, who groan and cough. Simon and John follow, but Simon notices

Matthew has hung back, covering his mouth and nose with a handkerchief. Finally, he joins the rest.

Jesus nods to the Pharisees as he passes them, all seeming to eye him guardedly. None return his nod. He approaches the man on the mat and says, "Shalom."

The man opens his eyes. "Me?"

Jesus smiles at him. "Yes."

The man shrugs, still prone. "Shalom," he says warily.

"I have a question for you."

The man raises his brows. "For me?" He sighs heavily as his neighbor rises on one elbow to see what's going on. "I don't have many answers, but I'm listening."

Jesus peers down at him. "Do you want to be healed?"

Simon is struck by what seems a ridiculous question, and he's not surprised when the man simply stares.

The man responds, "Who are you?"

"We'll get to that later," Jesus says. "But my question remains."

The man suddenly brightens, and he sits up, his back against a wood pillar. "Will you take me to the water?" he says.

Jesus shakes his head.

The man's smile disappears. "Look," he says wearily, "I'm having a really bad day."

"You've been having a bad day for a long time. So …?"

"Sir, I have no one to help me into the water when it's stirred up. And when I do get close, the others step down in front of me!" With a tremor in his voice, he looks away. "And so—"

Jesus kneels to face the man. "Look at me," he says. "Look at me. That's not what I asked. I'm not asking you about who's helping you, or who's not helping, or who's getting in your way. I'm asking about you."

The man begins to sob. "I've tried!"

Jesus nods. "For a long time, I know. And you don't want false hope again. I understand. But this pool, it has nothing for you. It means nothing, and you know it. But you're still here. Why?"

"I don't know."

"You don't need this pool. You need only me. So, do you want to be healed?"

The man tries to force a smile and nods.

"So," Jesus says, "let's go. Get up, pick up your mat, and walk."

Simon can't stop a grin as John pulls his journal from his satchel.

The man stares at Jesus, hope creeping into his visage. He gasps and slaps at his thigh, clearly feeling something. He laughs aloud, looking at his neighbor and drawing the attention of the Pharisees. He presses his hands to the ground and his back to the pillar and rises, giggling till he cries. Jesus smiles. Simon can barely contain himself as John scribbles and Matthew stares wide-eyed.

Jesus reaches for the man, cups his face in his hands, kisses him on the cheek, and pats his face before retreating.

"Who—?" the man says.

Simon approaches as Jesus slips away. "Time for you to walk, like he said. Don't forget your bed."

The man gathers the rotting shreds. "Why does this matter?"

"Because you're not coming back here," Simon says. "That life is over. Everything changes now."

The ranking Pharisee, Yanni, marches over. "You!" he bellows, pointing at the man. "It's Shabbat! What are you doing?"

Matthew says, "Torah forbids carrying a mat on Shabbat?"

"Not Torah," John mutters, still writing. "The oral tradition."

"Yes!" Yanni says, turning to John. "Transporting objects from one domain to another violates Shabbat."

"The man who healed me—"

John faces Yanni. "Do you not realize what just happened? Why are you trying to make this about Shabbat?"

"—he said to me, 'Take up your bed and walk.'"

"Who did? Who told you that?"

"He did!" the man says, pointing. But Jesus is gone. "I don't know. He didn't tell me his name."

"No, of course not," Yanni says. "He performs a magic trick and tells you to commit a sin! A false prophet. This will be reported."

"Report whatever you want! I am standing on two legs!" He hurries off with his mat, then turns back. "I'm sorry, I need to go find my brother."

Chapter 29

# THE STING

*The Upper City*

As darkness descends, marking the end of Shabbat, Simon the Zealot rushes into place. Any minute, Rufus and his wife, Octavia, will head for The Valerian for their customary Saturday night dinner. With his basket of fruit and in pedestrian attire, Simon blends in with the scant number of others in the square, the city not yet bustling following the Sabbath.

A Roman official and an obvious bodyguard step from an alley, appearing to scan the area. They nod to someone out of sight, and the Magistrate Rufus and his wife emerge in their finery, holding hands, heads hidden in hoods.

Though they're carefully guarded, it's time—now or never. Simon makes eye contact with his associates, one who will pose as a vendor and the other an irate customer—just as they have rehearsed dozens of times. As Ithran, dressed as a laborer, pulls the straw cart through the square, Simon is to collide with him and drop the basket of fruit. And here he comes.

Simon strides into him and the fruit goes flying, rolling

in the street. As he profusely apologizes and bends to gather it up, the vendor and customer loudly escalate their exchange, and the magistrate and his wife take notice. Simon sets his jaw. Everything rests on this, and his mind is finally clear. The timing is perfect.

"You think I'm a fool?" the bogus customer rages. "You think I don't know the difference between gold and brass? I curse you, your family, your children, and your children's children! And when they have children, I curse them too! You are an imbecile, huh? Scam artist! I will destroy you and your family and your children!"

The magistrate and his wife approach, appearing wary, their eyes on the argument. Simon surreptitiously reaches for his dagger, ready to pounce, as Ithran lights the hay. "Fire!" the customer shouts.

But just as Simon is about to lunge at the magistrate, his brother, Jesse, passes by, carrying his mat. What? How can this be? Simon's vow washes over him, having pledged to believe the Messiah has come if he ever sees Jesse whole again. As his brother moves out of sight, Simon looks back at his prey, only to discover that it's not Rufus at all—he has a stand-in! As the guards spirit Octavia away, Atticus—the *Cohortes Urbana* who had followed him the other day—lifts his hood and draws his own weapon.

Simon rises slowly. He'll defend himself if he must, but he has to get to his brother. "Jesse?" he whispers, and he runs off, leaving his companions to escape on their own.

He rushes around a corner to find Jesse striding away. Jesse turns and sees Simon, drops his mat, and points to his legs, breaking into a jig that makes them both howl with laughter. They embrace, but Simon quickly pulls away, knowing he must flee or die at the hands of Atticus.

• • •

Simon, John, and Matthew catch up to Jesus as he exits the Agora Gate. Laughing, Simon says, "That was great! Thank you for letting me see that!"

"Thank you for being with me," Jesus says.

"Well," John adds, "the Pharisees were pretty upset."

Simon says, "That was almost as much fun to watch as the miracle."

"This week should be fun, huh?" John says.

"I do have a question, Rabbi."

"Yes, Matthew?"

"Waiting thirty more minutes would not have mattered to that man. Why did you do this on Shabbat?"

Jesus stops and turns to face the three of them. "Sometimes," he says, "you've got to stir up the water."

# PART 5
# Spirit

## Chapter 30

# THE INTERROGATION

*Countryside between Jerusalem and Jericho*

Mary of Magdala loves the company of those she considers her new family—silently reveling in a life so different from her past. Her so-called friends from not so long ago were as desperate as she to merely exist, survive, tranquilizing themselves with alcohol and carnal pursuits, wasting their meager resources. Mary inwardly celebrates this new existence, unencumbered by raging headaches, demons, spells, and short-lived respites achieved through carousing, gambling, and drinking.

Following the man who redeemed her and called her by name—her real name—brings her joy unspeakable. Though the road is long and the journey exhausting, how she cherishes dining with an entirely new cast of acquaintances! Well, not entirely new. She had seen the fishermen—Simon and his brother, Andrew, and Big James and his brother, John—in The Hammer, the bar she frequented. But though they drank a little and gambled a bit, they were known as otherwise devout, observant Jews. And she had been aware of the tax collector, Matthew, but she avoided him—her income so meager she was not worth his pursuing.

But these men are now all following Jesus, and—like her—they abandoned their previous lives. No one can fully articulate what made them all do this. It was Jesus, of course, and when his identity was revealed, and proved over and over, it made sense. The man could see through you, into your soul. He knew you, really knew you, and when he called, you followed—end of story.

Even when the men squabble, and sometimes worse—seem to nearly come to blows—she feels privileged to be among their company. They all treat her with respect, deference. Care. They do not gaze longingly at her as have so many in the past. Oh, perhaps Matthew does—such an unlikely suitor with his precious quirks and sweet spirit, despite what all the others accuse him of and some still hold against him.

Mary has to admit that at times she enjoys drifting away from the group. As a woman, she is not referred to as one of Jesus' actual disciples—and yet he certainly treats her as one. She does not understand why a person of her gender had not been allowed to study Torah or attend Hebrew school as a child. But clearly Jesus honors her, treats her with the same compassion as he does any of the men. He even encourages her study of the Scriptures and urges her to help young Ramah in the same pursuit. Precious Matthew has been so helpful with that.

How different things seem today as she excuses herself to pick fruit alone. She takes with her a basket and a few scraps of parchment on which she has written the short Scriptures she and Matthew are trying to memorize and teach to Ramah.

Pronouncing a blessing over the citrus trees reminds her of her childhood and her dear father, a loving, devout man who often taught her passages to memorize. How she treasures the fact that her people had been taught to praise God for every detail of their daily existence. As she gathers the fruit, she peeks at her notes and recites, "'Blessed are You, Lord our God, King of the Universe, whose world lacks nothing and Who made the wondrous creatures and good trees, through which He brings pleasure to the children of Adam.'"

She sniffs a persimmon, which smells heavenly, but the other side feels mushy and proves to have rotted. Mary tosses it aside and moves to another tree, consulting her notes again. "'If I ascend to heaven, You are there. If I make my bed in the depths, You are there.'" She forces herself to look away from the parchment and recite the passage from memory.

But as she reaches the second phrase, the clip-clop of hooves on the nearby road distracts her. Over the rise appears a Roman soldier on horseback, his brilliant red attire contrasted with the field grasses and trees and sky. In an instant, Mary is transported to her teens, when just such a military man stalked her, chased her, forced her into an alley, and had his way with her.

Suddenly, she can barely breathe. She drops her basket and races behind a tree. As she peeks through the branches, stunned by the memory of the trauma and how it overwhelms her now, the soldier is met by another, galloping from the other way. Desperate to remain out of sight, Mary covers her mouth to silence her sobs, crumples the parchment, and tosses it away.

The soldiers trot off in opposite directions.

• • •

*The Chamber of Oils, Jerusalem Temple courts*

Jesse has been summoned to speak with two Pharisee leaders. Normally that would terrify him, yet now it merely proves he's no longer invisible. He has walked and skipped and run all over the city since he was healed, telling anyone and everyone what happened. He's more than happy to tell these two as well.

The one who had confronted him on the Sabbath for carrying his mat has brought another holy man from the Sanhedrin, Shmuel, and it seems Yanni is trying to show him how to aggressively interrogate Jesse.

"Did he tell you his name?"

"Just today, actually." Jesse paces, unable to suppress his grin. "Jesus!"

"Jesus who? From where?"

"Lineage," Shmuel adds. "Origin."

"Should I know his favorite food too? He told me his name, that's it." Jesse continues to pace and bounce on his toes.

"There were a million Jews here for the Festival," Yanni says, "thousands named Jesus."

"Jesse!" Shmuel says. "Stop pacing!"

"With all due respect, Rabbi, I've been still for thirty-eight years."

"Tell us exactly what he said," Yanni says. "Again!"

Jesse glares at them. "He found me again earlier today and told me to go and sin no more—that the result of sin is far worse than being crippled."

"And to pick up your mat," Yanni says.

"When he healed me, yes."

Shmuel says, "Was anyone with him?"

"Eh, three men? One was taking notes. Another said a few words to me as Jesus disappeared. I barely heard anything! My legs!"

"Jesse!" Shmuel says.

"The other said something. But by the time you finished yelling at me, they were all gone."

"Think!" Shmuel says. "What else did he say to you today?"

"They were going to see Jesus' cousin, I think."

Shmuel turns to Yanni. "It was him. It was Jesus of Nazareth."

Jesse giggles. "Nazareth?"

• • •

Atticus, the *Cohortes Urbana*, watches for the healed man to emerge from the Temple, having surreptitiously followed him to his meeting with the Pharisees. He grabs an apple from a vendor and blends in with the crowd near the Temple steps.

• • •

As Jesse exits into the sunlight, he can't quit looking at his fully functioning legs and feet and grinning. Will he ever get used to this? He hopes not.

Someone calls his name. He turns. A Roman, plainly, but in regular clothes.

"Yes? How do you know my name?"

The man is munching an apple. He looks Jesse up and down. "So it's true then? You're on your feet."

Jesse grows suspicious. He comported himself well with Yanni and Shmuel, he thinks, but now he faces the government? "Are you Roman?"

"Does my accent give me away?"

"I already told the Sanhedrin all I know."

The man chuckles. "I was born Roman, yes, but I'm just a man. I had to see with my own eyes." He leans close and whispers, "I believe it was a miracle."

Jesse becomes emotional. "I *know* it was."

The man lays a hand on Jesse's shoulder. "Ooh, life changing, hm? But forbidden. You must want to shout from the rooftops."

"I do!"

"Do you at least have anyone close to share the good news with? Friends? Family?"

"I encountered my brother almost immediately after leaving the pool."

"Incredible," the man says, smiling. "And what did he think?"

Jesse hesitates. What did he think? He believed it was of God, that it was proof ... But tell a Roman this?

"It's safe," the man says. "Jesse, you can tell me."

Jesse ponders this. Finally he leans forward, his voice low. "He believes the man responsible has to be our Messiah." They stare at each other, Jesse smiling broadly.

The man beams. "Messiah?"

"Yes!"

"Ramahrkable."

It takes little for Atticus to sound sincere, because, in fact, he *does* find the miracle remarkable—not to mention the sincere belief of many Jews that this preacher could be their prophesied Messiah. Having sworn to defend the empire, and in particular the emperor, at any cost, Atticus knows the Nazarene must die—or at the very least be exposed as a fraud.

Yet Jesus doesn't appear to be deceiving anyone.

## Chapter 31

# THE DEMONIAC

*Simon the Zealot's private campsite*

Simon misses the camaraderie of his mates, the years of training, the brotherhood. Banished from the catacombs for having failed to assassinate the Magistrate Rufus, he does not mind the alone time. He has been in perfect physical shape for ages, and his daily routines are required to keep things that way. A tuned, toned body is all part of a whole, fulfilling spiritual existence. He tends his campfire, kneels next to it, then lifts his hands. "My God, the soul You put into me is pure. You created it, You formed it, and You breathed it into me. You preserve it within me, and You will restore it."

Simon stands and steps a few feet from the fire, beginning his exercises with deep inhales and exhales, then rapid puffs. Invigorated, his body slowly warming, he runs through a series of precise drills, planting his feet, thrusting alternately with his fists. He parries with his dagger, swiping this way and that, imagining foes who don't stand a chance against the mastery of his body. Now leaping and kicking, he seems to defy gravity for an audience of only God.

When he has cooled, he dons his outer garments and cooks the flesh of a bird and small animals. Simon eats while poking at the embers. He blows on the flames, pondering his future. Will he ever be welcomed back into the Order? Who would believe his report? He'd been distracted by his brother's miraculous healing—bringing to life Simon's vow that if he ever saw Jesse on his own two feet, he would believe the Messiah had come. And Jesse believes his healer was indeed the Messiah himself.

But even had Simon followed through on his task rather than leaving his comrades to fend for themselves, it is clear the plot had been found out and Rufus had not been Rufus after all. Atticus had taken his place, ready to kill Simon before he could complete his mission.

That will be laid at Simon's feet too—the very fact that he had not eliminated the tail when first he detected Atticus following him about the city. So, no, perhaps there is no longer a future for him among the Zealots. But surely a man whose very body is a living, breathing killing machine will be of use to someone. Becoming a mercenary has never been even a temptation, but he will have to do something to survive.

Squatting before the fire, feeling physically fit but mentally conflicted, he starts at a howl in the distance. An animal? Might he be fortunate enough to increase his supply of meat?

The sounds draw near, so Simon pulls his weapon and looks where to hide, preferably upwind so whatever it is cannot sniff him out and escape. The smell of food and fire and smoke may attract it, but he must get out of sight. He deftly scampers up a tree, watching, listening. The original sounds seemed inhuman, but now moans and groans and screams change his mind.

A shabbily dressed man staggers into view, every step

appearing excruciating. Not much of a meal here, but Simon is intrigued. Curious, he drops to the ground without a sound, pulling his weapon and keeping pace behind the man, darting from one tree to behind another.

Suddenly the man stops, without turning around. "It can smell you, so I can smell you," the tortured man says. He faces Simon, who advances toward him in a crouch. This man will be no threat. "Come no closer," the man says, pointing.

"How did you know I was following you?"

"The demon that possesses me knew. Please! Please! It will hurt you!"

"That won't be easy." Clearly the man and the demon have no idea with whom they're dealing.

The man drops to his knees, face full of despair. "If you can kill me, do it!"

"Are you a Roman?"

"No."

"Tax collector?"

"Please!" the man says, lowering his head and sobbing.

Too bad, because slaying a Roman or a tax collector could be done with a clear conscience. But this poor man …

Simon relaxes. "Your body is temporal. A demon will go on, pass through the waterless places, and find someone else. If you're strong enough to have lucid moments, it's safer in you." Simon returns his dagger to its sheath. "Until you can find someone who can truly help you, God bless you."

He turns to leave, but the man crawls forward, shuddering. He pushes up his sleeves to show deep gouges in his forearms. "It makes me cut myself!"

Simon wishes he could help. But he also sees the irony. "Would you believe this isn't the strangest thing that's happened to me in the past week?"

The man groans, gags, coughs. "There's a smell on you. Something vile."

That's a compliment, coming from a demon.

"I hugged my brother goodbye yesterday at the end of the Feast. He's been lying in a pool of his own—"

"Is he a holy person?"

"Not for a long time."

The man glares at Simon. "It has a bad feeling about you."

Simon nods and smiles. "Thank you."

• • •

*The bank of the River Jordan*

Simon and his brother, Andrew, walk with Jesus and Philip, eyes peeled for John the Baptizer.

Andrew says, "He said that after the Feast we could find him near the Jordan outside Jericho."

"We passed Jericho a while ago," Simon says.

"*Near* is a relative term," Jesus says.

Philip says, "John's never where you expect him to be."

A crazy-looking man leaps out from behind a bush, screaming, and Simon nearly falls over backward, reaching for his knife as Jesus howls with laughter.

Andrew rushes to embrace his old rabbi—a scrawny man wearing animal skins and sporting a scraggly beard. They clap each other on the back.

*Creepy John,* Simon thinks.

Jesus says, "Come here," and the Baptizer hugs him.

"Hello, Cousin," John says. "I heard about the scandal at the Pool. I *love* it!"

"I figured you would."

"They're going to come after you so hard for that."

"Ahh, let them come. I see you're still not eating meat, huh?"

"Oy, the hassle of it all."

"Skin and bones," Jesus says.

"Listen," John says, "we don't have much time."

"Time?" Philip says.

"I left the rest of my followers in Jericho to preach repentance. I have to go back to Jerusalem."

"Jerusalem?" Jesus says.

"We were all just there," Andrew says.

"You didn't hear the news?"

"What?" Simon says.

"Herod divorced Phasaelis and is marrying Herodias, his brother's ex-wife. Someone has to call them out on this filth."

Jesus appears to study John. He turns to the rest. "Good men, will you allow me a moment with my cousin?"

Chapter 32

# THE LESSON

*Jericho campsite*

Mary of Magdala sits across from Ramah in an open tent. The young vintner's daughter first encountered Jesus at the wedding at Cana. Mary is teaching her to read and write so they can learn the Torah together. She finds Ramah an eager, bright student and longs to bring her along quickly. They have both benefited from Matthew's help and care, as he too expressed a lack in his scriptural training and has been consulting Philip on the best way to remedy that.

As the women pore over a passage Matthew has meticulously copied onto parchment for them, Mary is aware of the former tax collector's eyes on her from across the way. He and Thomas chop vegetables, having been left to prepare food while the others are off on errands for Jesus. Thomas, she knows, has eyes only for Ramah, but precious, shy Matthew is clearly enamored of Mary. She's flattered, though her affection for him is strictly sisterly. She secretly wishes Jesus would do something about the shabby way the others treat him.

Yes, there's no denying he used and abused his own race, siding with the Romans to tax them into poverty while lining his own pockets. But don't all of Jesus' chosen followers have pasts they regret? She certainly does. Mary, however, sees Matthew as simply a timid soul, unsure how to navigate his new station in life—his forgiven, restored, redeemed existence.

Today happens to be one of those days when she feels the weight of her past. She does not deny in the least that Jesus miraculously transformed her, and up to now, that has filled her with inexpressible bliss. But something niggles at her too. She had nothing to do with this change. She was speeding headlong in one appalling direction for years, even hiding behind an alias, when he called her by her real name, delivered her of demons, and chose her to follow him.

She wholeheartedly came to believe—as the others have—that he is truly the prophesied Messiah. But somehow that makes her feel all the more unworthy of his compassion, his care, his love. Perhaps immersing herself in the Scriptures will help it all make sense. Meanwhile, her sense of unworthiness threatens to rob her of that initial joy. And it distracts her.

Ramah, meanwhile, seems flush with excitement over this wholly new direction in her life. While it's clear she misses her home and family, she is also plainly in love with Thomas and anticipates a future with him. And any homesickness appears to have waned in light of the adventure of following Jesus. Not that it's easy. The women and all the disciples often mention the struggle of their daily existence now—laboring all day, it seems, to set up and break down campsites, find food for all, and walk. Oh, the walking! Simply following Jesus to random cities and towns and countrysides proves an ordeal. But what happens there—seeing him heal, hearing him preach and teach—seems to reassure them all that he is who he claims to be.

Ramah scratches notes into a wax tablet Matthew has given her as she slowly, tentatively sounds out the text before her: 'O Adonai, my God, in You—'" She stalls at the next word.

Mary points. "The root is in these three characters: *het, samek, heh.*"

"'To—seek—refuge,'" Ramah tries, looking up for approval. Mary nods. "But there's no *heh,*" Ramah adds.

"It's swallowed up in the ending characters."

"Oh! Why does it do that?"

Mary loves that Ramah wants to do more than simply learn by rote. "Well," she says, "th-the ending characters are, um—it's defining the action as, um—aah, I can't remember the rule."

"Oh, it's okay ..."

"No, it's really frustrating," Mary says, alarmed at her own impatience. "I know this."

Ramah sets down her stylus. "Let's take a break."

"No!" Embarrassed by her outburst, Mary sips water from a cup. "I'm sorry."

Ramah seems to look upon her with compassion, forgiveness, but she also appears self-conscious. She returns her attention to the parchment and sounds out, "'... from my pursuers and deliver me, lest they cut a lion—'"

"*Tear*, not *cut*," Mary says, again frustrated with herself, sipping again and knowing she sounds edgy. *What is wrong with me?* "And notice that the lion is not *receiving* the tearing, he's *doing* the tearing. The *caph* is the hint of that."

"'... lest, like a lion, they tear ...'"

• • •

Chopping cucumbers has become a new task for Matthew, something he tries to master as he stands next to Thomas, who's doing the same thing. For Thomas, this is old hat, having been a wedding caterer. But for years, Matthew had people for such menial tasks. Still, he's trying his best and does not feel above this. He's glad to do it, if only he could do it as effortlessly as Thomas. How long must it take to become so proficient? He feels exposed, conspicuous, and Thomas's looks of disdain are not lost on him.

Matthew keeps one eye on the interaction between Mary and Ramah, which makes his own task that much harder. He notices that Thomas also frequently takes in the teaching scene across the way. "It's not going well," Matthew says.

"I couldn't agree more," Thomas says.

"You see it too? How frustrated Mary is? When she needs a pause to compose herself, she takes a drink of water."

"No," Thomas says, "I meant staying behind with you while everyone else is out chopping wood or whatever."

Matthew takes this at face value, as he does everything. "Nathanael said he needs more posts for the new tent."

"I know!"

"They said that we are better suited handling food."

"Yes, Matthew! I was there. This is what I'm talking about." He chops in anger now.

Matthew agonizes over why everyone seems to treat him this way. Normally he would ignore this, pretend not to hear or to understand. But he forces himself to speak. "Is it because I was a tax collector?"

"You were a tax collector?"

*Now he's making fun of me.* "You knew that."

"I think you're arrogant."

*Arrogant?* Matthew laughs aloud, then grows serious. "I don't think you're right. I'm very humble."

Thomas stops and stares. "You're bragging about your humility!"

*Am I? I am!*

"And yes, it's because you were a tax collector. And why are you watching Ramah so closely?"

*Ramah?* "I'm not watching her!"

"You're collecting Torah verses for her, donating your tablets."

"They're easy to get!"

"Do you like her?"

*Not Ramah!* Matthew struggles for words. Dare he say who he *is* fond of? All he can conjure is, "You can be very illogical when you're emotional."

He turns back to his work, wishing he could dig a hole and climb in.

• • •

Simon the Zealot, with nothing else to occupy his time, follows the demoniac from a distance, wondering where he might go, what he might do. Simon moves silently through the underbrush but loses sight of the man. He scales a tree, knowing the possessed man can't be far, but what's this? Some sort of hastily built campsite for several people, though only a few are here at present. Two men, inappropriately dressed for the area but in garb that has seen better days, stand chopping vegetables. A young woman sits alone at a table in a tent across the way, and a slightly older one paces outside looking agitated.

Simon espies the demoniac several feet away, crouching by a tree. Now he stomps about, growling, hissing, fired up about something. The Zealot settles high in the tree. Is the man aware how close he is to this camp, whatever it is? That should become obvious soon enough.

## Chapter 33

# THE CONVERSATION

*The bank of the River Jordan*

John the Baptizer sits with Jesus on a log facing the water. How he loves his cousin! And what a privilege to have been chosen to bear witness that Jesus is the Light of God and to devote his life to persuading all to believe! John is well aware that he himself is not that Light—he is but a sinful man, after all. But his sole purpose is to bear witness of that Light.

Despite knowing exactly who Jesus is, John cannot deny that they seem to have entirely different approaches to reaching the hearts of men and women. Jesus heals and teaches. John pronounces judgment, calls people to repent, and baptizes them in water. Far be it from him to question Jesus and the Father's approach—how foolish would that be?—but at times he wonders and feels frustrated with why Jesus doesn't seem to take stronger stands against certain things.

Jesus' look of concern when John raised the issue of the

king's infidelities was obvious. And now John tries to explain. "It's right there in the book of Moses: 'If a man takes his brother's wife, it is impurity. He has uncovered his brother's nakedness; they shall be childless.'"

"I understand it's against the Law of Moses," Jesus says, "but I'm here for bigger purposes than the breaking of rules."

"You minimize incest? What of the Law of Moses can be minimized?"

"All of this will be addressed. I'm not ready to get into the specifics."

John realizes he's countering the Son of God himself, but he continues, "You appear to be not ready to get into the specifics of a lot of things. For instance—"

"Stay on topic, Cousin," Jesus says. "The romantic lives of rulers have been and always will be a subject of enormous fascination for people. It was covered at length in Torah. I don't see why you feel the need to focus on it now."

"He's a client king, or tetrarch, or whatever—he's one of us, and he's unlawful. I am not afraid of him. He may not be as bad as his father, but he is still bad. I'm going to march straight into his court and I'm going to tell him to his face. My followers will love it."

Jesus looks away, then back at him. "You do know how that's going to end, don't you?"

John shrugs. "I get arrested all the time. It's what radicals do. I'll be fine. Herod is afraid of me. The people hold me to be a prophet. Some say Elijah himself."

Jesus chuckles. "Well, maybe not *the* Elijah, but we both know of the Elijah-ness of your role."

"Do we? Because I'm beginning to wonder why you're taking this so slow. Why you're always running away after performing miracles. Tell me, why do you always go off to these desolate places?"

"I need solitude. I'm working on something. A sermon. A big one."

"Oh," John says, studying him. "You're the planning type." He smiles. "I always say the first thing that comes to my mind—in preaching and in life."

Jesus nods and smiles. "I remember from the time you started talking … And I heard about that 'brood of vipers' comment. That was classy. Do you know how the poets say vipers are born?"

"Yes! They hatch inside their mothers and eat their way out, killing their mothers in the process. I thought it was a pretty good line."

"Yes, but no one wants to be accused of killing their ima."

"Yeah, well, I'm not here to make friends with religious leaders. And judging by that stunt you pulled on the Sabbath, neither are you." John pauses as Jesus looks away. "Are you really going to be nice to these people?"

"I suppose not." He reaches to cover John's hand. "Just be careful."

"Now is not the time to be careful. Thirty years you've been here …"

Jesus sighs. "David was a shepherd, and in the wilderness, and on the run for thirty years before he became king."

"Yes, and then he ruled for forty years, he killed a bunch of people, made horrible mistakes, and then died in bed with a teenager he was not married to."

"Maybe not the best analogy," Jesus says, "but also, she was just there to keep him warm."

"I know, and I know what you mean, but what I'm saying is

that taking all this time, telling all these stories, I must confess, I'm eager for you to get to the point."

"Look," Jesus says, "I'm going to tell stories that make sense to some people, but not to others. And that's just how it's going to be."

John sighs. "I get it. It's not like I'm preaching stories for children either." He gazes out over the water. Finally, he says, "It's becoming real, isn't it? Everything we've prepared for."

Jesus nods. "It is."

"I mean, it's always been real, but it's one thing to preach about it and to hear my abba's prophecy growing up, and your ima's song. But it's heavy when it becomes real, no? Do you feel ready?"

"I'm always ready to do my Father's will. But that doesn't make it easy." Jesus looks sad, burdened.

John feels bad. "Listen," John says, "I was rude to you before, but it's only because we go back so far and I can tease a bit. But you know that my heart is yours. My life is yours. The sole reason I was miraculously conceived by two old people was to pave the way for you. I'm just impatient for you to get to work."

Jesus smiles wearily and grips John's shoulder. "I understand. And I'm grateful for your part. You have done God's work, albeit in a unique way."

"Guilty as charged," John says, then thinks better of it. "Perhaps a poor choice of words."

"Perhaps," Jesus says, and they share a laugh.

## Chapter 34

# TERROR

*The disciples' camp*

Mary Magdalene doesn't understand what has gotten into her. Since the day Jesus called her by name and delivered her from her torment, the change has been so stark, so radical, she cannot deny it. She had been transformed in an instant from a broken, wasted, and—even to herself—hopeless no-account, to a woman at peace, fulfilled. Everyone has noticed.

She remains a woman without means to speak of, but even simply cleaner clothes—neither new nor fancy—somehow flatter her, make her glow. Perhaps it is her smile, which had been so rare for so many years, and the absence of fear and foreboding in her countenance. Whatever it is, she feels the difference. She likes the person she has become.

Who would have thought that moving from scrabbling out a meager existence in the Red Quarter to becoming a vagabond following a controversial preacher would prove to be any kind of improvement? But of course Jesus is more than just a preacher. She has come to know him as the Son of God himself, the Messiah her people have longed for.

That makes all the new hardships worth it. She hates when the disciples squabble, of course, and she doesn't enjoy the occasional hunger pangs that come with this sort of lifestyle. But how she cherishes her new friends, and how she loves Jesus!

His choice of friends amuses and confuses her. From simple fishermen to disciples of his cousin, to an architect, a caterer, a tax collector … These aren't in the least perfect people, and no doubt she fits in the same category.

Her distraction and even burst of impatience today alarms her. Does it prove her new life is fake, that she doesn't qualify, doesn't belong? Perhaps she has reveled in the newness of it all for so long that she has grown complacent. The last thing she wants is even a vestige of her former self intruding.

Nursing her cup of water as she paces, Mary persuades herself to turn outward, to think of others, to quit being so introspective. She re-enters the tent and sits across from Ramah. "How's it going?"

Ramah's smile looks self-conscious. "It's hard work. How old were you when you learned this?"

The very question transports Mary back to her beloved abba and how he cherished her. "I was young. I think it's easier when you're a child, but I had a better teacher than you." Before Ramah can demur, Mary adds, "I'm sorry—about before."

"Don't worry about it."

"I just feel, um …" She wants to say *distracted,* but she doesn't want to get into a topic she'll have to explain. Mary doesn't want to plant any doubts in Ramah's mind when the young woman is even newer to Jesus and to all this. "I don't know." She decides to be forthcoming, to risk vulnerability. If nothing else, she can keep Ramah from idolizing her. She certainly doesn't deserve that. "I—so I saw a Roman on horseback this morning when I was picking persimmons."

Ramah looks alarmed. "Did he question you?"

"No. He didn't even see me. But just the sight of him made me—it filled me with …" Mary shudders. "I just dropped my basket and ran." Her voice grows wavery. "I totally ignored the prayers in my hands." She shakes her head, disgusted, disappointed in herself.

"This is hard," Ramah says. "Not just the readings."

"Do you want to try again?"

Ramah nods.

Mary senses something. A feeling washes over her she hasn't felt since—before. An ache begins behind her eyes. She presses a hand to her forehead and exhales sharply. She can't stifle a gasp.

Ramah looks up quickly. "What's wrong? Mary!"

A hideous screech in the distance terrifies Mary.

"What's that?" Ramah says.

• • •

Across the way, Matthew has just followed Thomas's lead and squeezes a lemon over his sliced cucumbers. "Did-did you hear …?"

The screech turns to guttural groaning, then a scream. "I heard *that*," Thomas says, wielding his big paring knife. Matthew grabs a huge ladle and shrugs at Thomas.

The growling sounds closer. Matthew shouts, "Mary and Ramah!"

The women emerge, looking petrified.

"Are you all right?" Matthew asks.

Mary freezes. Ramah screams as a bearded man in ragged clothes bursts into sight. Thomas displays his knife. The man wheels to face Thomas and Matthew. They stand shoulder to shoulder, immobile.

"That smell!" the man hisses, baring his teeth, eyes wild. "It's on all of you, but worse! Putrid!"

Matthew steps forward, ladle in hand. "Don't come any closer!"

The man sneers at him and advances as Little James and Nathanael arrive. To Matthew's shock, Mary steps directly in front of the man. Pale and horrified as she appears, she commands, "Stop!"

"Mary!" Matthew calls out.

"Lilith?" the man snarls.

She levels her eyes at him. "I don't answer to that name."

He whispers hoarsely, "They told me about you."

"Did they?" she says evenly.

"All seven of them."

She stares him down. "My name is Mary. It was always Mary."

"Oh," he says, his breath steaming as if in winter, "the stories they had." He moves closer, chuckling. "You're scared."

Not only does she not back down, but she also moves toward him. "What's your name?"

"Belial," he says, "spawn of Oriax, fifth knight of Legion."

She shakes her head. "What's your real name?"

He grimaces, gagging, choking. "That smell," he spits. "It's on all of you!"

"What did your mother call you?"

He holds his throat, groaning, and appears to try to answer. "C-Ca-." Finally he stops and smiles. "Can't say." He laughs.

"Please say your name."

At that he lunges at her, only to be tackled by Simon the

Zealot, who throws him to the ground and pulls his dagger. "Leave."

The man rises to all fours, breathing heavily and smiling wildly. Simon peeks behind him to be sure the others are clear and the man leaps to his feet and charges, knocking the dagger away and wrestling the Zealot to the ground. As Simon desperately reaches for his weapon, the man grunts and groans, wrapping his hands around Simon's neck and squeezing with all his might.

As the Zealot's eyes bulge and his breath is cut off, here comes Jesus. He advances on a dead run ahead of Andrew, Simon, John the Baptist, and Philip. Jesus shouts, "Out! Out of him!"

The possessed man lets go as his body goes rigid and he gags. He flops off the Zealot and lies in a heap, sobbing. Simon scampers away, coughing.

John the Baptizer raises a fist and shouts, "Yeah!"

Jesus kneels and turns over the weeping stranger. "It's all right," he says. "Welcome back."

The man stares up at him miserably.

"I know," Jesus adds. "It seemed like it would never end. What is your name?"

The man allows a smile. "Caleb."

"Well, it's over now." He caresses the man's cheek. "Let's get up, Caleb." He lifts the man and embraces him.

Meanwhile, John the Baptizer appears to study the other stranger. He cocks his head. "When did you pick up the Zealot?" he says, extending a hand to help him up. "I'm John."

Simon the fisherman addresses the Zealot. "Who are you?"

"Simon," the Zealot says.

"Yes?" Simon says.

"I'll stop you both there," Jesus says. "You're both Simons."

The Zealot stares. "Did you heal my brother in Jerusalem, Rabbi?"

"Yes."

"Then you are …"

"Yes."

"And where are your foll—"

"They're right here."

The Zealot takes them all in, appearing dubious. A few rugged guys, but mostly a scraggly bunch of little men and a couple of women.

"Not the fearsome warriors you pictured by my side when you were in the catacombs?"

The Zealot retrieves his elaborate sica dagger and slips it back into its sheath. He appears speechless that Jesus would know where he trained.

"And there are more," Jesus says, "not here at the moment. Let's go for a walk, Simon, son of Zebulon." Jesus turns to his people. "Boys," he says to Little James and Nathanael, nodding at the delivered man, "tend to his wounds. Thomas, some food for him. Ramah, check on Mary, please."

Chapter 35

# FORMAL INQUIRY

*Jerusalem Temple—the Bet Midrash study room*

Pharisee Yanni is nearly giddy with what he has been able to tell Shmuel about what happened at the Pool of Bethesda. Shmuel filed an official report with the Sanhedrin, and now they stand before a mid-level administrator.

The man does not stand to greet them but rather presses his lips together and raises a brow, as if to say, "Get on with whatever this is. I'm busy."

Shmuel clears his throat and gushes in one breath, "We need to update a report submitted last week about a man who performed a miracle on Shabbat and then told the healed person to commit a sin. And to file an addendum linking this report to my original petition."

"Wait," the man says. "Slow down. What changed about your report?"

"We have a name!" Yanni blurts.

"The offender is known," Shmuel adds.

The cleric sighs with obvious disgust and rises.

"The petition," Shmuel continues, "is in regard to an incident in Capernaum in which one Jesus of Nazareth performed a similar miracle and declared his authority to forgive sins—essentially claiming—"

"Ah, yes," the man says, returning to his desk with a box of documents. "I know about this case. It was escalated to the Sanhedrin, and the beginning stages of a formal inquiry were commenced. I processed the paperwork."

"That inquiry must be updated," Yanni says, "with what happened at the Bethesda Pool. We have significant evidence it was the same person."

"That inquiry was closed."

Shmuel recoils. "What?"

"It never advanced beyond opening arguments."

"Why not?"

"Those things are confidential."

"But this is a huge development," Shmuel says. "The inquiry must be reopened!"

"That doesn't happen."

"Why?" Yanni says.

The man looks bored. "All I can tell you is that a very prominent member of the Sanhedrin declared it a one-off incident by a rogue who posed no material threat. No further questions were asked. And none will be."

As the two Pharisees stalk from the room, Yanni says, "Well, we know who the 'very prominent member' was. The so-called teacher of teachers."

"Yes, him and his wordsmithing. He told me he would not oppose the petition itself, but he never said anything about what he would do if the case actually reached the Sanhedrin."

"Nicodemus has influence," Yanni says. "But he's not Caiaphas. Not even close."

"He closed the inquiry before it even got past opening remarks, and no one challenged him. You don't call that power?"

"I know some people above his station who may see things more clearly. Especially with this most recent development of violating Shabbat."

Chapter 36

# A BETTER SWORD

*The River Jordan*

Simon the Zealot, filled with wonder, walks along the bank with Jesus. He has no doubt he is in the presence of the prophesied Messiah himself but can hardly believe his fortune. For what possible reason could he be enjoying this singular privilege? The question on his lips is, "Why me?" but he asks it another way. "Why Jesse? Why my brother, out of everyone?"

Jesus looks as if the answer is obvious. "The man suffered unspeakably for thirty-eight years. That's a long time." He pauses. "And how else could I get your attention?"

"My attention?" *What could Messiah want with me?*

"Your Order trained you to be fearless, no?"

"'No Lord but God,' to the death."

"What I did with your brother—it's not the last of the trouble I intend to cause."

The Zealot steps ahead of Jesus and turns to face him. "You are Messiah, aren't you?"

"Yes."

*He sees my value as a warrior,* Simon thinks. *A fearless warrior.* He drops to one knee, realizing in a rush why the assassination plot failed, why he's been banished from the Fourth Philosophy—in essence, why he's suddenly between jobs despite his talents. "Then I will do anything you ask."

He stares up into Jesus' gaze as the man seems to study him. "I ask you to understand the nature of my mission, Simon."

"Yes," Simon says, nodding, certain he does understand. Clearly Jesus needs someone with his skill set to add muscle to his bunch of undernourished followers. They must bring something to the table—perhaps brains or compassion, something—but it doesn't appear to him that any of them, perhaps beyond the toned and taut fishermen, could handle a physical threat. Now he wants details. "How?" he says.

"How, indeed?" Jesus says. "It's not so easy with distracted humans, hm?"

The Zealot rises. "I have trained for years for this. I am ready to execute your mission today."

Jesus smiles. "We'll see." He hesitates. "Show me your weapon."

Simon presents the sica dagger with two hands. Jesus whistles as he receives it. "Impressive. That is something."

The Zealot smiles until Jesus deftly slings the weapon and its ornate sheath into the Jordan. Simon shoots him a double-take, and Jesus says, "You didn't see that coming."

Dumbfounded, Simon says, "You have no use for that?"

"I have a better sword. You'll see. We have much to discuss—just be patient. You've had quite a week."

"Without my dagger, why do you need someone like me?"

Jesus chuckles. "I have everything I *need*." He presses a hand to Simon's chest. "But I *wanted* you."

"But why?"

"You're not alone in misunderstanding. But not to worry. I'm preparing something to share with the world. For now, wanting you by my side will have to be enough. No one buys their way into our group because of special skills, Simon."

Simon remains confused. "Rabbi, after what you did at the pool during a High Holy Feast Day, there may be some who try to stop you. Even some from my former Order, especially if they find out you have a different mission."

"And what are you going to do? Stop them?"

"Well, I would be more likely to if you hadn't thrown my dagger in the river."

Jesus laughs. "Well, if that day comes, I guess we'll find out." He throws an arm around Simon's shoulder, and they walk on.

• • •

Jesus and Simon the Zealot have been followed. When they are out of sight, Atticus the *Cohortes Urbana* steps into the river, kicks the dagger free from the muddy bottom, and pulls it out.

• • •

*The road to Jericho, dusk*

Mary of Magdala sees through moist eyes the city looming on the fading horizon. She's on a mission, something she can't explain even to herself. What compels her? She doesn't know, except that this is bad for her—something she would not have even dreamt of doing yesterday. Seeing the Roman soldiers while in the persimmon grove? Facing down the demoniac? Had that been enough to push her over the edge?

She knows she doesn't look the way she did in her former life—at least she didn't before today. Her plain attire is fresh, her face clean, her eyes clear but for the tears. What does she want? What is she after? Familiarity—that's all she can make of it. What will a peek at her past gain her—even if it's only temporary? Or will it be? Can she not dabble in it for a reminder and escape back to Jesus? But how could she ever face him again after all he has done for her?

She turns at hoofbeats behind her and stiffens as a Roman soldier rides into view. But she doesn't panic, doesn't run, doesn't hide as before. Mary stands in the middle of the road, defying him to trample her—or worse. He glares as he trots by, and a sob in her throat disappears. Something satisfies her about that small triumph.

In town a few minutes later, Mary makes her way through a market where the merchants are packing up, dousing torches, closing up for the night. She moves directly to the top of a bank of stone steps leading to a tavern she remembers—The Nomad. Hesitating, she must decide. Turn and rush back to camp, to the disciples, to Ramah, Mother Mary, Matthew, and all the rest? To Jesus? Though she's done nothing—yet—he'll know. Won't he? He seems to know everything about her. Her having simply disappeared has to have already disappointed him.

Torn beyond logic, she can't stop herself and descends the dark stairway, lit only by a meager wall torch. As Mary approaches an imposing wood door, a massive bouncer rises. "We don't serve women here."

She sighs. "Tell Thro that someone is here to see him."

"Did someone put you up this?"

"Just get Thro."

He snorts. "Come on, you seem like a nice girl. It's late. Go home."

Mary pulls off her head covering, making it clear she's not going anywhere.

The man lifts his hands. "Okay, who should I say wants to see him?"

“Tell him someone from The Hammer wants to win back her money.”

“Well, you obviously know which button to push with Thro. Wait here.”

As the man steps in and shuts the door, Mary backs against the wall. There’s still time to flee, but she knows she will not.

• • •

*Near the disciples’ camp*

As darkness falls, John the Baptizer waits on the road, not wanting to leave without saying goodbye to his cousin. Jesus and the Zealot appear. Jesus says, “So you’re really going for it.”

“You know I can’t be silent,” John says.

“I know. Soon I will break my own silence as well.”

The Baptizer clicks his tongue. “Such a strange word, *soon.* Could mean anything.”

Jesus embraces him. “I love you.”

John holds tight, never knowing when or if he will see Jesus again. “And thank you for letting me see that today. I heard about the miracles, but I never thought I’d actually get to see one.”

“Well, timing is everything, I guess.” As the Baptizer pulls away, Jesus adds, “And John, what you are about to do—”

John spreads his arms wide. “I’ve lived my whole life with warnings. Warnings are how I know I’m on the right track.”

“It’s not a warning,” Jesus calls after him. “You’re doing what you’re supposed to do. I’m just reminding you to be sure to listen to God’s voice as you do it.”

“Always!”

And as John waves and turns toward the road, he hears Jesus sniffling.

• • •

Still trailing Jesus, Atticus watches from the shelter of a grove of trees. He wipes dry the sica dagger and slips it into his waistband. "The Baptizer?" he whispers. "Huh."

Chapter 37

# POLITICAL GOLD

*Yanni's office, night*

Yanni hunches over a sheet of parchment, writing by candlelight.

"An appeal is pointless," Shmuel says, pacing. "Nicodemus is too powerful."

"It's not an appeal."

"What Sanhedrin member would take up our fight against a fellow member?"

Yanni looks up. "Your thinking is too small."

"What then, go to Caiaphas directly?"

"Shmuel, think. There are two school of Mishnaic thought—"

"Hillel and Shammai, of course. But what does that have to do—"

"And when there is an issue presented to the Sanhedrin that could be interpreted two ways, the court …" Yanni spreads his arms, allowing Shmuel to answer. But the latter looks only puzzled. "Splits!" Yanni adds. "You're still a rube. When the court splits along Mishnaic traditions, it becomes political. Former allies become enemies."

"We can turn people against Nicodemus."

"Maybe," Yanni says. "But the right issues, especially those that appeal to emotion, can become political gold."

"But false prophecy is a moral imperative!" Shmuel says.

"To you, yes. And if we can make it emotional as well, you may find we don't even have to seek those who oppose Nicodemus. Nicodemus himself may have a change of heart."

Shmuel sits across from Yanni's desk. "What do we have to do?"

"Most Sanhedrin members follow the teachings of who?"

"Shammai."

"Exactly." *Maybe this rube is catching on at last.*

"Aah, and he's the most rigid interpreter of doctrine the Sanhedrin has known! This is exactly—"

"Now you're learning!"

"You can get this to him, Yanni?"

"That's not the hard part. The hard part is getting him to make it a priority."

"But if he understands the crime—"

"It's got no political weight," Yanni says. Shmuel looks blank again, so Yanni continues. "Here's what's important to Shammai right now: He's in a dogfight with Sanhedrin President Shimon—the son of Hillel, who is …?"

"The more tolerant teacher. Shammai's opposite school of thought."

"Shammai has the votes in the Sanhedrin, yes, but Shimon has the common people, *because* he's Hillel's son."

"Shammai wants the people?" Shmuel says.

"And Shimon wants the votes. If we could offer Shimon a way to beat Shammai at his own rigid game …"

"We pit the school of Hillel against the school of Shammai." Shmuel sighs. "Politics." He pauses. "So you're writing a letter to Shimon?"

"Shimon is too busy to read our letter. His personal scribe, however, is an old friend. He will have the time and Shimon's ear when the opportunity comes."

Shmuel rises. "Jesse gave us so little information."

"It's not entirely his fault. The miracle worker vanished right after."

"That's his pattern. Nicodemus himself was struck by the same curiosity. This preacher performs miracles discreetly and vanishes."

Yanni says, "What else do you remember from Capernaum?"

"A woman on the roof, an Ethiopian. She referred to an incident with a leper outside the city. I can go back to Capernaum and look for her."

"Excellent. If the case is reopened, it will have the full weight of the Sanhedrin behind it. There can't be too many Ethiopian women in Galilean backwater towns."

"That's my home you're talking about, you know," Shmuel says.

Yanni is about to cover with a feigned apology, but it appears something has occurred to Shmuel. "Cousin!" he blurts. "Jesus said he was going to meet his cousin."

Yanni shakes his head. "Jesse wasn't clear on that detail."

"But it's something! We can search the census records for relations. The population of Nazareth is so small, he will be easy to find. We can identify his father, mother, and their relatives. This is a census year."

"The numbers aren't in yet. How old did he seem?"

"Thirties, maybe forty. He must have been old enough to have been counted in that last census."

"Check on it yourself," Yanni says. "Don't draw attention. In the meantime, we need to re-create the events." Shmuel pulls up a chair again. "Argh! Shammai, Shimon, Shmuel—our people really need a better variety of names."

Chapter 38

# IN THE DEPTHS

*The Nomad tavern, Jericho*

Mary follows the bouncer inside. "Sorry for the delay," he says.

"Yeah, it's like you said. I look like a nice girl. How could you have known?"

The place is seedier than she remembers, a step down even from The Hammer. She spots the owner with his back to her from across the way. "Jethro?" she calls.

He turns, clearly startled. "Lilly!" He rushes to her. "You're back! I thought you were dead or something!"

She looks down. "Well, sort of." Mary had felt dead to her old life. At least for a while.

"Oh! But you look amazing!" He laughs and looks to the ceiling. "Somebody kill me!"

She needs to get on with this. "Look," she says, "I'm here for one thing. And I've got money this time. I can pay for it myself."

Mary hates his look of hesitation—and concern—but apparently he can see she will not be dissuaded. Jethro nods for her to follow and pours her a drink. "I've refined the recipe. It's even stronger." He leads her to a gaming table.

• • •

*The disciples' camp*

Simon the fisherman leads Simon the Zealot to the crackling fire, where many of the others sit warming themselves in the darkness. "Come, come," he says. "It's a nice little group. You will like them." He points to the former caterer, sitting next to his love. "This is Thomas. He overthinks things all the time, but he's growing on me."

"Hi," the Zealot says. "I'm Simon."

"That's Nathanael. He says the first thing that comes to his mind, so don't be offended."

Nathanael waves.

"I'm Simon."

"This is Ramah. She's an expert vintner, so any questions you have about wine, just see her."

"I'm Si—"

"Shh!" the fisherman says. "She knows. We all know." He scans the group. "Another woman we have—where's Mary?"

Matthew looks alarmed, as if he's just realized she's gone.

"I spoke to her earlier," Ramah says. "I haven't seen her since."

Simon the fisherman rushes off into the night, searching for Jesus, whom he finds pacing by the river. "Salt preserves from corruption," he's saying. "If it loses its saltiness, it doesn't do what it—no." Simon hangs back as Jesus begins again. "If salt has lost its flavor—its salty taste—its …"

*This can't wait.* "Rabbi," Simon says. "I-I'm sorry to interrupt. Mary's gone missing. Ramah thinks she may have been affected by the demoniac. Said she didn't appear to be feeling right all day."

Jesus groans.

"You don't think she could have gone into Jericho," Simon says. "Maybe I should go into the city, just to be sure."

Jesus nods, looking sad. "Yes."

Matthew runs up. *Great,* Simon thinks.

"I'm coming too," Matthew says.

Simon turns on him. "Are you spying again?"

"Simon," Jesus says. "Take Matthew."

"Rabbi, I think—"

"Simon."

Something about Jesus' look stops him.

Jesus says, "This is about finding Mary."

Simon pauses, nods. "I'll take him."

"Matthew?"

"Yes, Rabbi?"

"That passage Philip was teaching you …"

"Yes?"

"What is it?"

"'If I ascend into heaven, You are there. If I make my bed in the depths, You are there.'"

"Keep that in your thoughts."

Jesus turns back toward the water. Simon faces Matthew and feels the tax collector sizing him up with a look of despair. Simon resolves to put his animus aside for this critical task.

"Come on, Matthew," he says. "Let's find Mary."

# PART 6

# Forgiven

## Chapter 39

# THE PRESENCE

*Nob, Israel, 1008 BC*

Town priest Ahimalech tries to comfort his wife in the preparation room of the small tabernacle as she helps him dress for his duty during Shabbat. He too is worried about their eldest son, but he must not show it. She is clearly vexed enough for the both of them.

"His fever hasn't broken," she says, tidying another layer of his garments. "Five days now."

"He will heal, Yafa," Ahimalech says. "He always does."

"And what if he doesn't, hm?"

He knows what she's driving at. The family's legacy of the secret traditions of Aaron's priestly lineage would be jeopardized. If worse comes to worst, their younger son is next in line. But he's only ten. "I will teach Abiathar how to make the showbread today."

It's as if she doesn't hear him, her eyes showing she's still obsessed with their firstborn. "It's yet one more in our never-ending string of family curses."

He sighs. "You. Always thinking in catastrophes."

"And you, always thinking it's another sunny day."

"Send Abiathar to me."

When the boy arrives, he looks eager to learn, as if he's been waiting for such an honor. Ahimalech pulls a hot cake from the oven, showing his son how he can hold it with only a towel beneath it, because the heat rises. "Twelve cakes," he says. "One for each of the tribes of Israel."

The boy appears to study another dozen cakes, long cooled and dried, stacked on a table of wood and gold. "But if the bread is still here, Abba, why didn't God eat it?"

"God doesn't need food, Abiathar. It's called the Bread of the Presence because it's a reminder of His presence in our lives—a symbol that He sits at our table, dwells in our midst."

"What happens to the old bread?"

"In the Law of Moses, it was written that 'Aaron and his sons shall eat it in a holy place, since it is for him the most holy portion out of Adonai's food offerings, a perpetual due.'"

Laden with a stack of cakes now, the boy says, "I always wondered where you and Saba went every Shabbat."

"Yes, we came here to eat the bread that has been removed—provided neither of us had lain with his wife that morning." It was more than he intended to say, but there it was.

"Don't you lie with Ima every night, Abba?"

"Um—that is a discussion for another time. But for now, we must replace this with the hot bread as an offering to Adonai."

The boy sets the cakes on the table, and they take turns placing one atop the other onto a ceremonial plate. "Reuben," Ahimalech says.

And he's proud to see Abiathar knows what comes next. "Simeon," the boy says, placing the next cake.

"Levi."

"Judah."

The door bursts open behind Ahimalech, and he whirls to find a distressed man stumble in. It's none other than David, rumored to be on the run from King Saul. "Ahimalech!"

Shaken, Ahimalech tells his son, "Go home. Tell your mother I sent you and that everything's going to be fine."

The boy stares wide-eyed at the man and runs off.

"Listen," David says, "I—"

"Why are you alone? Where is your protection?"

"The king has sent me on a mission and said that no one is to know anything about it. I've arranged to meet my men—"

"David! It's my understanding that you and the king are not on friendly terms."

"No, I've been sent on a mission from *the* King—" he says deliberately. "Please. I haven't eaten in days, and I know my men haven't either. They're in hiding. We could make do with five loaves of bread, anything."

"I have no ordinary bread," Ahimalech says.

"What about that?" David says, pointing at the cold stack. "That was replaced by the hot bread."

"It's still holy bread. You know the Law of Moses!"

"And I know the *pikuach nefesh*. Saving a life overrides any religious law."

Ahimalech sighs. "Have the men kept themselves from women?"

"Truly they have, and always. They've been in hiding at Gibeah, waiting for me for days."

Ahimalech peers behind David out the door. "We must be quick." He stacks twelve cakes into a special linen cloth. "So remember, what I'm giving you is sacred."

"Life is more sacred than bread."

"If Saul finds out I helped you, I won't get to keep my life."

“I know.”

“But I’m not sorry, David. Something is going to come through you. I can feel it. Something bigger and more exciting—I don’t know what.”

David smiles as he turns to go. “There was nothing bigger or more exciting than that giant.”

“We’ll see.”

Chapter 40

# STAIRS

*A stable in Jericho*

Rousing from a bed he's fashioned from straw in an empty stall, Simon the former fisherman squints in the morning light. "Matthew?" he calls out, then closes his eyes again and sits up. "I am thankful before You, Lord our King, for You have mercifully restored my soul within me. Great is Your faithfulness."

He rises, brushing himself off.

"Are you hungry?" Matthew says, leaning over parchments on a crude table, apparently unaware that his once-pristine tax collector apparel—already frayed and faded from his days on the road with Jesus—is smeared with horse dung.

"What did you do to yourself?"

Matthew looks puzzled, then notices the filth, gags, and whips off his tunic.

"That's disgusting!" Simon says. "Did you not put down new hay before lying down?"

"No! Did you?"

"Of course I did."

"My mind is racing," Matthew says, vigorously washing his hands in a bowl of water. "I guess I wasn't paying attention." He dries them and turns back to his parchments, crude maps of the city. "If we split up today, we'll be able to cover more ground."

*That's a laugh*, Simon thinks. *Does he think Jesus would want me to let him out of my sight?* "We're not splitting up."

"It would be more logical."

"Jesus wants you back in one piece." Matthew can't argue with that. "Did you say there was breakfast?"

"No," Matthew says. "I asked if you were hungry. Do you know how to make eggs?"

"No."

Matthew finds a pot. "Boil water. Put the eggs in the water."

"No, no, no, no."

"What is it?"

"Well, I'm not a cook, for starters."

"Neither am I," Matthew says. "But we must sustain ourselves. While you make eggs, however you like them, you can also devise our plan for the day—with me."

Simon stares. "Fine." They are, after all, on a mission. He sets the pot on a small fire. "You know, we have to consider the possibility that Mary went somewhere other than Jericho."

"Ephraim or Bethel? No, too much wilderness to cross between camp and either of those places. She's most comfortable in cities."

"Ah," Simon says. "You think she's still here?"

"I do. We must analyze her history, what she normally does …"

"Lately, before this, all she did was study Torah with you and Ramah."

"I checked the synagogue. The officials said they hadn't seen her."

*Interesting,* Simon thinks. "How did you describe her?"

"How would you?"

"She's got black hair," Simon says.

"Long, black hair."

"All our women have—"

"Sometimes she can't even cover it all," Matthew says. "She might be inconsolable, or distressed."

Simon looks at Matthew with new eyes. "Anything else?"

He seems to concentrate. Finally he says, "Unusually pleasant to look at?" Simon grins, but before he can tease, Matthew says, "You want to add water to the pot before it heats up."

"Okay, Matthew."

A tottering Roman soldier, helmet in hand, staggers to the stable. Simon rises. "You all right?"

He looks up with a stupid grin. "Jes' another night at The Nomad."

"The Nomad?"

"I can't believe I made it up the stairs. Dionysus carried me." The soldier looks as if he's about to go down. Simon rushes to help him. "Hey!" the man growls. "Paws off, rat!" He lurches away.

Simon glares after him, then turns to Matthew. "Anyway, where were we? Oh, yeah, you gave a description of Mary to the official at the—"

"What did he say about the stairs?"

*Hmm,* Simon thinks, and they both peer down the alleyway from which the soldier had come. It's worth a shot.

• • •

*Jericho countryside*

Ramah feels it a privilege to have been assigned to accompany Mother Mary to take baskets and forage for edible vegetation, but she's distracted. Worried about the other Mary, she has to force herself to concentrate on the task—so many mouths to feed. "What flowers *can* be eaten?" she says.

"Rose, borage, dandelion," her elder says. "A little tangy, but who's going to complain?"

"How do you know so much about edible flowers?"

"My family has been poor my whole life. You learn what the earth can give you."

"But your son is ..."

Mother Mary smiles wryly. "My son is a homeless nomad who no longer brings in income from carpentry."

"And you're smiling about it."

"I'm smiling because he is doing what he was born to do. Maybe sometimes that means we will be hungry for a few days, but at least his time has come."

Ramah feels she can learn as much from this precious woman as she's been learning from Torah. "If his time has come, why doesn't he just bring Mary back?"

"It doesn't work that way."

"How does it work?"

Mother Mary stops and faces her. Kindly, she says, "Sometimes he is as much a mystery to me as he is to you."

Ramah ponders this, then notices. "Oh, berries!" She picks one, pierces it with a fingernail, and sniffs it. "Poison."

They walk on in silence. Finally Mother Mary says, "We lived in Egypt when Jesus was a boy. One of their gods was called Thoth, whom they believed they could compel to grant their wishes if they performed rituals. It's not like that with our God, so why would it be with Jesus?"

*Because he's God's son, yes,* Ramah thinks. But ... "Nothing good can come from Mary disappearing like this."

Mother Mary seems to study her. "Do you know that?"

"Well, she was already upset about something even before the possessed man came into camp."

"Simon and Matthew are competent searchers."

"That may be, but they do not like each other."

Mother Mary says, "They'll have to work together."

Ramah surprises herself with an outburst she doesn't intend to sound so harsh. "She could be dead or dying in a ditch somewhere! Why would Jesus use her pain to unite two men who are annoyed by each other?"

"We do not know that she's in danger," Mother Mary says.

"She's a woman alone! She's either in a savage wilderness or a depraved town patrolled by Romans."

"Ramah, 'Some trust in chariots and some in horses.'" And Ramah joins her in unison to complete the Scripture: "'But we trust in the name Adonai our God.'"

As they move on, Ramah says quietly, "I want to be a teacher like Mary some day. I want to be able to write my thoughts."

"You will."

"Not if she doesn't come back."

"We can't fix anything by worrying about it," Mother Mary says.

*Wisdom*, Ramah thinks. Pure and simple.

The older woman points. "Lavender!"

"Can you eat lavender?"

• • •

*The Nomad*

Mary of Magdala sits at a table full of gamblers playing knucklebones. She can hardly fathom how it has all come back to her in a rush—not only the game and her taste for strong drink, but also her tone and bearing. She's one tough wench, she decides, in a room full of swarthy men. A pile of coins lies before her. One player dozes and another scowls, grumbling about his losses. Shoob and Hohj are immersed in the game with her. The others toss in their meager bets.

"Nine for Shoob," she announces to a chorus of *oohs*.

An onlooker says, "Nine is too much."

Mary turns on him, sneering. "I came in here with a single shekel to my name, and now look at this pile, huh?"

"How did you get the first one, woman, hm?" the onlooker says. "What'd you do for it?"

"Wouldn't you like to know?" The new Mary hardly recognizes herself. But her old self knows her all too well.

Hohj, facing her from the other end of the table, says, "Hey, are we going to play or what?"

"Get on with it," Mary says.

Hohj shakes five knucklebones in his palm. "Watch and learn, boys. Watch and learn. Hie!" He tosses them in the air and tries to catch them on the back of his hand. Three scatter across the table. He slaps the table as the others groan. "Mother of a dog!"

Mary shoots him a look, drink in hand. "First time, Hohj, yeah?" She catches Jethro's eye and lifts her cup. "Hey, another." Hohj tries to shoot an angle, and she says, "Ah, no sweeps on twos."

"That's a loose rule," the onlooker says.

"Well," she says, "we're playing by …" And suddenly she falls silent, awash with where she is—and where she is not. She scans the table and sees laborers, crooks, ruffians. For all her complaints and misgivings about her new friends and their constant squabbling, at least they're wholesome, well-intentioned men who seemed to care for her. How has it come to this? What is she doing here? It's the last place she wants to be, but she feels helpless, as if possessed again.

A sob rises in her throat, and she has to get out. The men look to her expectantly. "We're not playing," she says. "We are done." She begins filling a bag with her coins.

"Hey!" Hohj hollers. "You can't do that! I'm going to win my money back."

"Yeah?" she says. "When?"

"Now!"

"I see," she says. "Hohj was just slow-playing us, everyone. He's actually a lion." The others laugh, and she can see he's boiling. "You want to win your money back?"

"Seriously?" he says.

"Mm-hm. It'll be behind the bar." She looks for Jethro again. "Another!"

Hohj stands, serious as a stoning. "A woman should know her place."

Mary slaps her moneybag onto the table and, with less bravado now, says, "I suppose you're going to show me?"

Hohj glowers and marches toward her end of the table. What now? Why had she been so brazen? Petrified, she closes her eyes and is transported to her childhood when her beloved father comforted her in the dead of night. "What do we do when we are scared?" he asks her.

"We say the words," her tiny self responds, and the adult Mary finds herself whispering this now.

Jethro moves boldly into Hohj's path. Mary, sobbing, leaves her bag on the table and rushes out.

Chapter 41

# 613 RULES

*The disciples' Jericho campsite*

Thomas misses Ramah, even when she's just on an errand, but to admit this would open him to unending teasing. The others are just jealous, he knows. Which of the single men would not trade places with him in an instant?

Of course, he promised Ramah's father he would take care of her at all costs. But that means making sure she is fed too, and right now he's worried about food for the entire entourage. As the former wedding caterer, it's fallen to him to keep track of the inventory for meals. He sits next to Andrew, sorting the last of the food. It's down to lentils now, each handful enough to feed one person for one meal. "Nineteen servings," he says. "And there are fifteen of us."

"Fourteen," Andrew says, "if Philip doesn't make it back today."

"That's true. And eleven if Simon and Matthew don't come back with Mary. We could split the rest, but what if they *do* return?"

"Maybe Philip stayed an extra day to visit his brother ..."

"Why are you so troubled about Philip? This is literally our last meal. We don't even have half a beitza of flour or yeast."

"Ramah and Mother Mary might find berries," Andrew says.

Thomas shakes his head. "Jesus can make people walk. He can heal lepers. Why can't he make food appear?"

"When I was following John," Andrew says, "sometimes we would go for days without food. Other times a person he baptized would give us money, and we would eat like kings—for a day."

"He doesn't sound like much of a planner," Thomas says.

"We never thought about it. John doesn't believe in money."

"Doesn't believe in it?"

"He says it's a manmade construct—designed to assign value to and take ownership of things that belong to God."

Thomas chuckles. "Sounds like the guy needs an accountant. Maybe we should send Matthew to him."

"Right now isn't the best time for jokes."

• • •

Across the way, John chops wood with his brother, Big James. It's different work from fishing every day on the Sea of Galilee with their father, Zebedee. But John is getting used to it. It took him a little longer to get into the rhythm than his brother, but then James has always been brawnier. John hacks away at logs, producing blocks James deftly splits, sending the halves flying with one chop of his ax.

James suddenly stops, his attention apparently drawn by Simon the Zealot—whom the rest have taken to calling Zee to differentiate him from Simon the former fisherman. Zee has emerged from his tent and begins his day by running through a vigorous exercise—spinning, kicking, leaping, shadow punching.

John joins his brother to watch. “I once thought about joining the Zealots,” John says.

“What? You never told me that.”

“You never asked.”

“So, why didn’t you join them?”

John points. “This very thing he’s doing. We have enough rules from Torah to follow as it is without adding all this.”

“Six hundred and thirteen rules,” James mutters.

John repeats the number and adds, “All these prayers we have to recite, and all these things we can and can’t do. Add a bunch of bodily exercises to that each morning? Not me.”

“They have to be in prime shape, you know?” James says.

John brandishes his ax. “To kill people.”

“Yes.”

They stand staring, sweating from their own labor, as Zee seems to effortlessly fly through the air and land lightly on his feet.

“But when I considered it,” John says, “rolling out of bed each morning to Ima’s breakfast and going out on the boat with you and Abba seemed pretty great.”

“But now that Zee’s with us,” James says, “he’s technically not a Zealot anymore, right?”

“I have this theory,” John says, “that for some people—like Little James and Thaddeus over there—they’re called to follow our rabbi, and they just somehow know it is a better path than the one that they were on.”

“And then there’s Zee,” James says.

John nods. “Decades of training to do one thing? That cannot just go away overnight.”

“I’m more worried about *our* Simon than Zee.”

John chuckles at the thought of Simon trying, and often failing, to get with the program. “And we’ve had our moments too.”

"Ah, yes, Jesus calling us the Sons of Thunder. What would Ima think of that?"

"I don't know," John says. "Maybe she'd be glad we got a title!"

James laughs, then sobers. "I wonder how Mary's doing."

John says, "I just don't understand why Jesus would pair up Simon and Matthew to go and find her. Matthew! It's like asking a fox and a fish to go and team up and do something productive."

"What?"

*Is that so hard to understand?* John wonders. "Because they could never work together. It's a saying."

"Nobody says that."

*Always the big brother.*

"Anyway," James continues, appearing to search for words, "I actually don't understand most of this—what we're doing. Just pieces here and there when good things happen. But the rest? I'm just following."

John nods, appreciating his brother's honesty. "I have a sinking feeling that it's going to take a long time to understand."

"For us?"

John shakes his head. "For everyone."

• • •

*Jericho*

Simon sees sides of Matthew he's never seen before. The despised former tax collector has scrubbed his tunic to at least get the smell of horse dung off it, but still carries a kerchief and is quick to press it to his nose and sometimes over his mouth as they encounter the odors of the bustling city. Matthew is young and spry enough to keep up, but he still seems delicate, hardly rough and tumble. It's as if he were born for the tax booth, an office, his luxurious home. Simon imagines himself one day preaching the kingdom as Jesus does, maybe even performing miracles as the Rabbi has promised. But he'll always be an outdoor guy.

"You familiar with The Nomad?" Simon asks a merchant in the market while Matthew keeps his distance.

"I'm familiar with a lot of nomads, my man. Can you describe him?"

"No, sorry, I mean an establishment. A tav—"

"The bar? Sure! Too familiar with it, if I'm honest. Down there and to the left. You'll see the stairs. A little early in the day, isn't it?"

"Oh!" Matthew says. "We're not—"

Simon pulls him away, thanking the man, and they find the steps minutes later. He stands next to Matthew at the top, strategizing. If Mary has been here, someone will know. Should he pretend to be her brother? A long-lost friend?

Matthew begins to descend, but Simon yanks him back. "Huh-uh," he says. "I know places like this." He leads the way down.

Matthew recites, "'If I make my bed in the depths, You are there …'"

"Just stay behind me," Simon says, entering to find the place busy. Men are crowded around a table gambling, shouting, trash-talking each other.

From a table full of Roman soldiers, a guard stands. "Keep it civil over there, Hebrew dogs!"

The gamblers fall silent but keep tossing in their bets. Simon is about to ask for the proprietor when Matthew shouts, "Excuse me!"

*Oh, no,* Simon thinks. *Here we go.*

The place goes quiet, and the ragged men at the gambling table turn and stare.

Matthew calls out, "Have you seen a woman with long, dark hair?"

Simon lowers his head, wishing he could disappear.

Matthew adds, "She may be distraught."

"Tell 'im, Hohj," someone whispers, and a big, bearded man rises from the end of the table.

He folds his arms. "Are you friends of Lilith?"

*Lilith?* "No," Simon says.

"That sounds like Lilith. That witch took me for everything I have at knucklebones."

Remembering her prowess at the game at The Hammer, Simon whispers to Matthew, "It's Mary." He turns back to the man. "Do you know where she is now?"

"I don't keep track of her. All I know is she staggered out and left her winnings here. You can tell her she's not gettin' a shekel back."

Outside, Simon has no idea where to start looking.

"She can't have gone too far," Matthew says. "We'll cover more ground if we split—"

"We're not doing that," Simon says.

"We can meet at the stables."

Simon turns on him. "Didn't you learn anything in there? Mary can obviously take care of herself. *You* can't."

Matthew looks hurt.

*Great,* Simon thinks. *Now I have to worry about his feelings.*

The tax man appears to muster his courage. "What if you were cut off from Jesus by something in your past? Wouldn't you want help getting back to him as soon as possible?"

For once the quirky little man has stopped Simon. *Yes!* He thinks. *Yes, I would!* He finally gives in. "Okay, we split up." He points to the north, the east, the south, the west. "I go north, you—"

"Boys?"

He starts at the voice of a woman at the end of an alley,

looking tattered and spent. Simon follows as Matthew rushes to her. "Mary!"

"I thought I was dreaming you," she slurs, eyes lolling.

Simon would not have recognized her—her tender beauty and grace camouflaged under tangled hair and in soiled clothes. And she smells. "Can you walk?" he asks her.

She appears to force a smile. "I'm not going anywhere."

"We have to go back," Matthew says.

Her smile fades. "No! I can't."

"C'mon, Mary," Simon says. "He told us to come for you."

She sounds pitiful, a sob in her throat. "No. No. He already fixed me once, and I broke again."

Simon doesn't know what to say, and Matthew wrings his hands.

"I can't face him," she whines.

Matthew looks to Simon, as if he hopes he will say something. But Simon is at a loss too. Matthew steps close and whispers, "I'm a bad person, Mary."

That seems to get her attention. She shakes her head. "Matthew …"

"No! My whole life, all for me. No faith."

"I do have faith in him," she manages. "Just not in me."

"I'm learning more about Torah and God because of you, Mary. I'm studying harder because *you* are such a great student."

Her face is a mixture of appreciation and despair. Matthew nods at Simon as if to say, "Your turn."

Simon thinks Matthew was doing so well. *What can I add?*

"Uh, r-remember when we were at Zebedee's, and they lowered that man after breaking Zeb's roof?" That actually draws a smile, so Simon plunges on. "We did that together. And they got to meet Jesus because of your care for them, and your good ideas."

Matthew chimes in, "Ramah is beginning to read and write

because of you," and he sits next to Mary, despite everything. "He saved you to do all these things."

She seems to smile at the memories, then gags and retches. Matthew leaps to his feet but shocks Simon by not fleeing. Instead, he reaches to hold back her hair, telling her, "It's all right. It's all right."

Simon suggests Matthew use his own handkerchief, but Matthew asks him to find some water. As he goes in search, he realizes this is an entirely new Matthew. And there's no way they'll head back to camp without Mary.

Chapter 42

# POLITICS

*Solomon's Temple, Jerusalem*

Shmuel is frustrated, trying to keep up. He and Yanni have come to speak with an elder Pharisee, Dunash, who clearly doesn't have time for them. As the older man rushes between the columns, he barks over his shoulder, "So, all you're telling me is that he told someone to carry his mat on Shabbat?"

"And invoked the title 'Son of Man' from the prophet Daniel," Shmuel says, "for himself!"

"Yeah, many have. And you say *maybe* something happened at Capernaum, but you're not sure it's the same person."

"I *am* certain," Shmuel says.

"Right," Dunash says, "and your second witness …?"

"My colleague Yussef."

"… who was not at the pool, and neither were you."

"I was there," Yanni says.

Dunash stops and turns to face them. "I'm sorry, but this case is very thin. President Shimon does not preoccupy himself with minutiae."

"Minutiae!" Shmuel cries.

"If I may be so bold," Yanni says, "which violations of God's immutable Law *does* President Shimon deem worthy of his attention?"

The elder smirks and shakes his head, pointing to his ear. "You're not listening, Yanni. Just like you haven't in the past. That is why you still hold a low station."

"I would like to know as well," Shmuel says. "If Shabbat violations are not worthy of Shimon's time, what is?"

Dunash sighs. "Of six hundred and thirteen commandments, there are some which, when pitted against one another, under certain circumstances create pain for people who are already suffering."

"But," Shmuel says, "the Psalmist says, 'The Law of Adonai is perfect, reviving the soul …'"

"Let us return to the matter of witnesses. In the Torah, how many witnesses are required to judiciously establish a fact? Hm?"

"Two," Shmuel says.

"And if a husband dies," Dunash continues, as if teaching children, "and his wife is the only one to witness his death, what does that make her?"

Shmuel knows where this is going, but it's obvious Yanni can't stop himself. "A widow?"

Dunash is not amused and shoots him a look.

"An agunah," Shmuel says. "An abandoned woman, because there was not a second witness to his death."

Dunash nods. "And if she remarries?"

"It makes her an adulterer and her children illegitimate."

"Well," Dunash says, plainly pleased with himself, "can you not see the cruelty of that? *These* are the laws that Shimon, like his father Hillel before him, is seeking to reform. His care is for women, for widows, for the undervalued, for the vulnerable. Yours seems to be about people carrying mats on Shabbat."

Shmuel knows they've been trapped, but Yanni again speaks up. "Blasphemy is not harmless. Dunash, think of the political value."

Dunash shakes his head again as if they will never learn. As he strides away, he says, "I'm only telling you that Shimon is extremely focused. He will not expend energy on this case. Shalom."

Feeling as if he has been run down by a loaded wagon, Shmuel glumly follows Yanni to his office. As soon as the door is closed, Yanni, pacing, says, "Thin? Blatantly commanding someone to violate Shabbat, in addition to blasphemy! President Shimon would call that a thin case?"

"Dunash was totally dismissive."

"He is arrogant because he believes he's the final word. He thinks there's no consequence for talking down to us."

"It's hopeless," Shmuel says.

That stops Yanni. "No!" he says. "It's just getting started. Now we go to the other side. The rigid one."

*Seriously?* "Shammai?" That seems a radical move.

Yanni lurches ahead. "I was hoping to create more chaos by working through Shimon, but perhaps Shammai will respond to our stories with such fury that this will work better anyway."

Shmuel can't hide his angst over the idea, but Yanni is not finished.

"Once," he says, "during the Feast of Tabernacles, Shammai's daughter gave birth to a son. Shmuel, Shammai climbed up onto the roof of the chamber where she and the boy lay and tore open a hole in the plaster, just to make it a sukkah."

"Yes, and his philosophies have weight in the Sanhedrin,

which helps. But what if he finds out we sought President Shimon first?"

"Not what if, Shmuel. We spell it out for him. Shammai and Shimon are philosophical rivals. Here we have a matter of law that President Shimon doesn't have time for. It's a perfect issue for Shammai. Shimon will have no explanation as to why he didn't take this seriously."

Shmuel foresees nothing but endless partisan wrangling ahead, when these things should be clear to all. "Why does it take all this?"

## Chapter 43

# FORGOTTEN

*The disciples' camp*

Mary feels at the end of herself and hangs back with Matthew as Simon leads the way. How can she face her friends? How can she face the Rabbi? It's bitter medicine, but she must see it through or abandon this new life and run back to the old. It's all she can do to put one foot in front of the other. She trudges on, arms folded, feeling as low as she looks—and smells. As kind as the boys have been to her, she's still grimy and wishes she could plunge herself into a river before seeing anyone else—but especially Jesus.

She can tell, even from behind, that Simon strides with that certain bounce, eager to show that he and Matthew have succeeded in finding her, bringing her back. How she wishes to disappear! How has she gotten herself into this mess?

As they come into view, Simon's confidence seems to evaporate. He must see what she's seeing—the others sitting gloomily. Has she caused this? Are they mourning her, worried about her?

Ramah notices her, leaps to her feet, and comes running,

Jesus' mother right behind and trailed by John and Big James. Ramah gathers Mary in. "Thank heaven you're alive!"

In many ways, Mary would rather be dead. But she's overcome as the elder Mary pulls a shawl from around her waist. She gently covers the younger Mary's hair, looking so concerned and relieved that Mary feels even worse for causing all this trouble. As they tend to her, Simon approaches John and Big James, and Mary notices their stony expressions. This has to be about more than her return.

"What happened?" he asks them.

"Philip returned with news," John says. "The Baptizer was taken into custody."

Big James adds, "He's in Herod's most heavily blockaded prison."

"I guess it was pretty bad," John says. "They were rough. They hurt him."

"Does Jesus know?"

"Mm-hm."

"Has Andrew heard?"

They nod and look to where Philip is talking to him. Mary can see that Andrew looks as if he's about to burst. As Simon rushes to him, Ramah and Mother Mary continue wiping her eyes, smoothing her hair and clothes. "Do you need anything?" Ramah asks.

"No," Mary whispers, dreading what comes next. "Where is he?"

"In his tent," Mother Mary says.

Mary knows she must face him but is torn between stalling and getting it over with. What can she possibly say? "Should I wait?"

"No," Mother Mary says. "I will take you to him."

How thoughtful of her! To not have to go alone is the best

she can make of this. As she follows his mother, she's aware that Matthew quietly follows and waits outside. How kind he has been!

Mother Mary opens the tent. Jesus is kneeling, his back to them. Mary hears him weeping and fears she is the cause. She never, ever, wanted to become a burden to him.

Jesus says, without looking, "It's not you. There's quite a lot going on right now."

He turns to face her, and she has never felt so ashamed. She wraps her arms around her own waist. If only she could make herself smaller.

He sniffles and wipes his face. "So, it's good to have you back."

She knows he means it, but it makes her feel only worse. His look is so loving, so compassionate. And she feels so unworthy of it. This is the way he looked at her when first they met, when he delivered her from the demons. She looks away. "I don't know what to say."

"I don't require much," he says.

Staring at the ground, she says, "I-I'm just so ashamed." At his silence she whispers, "You redeemed me, and I just threw it all away."

"Well," he says lightly, "that's not much of a redemption if it can be lost in a day, is it?"

She chuckles miserably but still can't meet his gaze. "I owe you everything. But I just don't think I can do it."

"Do what?"

"This. Live up to it. Repay you. How could I leave? How could I go back to the place I was? And I didn't even—I didn't even come back on my own. They had to come get me." She shakes her head in despair. "I just can't live up to it."

"Well," he says, "that's true. But you don't have to. I just want your heart. The Father just wants your heart. Give us that—which you already have—and the rest will come in time."

*How can he say this?* Mary thinks. *How can he not show his frustration, his impatience?*

"Did you really think you'd never struggle or sin again?"

It's more than she can take in.

"I know how painful that moment was for you."

*But why did I do that? Why?* "I shouldn't—"

"Someday you won't," he says. "But not here."

*I have to wait for heaven before I can do this?* "I'm just so sorry," she says, shoulders heaving. Mother Mary puts a hand on her back.

"Look up," Jesus says.

"I can't."

"You can."

"I can't." Tears splash at her feet.

"Look at me."

She forces herself to peer up at him, into a look so tender she can hardly bear it.

"I forgive you," he says, stepping closer. "It's over."

Sobbing, she reaches for him, and as he embraces her, he whispers, "It's forgotten."

Chapter 44

# NOTHING LEFT

Interesting. That's the best Thomas can say about these four of his new friends—Simon, Andrew, Philip, and Zee, the newcomer. He's approached them to discuss the latest crisis, for which he somehow—stupidly, he knows—feels responsible. It made sense for Jesus to put a former caterer in charge of food inventory, meal planning, everything but final preparation—that remained the task of the women, though he and Matthew often helped.

How can he tell the Rabbi he has run out of food? Well, *he* hasn't, necessarily. It is not his job to buy it, but for days his list of needed supplies has been ignored because there is no money. He never would have let things get to this point in his business, and he can't shake the feeling that there must have been something he could have done.

But now is clearly not the time to discuss this with his mates. While Jesus is in his tent dealing with Mary, Simon is massaging his brother's shoulders, trying to console him. The news from Herod's court has them all exercised, but to Andrew and

Philip—the Baptizer's former disciples—it's personal. Thomas is impressed that Simon, known to refer to Jesus' cousin as Creepy John, is clearly sensitive to Andrew's distress.

"You're certain Herod said forever?" Simon asks Philip.

"I think that's what life imprisonment means. He signed the declaration on the spot—in blood."

Andrew shakes his head. "We'll never see him again," he says, choked with emotion.

"We can break him out," Zee says. "I know some people."

Thomas is stunned. *He's serious!*

Philip turns. "The Zealots against Herod's army? That's a fight I'd pay to see. It's maximum security up there."

Zee, looking more intimidating than ever, says, "That would make it more fun."

Philip glances at the others, then back to Zee. "No. No. You're not a part of that Order anymore. You're a part of this one."

"We shouldn't limit our options is my point."

Simon says, "Now isn't the time for that."

*Maybe it* is *the time*, Thomas thinks. He can withhold his news no longer. "I'm afraid the situation is worse than you know."

"What could be worse?" Andrew says, and Thomas wishes he didn't have to say.

Assuming they know what he's referring to, he says simply, "This never used to happen to me before I met you guys."

He heads to Jesus' tent where Matthew pulls open the flap and says, "I'm sorry to interrupt, Rabbi. It seems that there's, uh, a prob—"

"Yes, let him in, Matthew," Jesus says as the two Marys leave.

Thomas steps in. "Rabbi?"

"Thomas."

"I recognize there is a lot happening, and right now may not be a good time."

"What is it?"

"We only have lentils left to eat for tonight's Shabbat dinner, and after that we are completely out of food."

"Nothing left?"

"I'm so sorry, Rabbi."

Jesus sighs. "Seems like something we should seek my Father about."

*Wait. He turned water into wine. He can't make food appear?* "Pray?" Thomas says.

"Well, it is almost Shabbat, after all. I know of a synagogue nearby."

"The nearest settlement is Wadi Kelt, and I don't think they give out free meals."

"Tell everyone we head out in the morning."

Chapter 45

# CONFRONTATION

Simon finds himself curious. Intrigued. Thomas seemed honored to have been assigned to pass along a message to the rest directly from Jesus. Nothing earth-shattering. Just that they would all be going to a nearby synagogue. But they're in the middle of nowhere. How significant can this synagogue be?

The entire entourage follows Jesus along a path through vast wheatfields, ripe for harvest. Simon strides next to him with John and Big James a step behind. Trailing the rest of the disciples, several paces back, are Mother Mary, Mary Magdalene, and Ramah.

As the tiny village comes into view, the synagogue appears to be the main attraction. But as he feared, Simon finds it not much to speak of. "Have you been to this synagogue, Rabbi?"

"No, I have not, Simon."

John speaks up. "Why this synagogue, Rabbi? It's not on any of our maps."

"That's a good question," Jesus says. "Have you noticed

that no matter where we go recently, we are more and more misunderstood?"

"Definitely," John and his brother say in unison.

"It's a very complicated time," Jesus adds. "It grieves me that Mary was not welcomed in the synagogue in Jericho when she first arrived in distress."

"They turned her away?" Simon says. "She didn't mention it."

"Come on," Jesus says. "She's a woman. She didn't expect their help, but she needed it. Add to that my cousin John's arrest. You could say I'm feeling nostalgic for a small town."

They enter the synagogue, and as they pass the showbread preparation kitchen, it is obvious the oven has not been fired for years. In the sanctuary, the service of worship has already begun. Simon is not surprised to see that he and his compatriots have nearly doubled the attendance.

They settle into place, men on one side and women on the other, as usual. The more elderly of two rabbis, Madai, sits behind the younger, Lamech, who stands at the almemar, reading from the Torah scroll. "'No one born of a forbidden union may enter the assembly of the Lord. Even to the tenth generation, none of his descendants may enter the assembly of the Lord.'"

Simon spots a dark-complexioned man about his own age, sitting alone, head down, his left hand grotesquely curled in his lap. Jesus approaches the man, and the presiding rabbis appear to notice. Lamech pauses, then continues. "'No Ammonite or Moabite may enter the assembly of the Lord. Even to the tenth generation, none of them may enter the assembly of the Lord forever!'"

The man with the useless hand suddenly notices Jesus and the others and appears puzzled, concerned.

Lamech continues, "'Because they did not meet you with

bread and with water on the way. Even to the tenth generation, none of them may enter the assembly of the Lord forever.'"

Madai rises from his seat. The younger rabbi stops and uses his stylus to keep his place, glaring as Jesus reaches the man, lays a hand on his shoulder, and says, "Shalom."

The man looks alarmed.

Jesus nods at his hand. "May I see?"

Lamech shouts, "Excuse me! What are you doing?"

Jesus whispers to the man. "What is your name?"

The man looks to the two Pharisees and back at Jesus. "Elam."

Jesus addresses the rabbis. "Your friend Elam has a withered hand."

Madai rushes forward. "Are you a healer?"

"It is not lawful to heal on Sabbath!" Lamech shouts.

Jesus sighs, and it strikes Simon that he has never seen the Master so exercised. "Which one of you," Jesus says to all, "who has a sheep, and it falls into a pit on the Sabbath, will not take hold of it and lift it out?"

Madai points and roars, "Who are you to speak to our congregation in such a way?"

"Of how much more value is this man than a sheep?"

Lamech comes from behind the pulpit. "Stop this at once!"

"Come here," Jesus tells Elam. "Come stand here. It's okay."

The man rises to follow, but Madai barks, "Elam, sit down! We don't know this person. He could be a shaman."

Elam remains standing next to Jesus.

"Is it lawful on Sabbath to do good or to do harm?" Jesus says. "To save life or to kill?"

"This affliction does not threaten his life," Madai says.

"It does not even affect his health!" Lamech adds.

"Lift it," Jesus tells Elam. Jesus takes the withered hand in both of his and breathes deeply. He releases the hand. "Stretch it out. It's good, huh?" The room is stunned to silence, and Elam beams.

Lamech rages, "If he was supposed to be healed, God would have done it Himself!"

*If he only knew,* Simon thinks.

"Interesting point," Jesus says.

"Get out!" Madai shouts.

"Gladly," Jesus says.

As Simon and the others follow him out, Lamech shouts, "Blasphemer!"

"What is wrong with you?" Madai adds.

Jesus turns back. "Apparently everything."

A moment later Lamech shouts, "Wait! Come back! How dare you?"

Simon and the rest follow Jesus back out onto the path through the wheatfields. Ramah says, "Are they going to send the town guards after us?"

"I think those guys *are* the town guards," Thomas says.

Simon, at the front with Jesus but walking backward to face the others, can't stop chattering. "All right, so for those of you who weren't close enough to see, first Jesus interrupted the reading simply by standing next to this guy with a paralyzed hand." He laughs and pulls a handful of kernels from the spike of a wheat plant, shoving them into his mouth. "And then the priest, he just went cr—"

He suddenly stops, mid-chew, realizing what he's done. The others stare wide-eyed.

"What?" Matthew asks Philip.

"Reaping or harvesting on Shabbat."

"Oh, yes."

Humiliated, Simon spits everything out and turns to Jesus. "I'm sorry. I've been so hungry, I forgot what day it is."

Everyone seems frozen in place as Jesus seems to study them. Finally he says, "You may."

Simon hesitates, then shoves another handful into his mouth. The rest immediately grab wheat stalks, rolling the spikes between their palms to release the kernels. As they eat, Madai and Lamech catch up to them. They elbow their way through the women and shoulder their way up to Jesus. Madai says, "You have made a mockery of our little synagogue and of Torah!"

Pointing in Jesus' face, Lamech says, "You will tell us your name, your lineage, your—" He whirls, staring at Jesus' followers. "First you, and now your disciples, are doing what is not lawful to do on the Sabbath!"

"Have you not read," Jesus says, "what David did when he was in need and was hungry? He entered the house of God, in the time of Ahimalech the priest, and ate the Bread of the Presence, which was not lawful for him to eat, but only for the priests."

"You would compare yourself to David?" Lamech says.

"It was an emergency!" Madai says.

"Or have you not read in the Law how on Shabbat the priests in the Temple profane the Sabbath but are guiltless?"

"That's for Levites! Are you a Levite? Of priestly lineage?"

"Listen carefully. Something greater than the Temple is here. And if you had known what this means—'I desire mercy, not sacrifice'—you would not have condemned the guiltless. Sabbath was made for man, not man for the Sabbath. So the Son of Man is Lord even of the Sabbath."

Madai looks stricken. "The Son of M-m ..."

"Let's go," Jesus says, and Simon and the others leave the priests running back down the path to their synagogue.

• • •

*That night*

Madai paces before Lamech's desk as the younger man furiously writes. "They probably won't even read it," Madai says. "This is Wadi Kelt, not Bethany or Jericho. They routinely forget to send us memoranda of liturgical changes for synagogue practice."

Lamech looks up. "And if we don't alert the Sanhedrin?"

"Then we sin by omission."

"He even had women following him. Three!"

"Be sure to add that."

"If that doesn't catch their attention …"

"But the Sanhedrin is distracted," Madai says. "Between Rome and the factions and reforms and the protests, and the Zealots and Herod and Caesar—their attention is diluted."

"Who would have dreamed," Lamech says, "that someone claiming to be the Son of Man—"

"The one who approaches the Ancient of Days …"

"And Lord of the Sabbath. Walking into our tiny synagogue."

"Wadi Kelt versus Jerusalem is like David versus Goliath. Maybe there *is* hope for the little, the overlooked."

"Or maybe," Lamech says, "they write it off as just another lunatic in the wilderness, spewing blasphemies and trying to get attention."

"And it will end up at the bottom of the pile on some secretary's desk." Madai pauses. "We could go to Jotapata where this man is supposed to speak next. There will be people of import among the protestors. We could tell them as well."

"Yes, we will do both. Who knows? All we can do is fulfill our duty to report the facts. And pray."

"For what?"

"Justice."

# PART 7
# Reckoning

## Chapter 46

# PREPARATION

*Capernaum*

Caesar's *Cohortes Urbana* Atticus makes his way through the bustle of the marketplace, cloak covering the SPQR insignia on his chest that identifies him with the *Senatus Populace Romanus* (Senate and the Roman people). The troublemaker he's been tracking may be from Nazareth, but this is where everything seemed to begin—where the preacher and seeming magic man started gathering his gaggle of fishermen, a cripple, a tradesman, a woman of less than stellar reputation, one of the followers of his own weird cousin, and even a tax collector forevermore.

Where would it end? The man had added a wedding caterer, a failed architect, even a Zealot to his menagerie of misfits! What might he be up to? No question he has pulled off some impressive stunts—rumors flying about healings and all the rest. Tricks? Mind games? Who could say? Despite the ragtag lot he has chosen, the result is a growing following who believe he might be the Jews' long-prophesied Messiah.

That this so-called prophet and teacher has proved

interesting enough to attract the attention of Rome makes him Atticus's business. To be in the very city where he might seek out and interview the parents of two of the fisherman followers, the wife and mother-in-law of another, perhaps even the guard who had been assigned to the tax collector … Well, if nothing else, Atticus can feather his own nest with the emperor. Besides, he can't deny his own curiosity. Might there be something deeper, something real about this strange itinerant?

All about Atticus, Roman guards in their brilliant red tunics nail signs on walls and posts. He waits until one moves on, then approaches to find the announcement: *Jesus of Nazareth sought for questioning.* It adds that anyone with knowledge of his whereabouts is to get word to the local praetor.

Aah, the praetor! Slimy Quintus, who wears his title and station like peacock feathers but who in reality—Atticus knows—would trade it all to be a true confidant of the sovereign himself, Tiberius Julius Caesar Augustus. In short, like all mid-level Roman operatives, Quintus can't hide his jealousy of the *Cohortes Urbana*. Everyone beneath Quintus may fawn over him or fall quaking at his feet, but not Atticus.

He tears down the sign and stuffs it into his cloak. How it will gall Quintus to have him be the one to deliver the Nazarene on a silver platter!

Moments later, he approaches the desk of a scribbling underling who doesn't even bother to look up. "Yes?"

"I'm here to see Quintus."

Finally the man deigns to pause. "That's *Praetor* Quintus, and you may request an audience only via formal—"

Atticus slaps the torn sign atop the man's work.

"—application." The lackey looks horrified. "Did you deface and remove a public notice?"

Atticus finds this delicious. He lifts his cloak to reveal his insignia. "How 'bout now?"

The man leaps to his feet, ushering Atticus to Quintus' office, where the praetor stands gazing out the window. He turns, and his eyes widen. "Atticus Aemilius Pulcher? Sent all the way to the Upper Galilee?"

"You're behind the times, Quintus. I've been up and down Judea. Practically under your nose."

"I thought you retired."

"*Cohortes Urbanae* don't retire."

Quintus looks gleeful. "That's right. They ship you off to Gaul."

"Question for you: How do you hold up all that armor with no spine?"

"Don't be salty, Atticus. Gaul's not a bad place to retire. I hear the women all have red hair, and the music—"

"I'm not here to talk about women and music, though I'm sure you have plenty of time for both."

"Yes, I do," Quintus says, "because I keep things so tight around here. It's how I have time for you. Oh, and Hail Caesar! Did I hail already? How can I serve him today?"

Time to get down to business. "I come bearing intelligence."

That appears to get the praetor's attention. "I bear ears."

"Good. Open them wide, Quintus. I've got news. It's about Jesus of Nazareth."

Finally, a smile from the praetor that appears genuine. Atticus trades information on where Jesus and his disciples can be located for the privilege of accompanying the *contubernium* assigned to bring him in. "Just don't interfere," Quintus says. "I'll assign Primi Gaius to lead them and make the arrest."

"Wait," Atticus says, "the same Gaius who—"

"Had been assigned to my best tax man, yes. You do your

homework, I'll give you that. I'd like to throttle this Jesus for stealing that quirky little guy alone."

• • •

*Southwestern shore, Sea of Galilee outside Tiberias*

Standing here with his brother, Andrew, and the brothers John and Big James, reminds Simon of home. He fights off the nostalgia to keep from dwelling on how much he misses his beloved Eden. The days—the lives, really—of fishing are over for these four, but the anchored boat, the lapping waves, and the smells bring it all back. Days in the sun with John and James's father, the gregarious Zebedee …

Yet he's here not to fish, but to get out of fishing. Each of the four has chosen a stone from the beach, having agreed that whichever pair of brothers throws the farthest gets to return to where Jesus is preparing the others for his next big sermon. The other pair must complete the task Jesus has assigned, restocking the disciples' stores of food.

"All right," John says, "I'll go first," and rears back to throw.

"Whoa! Whoa!" Simon shouts, and John stops, clearly annoyed. "How are we gonna measure it if you throw it into the sea?"

"By the splash."

"Throw it on the shore," Andrew says.

Big James says, "I'm going to win anyway."

"We'll see," Simon says. "If it's between fishing or hearing Rabbi's instructions about the sermon, I'll throw this thing to the Mediterranean."

"We should *all* be fishing!" Andrew says. "Try to avoid anything like what happened at Wadi Kelt."

"So," John tells him, "throw it, big guy."

Andrew winds up and launches a rock into the sea. Simon

throws one even farther. John and Big James throw almost simultaneously, and both their splashes far outdistance Simon's and Andrew's. The sons of Zebedee laugh and crow. James, the winner, says, "The sons of Jonah fish today!"

"Great," Simon says, picking up another rock. "Two out of three." The others look at him with such disdain that he drops the stone and says, "What if we arm wrestle?"

"Why are we deciding anything?" Andrew shouts. "We should all be fishing like Jesus asked! We can't risk messing up his sermon plans."

"Andrew!" John says with a wry smile. "I never took you for a sore loser."

"Easy, Little Thunder," Simon says. "You two go listen to Rabbi and catch us up when we come back."

"No!" Andrew says. "I mean it! Rabbi has told four of us to find food. We should do as he says or bad things will happen."

James folds his arms. "Sore loser *and* superstitious. Not a good look."

As John and James leave, John says, "Oh, and Simon, we can arm wrestle next time."

"No problem!" James adds.

When they're out of earshot, Andrew says, "That was a terrible suggestion."

"You don't think I could take at least one of them? Have some faith, man."

"Faith isn't my problem!" Andrew says as he trudges to the boat.

• • •

*A knoll outside Jotapata*

Matthew feels he is getting better at keeping up with his furiously scribbled notes, even though others in the group—like

Simon—keep warning that such documentation, in the wrong hands, could ruin everything. But who's going to be interested in the hen scratchings of a former tax collector, still dressed in his old finery, now dingey and worn from traipsing around the dusty countryside?

Jesus is telling his mother, Philip, Nathanael, and Matthew that everyone has a part to play in the execution of the upcoming sermon, which he expects will draw a crowd much larger than ever. That's how fast word is spreading about Jesus not only performing a miracle here and there, but also healing *everyone* wherever he goes.

When John and Big James arrive, Jesus says, "Sons of Thunder! Aren't you supposed to still be fishing?"

"We decided they could handle it," James says. "We wanted to learn more about what you are planning."

"Hmm," Jesus says. "You won a contest, huh?" They nod, and all chuckle. "How is Andrew?"

"He'll get over it," John says. "So what have we missed?"

This is where Matthew feels valuable. He reads from his notes. "Zee is working on a security plan. Mary and Ramah are back at camp working on—"

"Thank you, Matthew," Jesus says. "They don't need to hear all the details. Here's what I want each of you to understand, and what I want you to make sure that everyone else understands as well: It's the *why* of this sermon, hm? It's not because we need to make our presence felt here in the region, and it's not about the details of how we make this happen." He looks at Matthew as if to reassure him. "The details matter, yes, and all of you will make sure that this is executed well. But what makes this sermon so important is each person who will be there. Philip, what makes John's sermons so memorable?"

"The volume."

Jesus laughs. "Well, yes, that too."

"He spoke directly to whoever was there. It was personal."

"Yes, good. But this sermon will have thousands of people, so I won't be directing it to one group over another. But what I will say will be for each and every one of them. They're coming because word is spreading from the signs and wonders. But what I'll be giving to them will be far more important: truth. This will define our whole ministry. That's what we need to focus on."

Chapter 47

# DANGEROUS

*Capernaum synagogue*

Yanni agrees with Shmuel that they must find the woman who brought her friend to Jesus for healing. He insists that Yussif will know who she is, and he talks Shmuel into returning to their home synagogue. "Isn't it customary to send word ahead?" Shmuel says.

"Let's just see what happens."

They enter a dimly lit room where the local Pharisees sit praying or quietly conversing. Yanni clears his throat. "Rabbi Shmuel bar Yosef of Capernaum!" he announces. To his delight, a buzz runs through the assembled, and they break into enthusiastic applause. Shmuel looks embarrassed—and relieved.

Yussif emerges from a corridor. "Shmuel!"

"Shalom!" Shmuel says.

Yussif addresses the room. "The learned Shmuel returns from Jerusalem! For what reason we cannot say, but we are honored!"

"For the sardines!" Shmuel says with mirth. "Where else

would I go?" The two laugh and embrace as the others seem to catch on.

Yanni says, "We do have them pickled in the Holy City as well."

Yussif roars. "I think Nicodemus made a fish joke upon his last arrival too." He turns to an underling. "Prepare the seat of honor—"

"No, no, Yussif, I've done nothing to—"

"You were accepted by the Great Sanhedrin of Jerusalem for special research—a privilege few are granted. Please—"

"I'm flattered by your gesture, Yussif, but this is no time for sitting. May I speak with you privately?"

Yussif appears flummoxed. "Well, yes, of course."

Shmuel leads him to the Bet Midrash study hall, and Yanni follows, detecting curiosity on the faces of the others.

As soon as they're settled in private, Shmuel reminds Yussif of the beautiful Ethiopian woman who managed to get her crippled friend through the roof of a local home so Jesus of Nazareth could heal him.

"Tamar, yes," Yussif says. "At the house of Zebedee the fisherman. What about her?"

"That day she appealed to Jesus by saying she'd seen him heal a leper on the road. Remember?"

"Yes, but there is no law against healing a leper."

"But if it was on Shabbat, like Yanni saw him do at the pool, then a pattern has emerged. She could be the key to confirming two incidents."

"But a woman's testimony is automatically disregarded."

"Not if she leads us to the leper."

"You think someone healed of leprosy would turn over damning information about his healer?"

Yanni jumps in. "To do otherwise would violate the commandment against bearing false witness."

Yussif appears conflicted. "With all due respect, Teacher, I thought you went to Jerusalem to investigate false prophecy, not hunt down this one man from Nazareth, of all places."

"One and the same errand, Yussif," Shmuel says.

"I know he spends time with sinners, but—"

"The Ethiopian, is she still in Capernaum?"

"Not in Capernaum. The last I heard of her was from Yehuda. He encountered her in Migdal."

"Why would Yehuda bother to mention it?" Shmuel says.

"She was offering testimony on the street."

Yanni shakes his head. "A woman?"

"Blasphemy!" Shmuel says. "It's like a wildfire with this man. Everywhere he goes! We must find her."

Yussif says, "And if you discover the healing was not on Shabbat?"

Yanni shares an awkward glance with Shmuel. That would be disastrous, besides making them look like fools.

Yussif brightens. "I hope you will consider sharing with us your experience in Jerusalem."

"I would like that, Yussif," Shmuel says. "But there is one other I must speak with."

• • •

*The Sea of Galilee*

As much as Simon bickers with his brother, there's no one he'd rather spend the afternoon fishing with than Andrew—even when he's more agitated than ever. "I don't know why the grain thing bothers you so much," Simon says. "Jesus didn't mind."

"The Wadi Kelt Pharisees sure did! And you know they'll report him now."

"Jesus knows what he's doing. You don't have to ride to his rescue all the time."

Andrew looks up from his net. "Seriously? You? The master of riding to his rescue?"

"Yeah, all right, I did that a few times. I know it doesn't help."

Andrew pauses. Then, "You know what they're doing to John. We can't let them do that to Jesus."

"We won't!"

"Then let's not make a scene everywhere we go! That's all I'm saying. It's common sense."

His brother seems more exercised than ever. Simon says, "I think he's more of an uncommon sense guy, don't you? Get used to different, brother."

"I'm being smart."

Simon shoots him a look.

"What?"

"Leave smart to Matthew and Thomas," Simon says.

"So Matthew's smart now? The Messiah really has come!"

"Forget I said anything. Let's just fish."

• • •

*The Roman Authority headquarters*

Yanni and Shmuel approach the clerk at a desk in the vestibule. A guard stands nearby.

"I'm here to request an audience with the praetor," Shmuel says. "It's urgent."

The clerk turns to the guard with a smirk. "He says it's urgent, Marcus." He turns back. "That's what everyone says."

"Well, there are signs all over Capernaum saying the man known as Jesus of Nazareth is sought for questioning."

That seems to sober both Marcus and the clerk. "I can take your statement," the clerk says.

Yanni was hoping they could actually talk with Quintus, but he raises a brow to Shmuel, as if he should proceed.

Shmuel hesitates but says, "I believe he was last seen in Jerusalem for one of our pilgrimage festivals."

"When was this?"

"Five days ago."

Both guard and clerk relax. "That's outdated intelligence," the clerk says.

"What?"

Marcus speaks up. "We'll have him in our custody by tomorrow."

"What's happened?" Shmuel says.

"On what charge?" Yanni says.

Marcus says, "Do you have anything else to report?"

"With all respect, officer," Shmuel says, "I must know the nature of the charges. If he broke Jewish law, then we must know."

"We?" the clerk says.

"What do you know of the Order of the Zealots?" Marcus says.

"The Fourth Philosophy?" Shmuel says. "I-I don't understand."

"Stories and rumors," Yanni says. "They are outsiders."

"What have the Zealots got to do with Jesus of Nazareth?" Shmuel says.

"Thank you for coming in," Marcus says. "Can you see yourselves out, or would you like me to show you the way?"

"No, no," Shmuel says, "you're on the wrong track. Jesus *is* dangerous, but he's not—"

"We can decide for ourselves who's dangerous," the guard says. "Thank you."

Yanni is not about to give up. "May we question him? Once you have him in custody?"

"Yes," Shmuel adds. "I would very much like to speak with him on behalf of the Capernaum synagogue."

"We'll pass that along," the clerk says flatly.

"Will you really?" Shmuel says.

"No."

Marcus steps toward them. "Out!"

At the door, Shmuel turns back. "Mark my words: Do not underestimate him."

Marcus unsheaths his sword. "Do not underestimate this."

Chapter 48

# A WORD TO THE WISE

*Outside Jotapata*

Gaius and his small band of legionnaires leave their horses in the woods and march through the wilderness to where he has been told he might find Jesus. That one of Caesar's own *Cohortes Urbanae* has somehow finagled his way to accompany them feels like yet another political distraction he must navigate. For now, Atticus is at the back of the pack.

Gaius has no idea what to expect from the roving so-called prophet, but beyond the potential threat of a former Zealot and one oversized former fisherman, he anticipates little trouble for his nine muscled, armed, and uniformed troops. He will be swift and authoritative, giving the preacher no recourse but to surrender.

Gaius turns at rushing footsteps. The interloper is moving up. Great.

He overtakes Gaius. "So what's your plan, Primi?" The man sounds genuinely curious, not condescending.

"Plan?" Gaius says. "We're gonna walk through that city like we own it, arrest our man, and be home by breakfast, *Cohortes*. That is the plan."

"Have you been to Jotapata?"

"I've seen schematics."

"It's a very, um—intense place."

"Meaning?"

"Well," Atticus says, "let's just say the praetor in Jotapata doesn't have the kind of control Quintus has in Capernaum."

"How do you know that?"

"I used to have some reliable informants there."

"Used to? What happened, they stopped talking?"

"They stopped living. Tortured to death. One by one. Rome is the enemy in Jotapata, Primi."

"But it's named after a Roman emperor."

"Exactly," Atticus says. "Herod built it on top of Jewish tombs, no less, and forced many Jews to settle there against their will. How do you think that's going?"

"Not great."

"Yeah. You know the guys in black and white?"

"Pharisees."

"They've got a lot of 'em. And the other ones?"

"Sadducees," Gaius says.

"Yeah, some of those too. And preachers, like this Jesus, all over the place. Pretty much everyone in the town is on a mission of protest. You know what I mean?"

"I'm starting to get the picture."

"Jesus' camp is just south of the city."

"Maybe we'll take the long way around," Gaius says, drawing a smile from Atticus.

"Now *that* sounds like a good plan."

"Is that why you came along?"

"I wanted the exercise. But mostly, your praetor is about the most detestable guy in all of Galilee."

Gaius can't argue with that, but he's also made a career of subordinating himself to Quintus. "You sure that's the only reason you've come? For exercise you could have walked along the seashore. If you wanted to avoid Quintus, there's always plenty to drink in a fishing city."

This brings a chuckle from Atticus. "You've got good instincts, Primi. All right, if you must know, I admit I am intrigued by your prey."

*Seriously?* "Intrigued by Jesus of Nazareth?"

"I saw a man who had not stood on his own two feet in decades bounding like a boy. I saw a Zealot surrender his weapon and take a knee. And let me tell you this, Gaius: I watched in secret as a madman attacked that former Zealot in the group's camp, and easily overpowered him with supernatural strength, until the teacher merely spoke to him. The lunatic's eyes went clear, and he collapsed in joy. Jesus of Nazareth did those things. He doesn't strike me as at all threatening. And *that* scares me."

*Of course,* Gaius thinks, *I myself saw a ridiculously wealthy Jew abandon his privileged position and opulent lifestyle in an instant to follow this man.*

Atticus continues, "Maybe I'm just interested to see how he'll take to wrist irons."

If the rumors of healing miracles have any validity, Gaius will have to execute this arrest entirely by the book and see what happens.

## Chapter 49

# APPREHENDED

*The Sea of Galilee*

Agitated as his brother seems, Simon still enjoys working with him. With Jesus and a few of the others in sight far across the beach to the knoll, Simon and Andrew deftly untangle their nets. If anyone can bring in the seafood for sustenance, they can.

"Like old times, huh?" Simon says.

"As Jesus says, no one ever has to guess what's going on in your head."

"There's nothing in my head. This kind of work is in our bones. Don't have to think."

"Must be nice," Andrew says, "having nothing in your head."

"Don't be smart. It's just a saying."

"Was certainly true when you plucked the heads of grain at Wadi Kelt."

"C'mon! Everybody did that—well, except Mary."

"She'd already done her part," Andrew says, his disgust obvious.

"You think you're never going to make another mistake in your life?"

"She was gone for days!"

"Two days," Simon says. "Don't exaggerate."

"*Me* not exaggerate? Are you telling *me* not to exaggerate? That's-that's … wow."

"Look," Simon says, "she went through something horrible and terrifying, and she dealt with it the best way she knew how."

"She should have gone to Jesus."

"She knows that now, Andrew! If you remember, Jesus was busy disarming crazy Simon of his dagger."

"Oh, *he's* the crazy Simon?"

"Compared to me? I'm a married man who worked an honest trade …"

"Worked an honest trade dishonestly!"

"It's how I met Jesus," Simon says. "Unexpected roads."

"Gambling. Brawling. Was that also unexpected?"

"You gambled too, brother."

"And I'll never do it again. And if I'm ever tempted, I'll ask the Rabbi for help. Certainly, I won't do anything selfish that leaves the group stranded at camp for two days, starving, or puts Jesus on edge, makes him snap at the Pharisees—who are hunting us down now!"

"He was grieving his cousin's arrest. And they're not hunting us down. You're so dramatic."

"When word reaches Jerusalem," Andrew says, "that he claimed the title 'Son of Man' and 'Lord of the Sabbath,' they'll hunt him down and put him away. And it could completely ruin all the plans for the big sermon, erase all the momentum we've gained. That's what I'm afraid of."

Simon shakes his head. "Jerusalem doesn't even open the mail from Wadi Kelt. Andrew, this is just your fear talking."

"I've been at this longer than you. When they decide they don't like you, it's over. John the Baptizer might spend his *life* in prison!"

"But Herod arrested John, not the Sanhedrin."

"The Sanhedrin arrests people all the time!"

Simon studies his brother. "You're the one who told me he was the Messiah. Am I gonna have to be the one to remind *you* now?"

"The very fact that he's the Messiah means there's going to be trouble. You get it? Maybe even a war."

*A war? Is he serious?* "Andrew, if you were building an army, would you start with Little James and Thaddeus?"

"Simon!"

"You think he's drawing up military plans when he goes away to desolate places?"

"He never comes back with anything."

*How can he say that?* "You know what, let's just fish. All right? Can we?"

As if he can't stand the sight of his brother, Andrew quickly moves to the other side of the boat. Simon ties off his net and breathes a huge sigh. Blessed silence. But then his attention is drawn to the shore, where Matthew's old guard swiftly marches a small band of soldiers—and a civilian—toward where Jesus and the others are huddled.

"Andrew? My little brother whom I love very much ..."

"What?"

"I need you to take a very long, deep breath. Can you do that?"

"What? Why?"

"Just please. Ask God to give you peace before—"

But Andrew finally turns and sees what Simon sees. "I knew it!" Andrew rages. "I knew it!"

"Hey! Keep it together, man!"

They frantically prepare the boat to head for shore.

• • •

Sitting before Jesus with Big James, along with Mother Mary, Matthew, Philip, and Nathanael, John feels guilty for having schemed their way out of the task the Rabbi assigned them and the other pair of brothers. But on the other hand, he never tires of hearing Jesus instruct and plan.

Jesus says, "Now, a few days will be plenty of time to make sure everything goes smoothly. Nathanael, take Thaddeus and Little James to find a suitable location, and decide if it makes sense to build some sort of a platform."

He suddenly stops, staring past his followers. John turns to see Gaius and his troops approach. He and Big James leap to their feet as the others stare, fear etched on their faces.

Jesus puts a hand on Matthew's shoulder and tells him and Philip, "Don't be afraid. Tell everyone to keep planning. I'll be back."

The pair hurries off toward camp.

Jesus holds up both hands to calm everyone, and John senses the terror in Jesus' mother. Nathanael pulls her close as the soldiers arrive and form a circle around the Rabbi and his followers. John and Big James flank Jesus.

"Jesus of Nazareth," Gaius says, "you're sought for questioning by a Roman authority. Will you surrender peacefully?"

"Yes."

"Jesus, no!" John whispers.

Jesus shushes him.

"Are you armed?" Gaius says.

"I am not. But some of my followers are."

The soldiers pull swords from their sheaths in unison. "Tell your followers to drop their weapons," Gaius continues, "and step back ten cubits."

"I will. May I say goodbye to my ima?" Gaius stares and Jesus adds, "*Mater mea,*" in Latin (*My mother*).

Gaius appears to be trying to remain severe without acting the monster. "Yes," he says flatly.

Jesus embraces her. "Don't be afraid, Ima." She nods, but John can tell she's petrified. Jesus turns back. "James and John," he says, "drop your weapons and step back ten cubits."

Gaius nods to two troops who retrieve the knives. One soldier binds Jesus' hands behind his back.

The primi looks conflicted, as if he simply wants this over. Jesus appears to gaze at him knowingly, and Gaius is plainly uncomfortable.

"Matthew is safe and doing well," Jesus tells him. "He's back at the camp."

Gaius steps closer. "You all look underfed. Filthy."

"We had a bit of a hungry spell," Jesus says. "But we have men out on the water now, stocking us up."

Gaius leans in and whispers, "Matthew's used to eating well. What do you have to offer him?"

"Should we talk about this later?"

Gaius pauses, seeming to assess the man. He raises his voice. "Move out!" And they lead Jesus away.

Chapter 50

# DESPERATION

*The disciples' camp*

Simon can hardly believe Andrew has been right. He expected trouble down the road but assumed it would more likely come as a result of the massive crowds they expected at the upcoming sermon. To see the man they had virtually given their lives to led away, his hands bound behind his back, is more than he can bear. He and Andrew race toward the camp. Big James and John had been among those who appeared to stand by passively as the arrest was executed.

Simon has never been able to keep up with his little brother, and as he follows, he determines what to say to the others. Of one thing he is sure: He will *never* abandon Jesus in such a situation. Does no one else have an iota of backbone?

He finds the group huddled under the canopy where they usually eat together. Even from a distance, they look shaken, stunned, heads down. Simon and Andrew charge into their midst. "What happened?" Andrew demands.

Simon shouts, "You stood there and did nothing while he was arrested!"

Philip holds up a hand. "He was specific."

"Detained," Big James says. "Not arrested."

"Those are just words!" Simon says. "Have you no experience with Rome?"

Andrew looks as if he's about to burst. "We have to go after them."

"He surrendered peacefully," John says.

"No!" Andrew rages. "No! What if they change their minds? Have you forgotten what they're doing to the Baptizer?"

Mary puts a hand on Mother Mary's shoulder. "Andrew! You're terrifying her."

"I will be fine," the elder whispers.

"Well, I'm going," Andrew says. "They're headed north. I'll catch them in Jotapata and petition for his release."

"Andrew," John says, "he didn't ask for your help."

Near tears, Andrew says, "He shouldn't have to! I don't recognize any of you."

Simon leans close and whispers, "Brother, you're not yourself."

Andrew pushes him away.

"Maybe I should come with you," Mary Magdalene says. "I feel responsible."

Andrew whirls to face her. "You might *be* responsible!"

"Andrew!" Simon scolds.

But his brother continues. "How *could* you leave?"

Simon hollers, "Stop this right now!"

Andrew glares and stalks toward his tent.

Mother Mary says, "It isn't anyone's fault."

Philip addresses young Mary. "Please stay. I'll accompany Andrew. I have lots of experience waiting for my rabbi outside jails."

"Why wait?" Zee says. "Let's break him out."

Andrew rushes back through them, a traveling pack over his shoulder. Philip follows, calling back over his shoulder, "Don't wait up."

• • •

*Jotapata*

Leading Yanni into the city, Shmuel finds the place a bastion of orthodoxy—Pharisees davening in every street and alley—loudly reciting liturgical prayers, rocking from the waist. On one corner he encounters an ornately attired priest calling out the Amidah as if performing on a stage. "You graciously bestow knowledge upon man and teach mortals understanding! Graciously bestow upon us from Your wisdom, understanding, and knowledge …"

"Excuse me, friend," Shmuel says gently. "Shalom. We're trying to—"

But the man holds up a hand for silence and continues, "O behold our affliction and wage our battle, for You are God, the Redeemer, the mighty One!"

"We're from Jerusalem, and we're looking for—"

Another hand. "Cause us to return, our Father, to Your service and bring us back …"

"He does this every day," a beggar woman calls to them from the entrance of the alleyway, her coin cup in hand.

"It's okay," Shmuel tells the man of prayer. "We'll find someone else." He approaches the woman.

"They're all like that in this city," she says.

Yanni says, "Have you seen any Ethiopians around here?"

"Not many," she says, looking away but thrusting out her cup.

Shmuel drops in a shekel and says, "What about a woman, impossible to miss? Lots of jewelry, very striking, very loud."

"Gets men like you upset?"

"Yes," Shmuel and Yanni say in unison.

"If you're talking about the woman who rattles on about a healer from Nazareth, she's probably not far."

Shmuel hands her another shekel. "Tell us everything you know."

• • •

*Disciples' camp*

Young Mary worries what this must all sound like to Jesus' mother—the men arguing over what to do next.

Nathanael says, "I'm not sure what could be clearer than the three words, 'I will be back.'"

"That's four," Matthew says.

"How can you dispute that?" Big James says.

Zee says, "Maybe it was a hint. That *we* are supposed to be the fulfillment of those words."

"You Zealots," Nathanael says, "with your secret handshakes and codes!"

"I am not a Zealot anymore," Zee says. "Just zealous. There's a difference."

Nathanael is having none of it. "You just interpreted plain speech about trust and peacefulness as code for insurrection!"

"I think he's onto something," Big James says. "Rabbi told us how important this sermon is. We can't let anything stop it. Maybe it *was* a hint."

"You're not going to keep me from another obvious fight, are you?" Zee says.

"With Zee's skills," John says, "we could do it."

Mother Mary says, "James and John, be mindful of what he named you."

"Seems perfect for a time like this," John says.

Young Mary is alarmed. "I think we should do what he said and wait here for him."

"Oh, yes," John says, "great advice, coming from someone who disappeared for two days."

"How dare you?" Ramah says.

Matthew jumps in. "Don't talk to her like that!"

John turns on Matthew. "Oh, now he speaks. Suddenly he has a voice when it's about her."

"You've made mistakes too, John," Simon mutters. Mary is pierced but grateful that even Simon defends her.

"Boys!" Mother Mary says. "Stop it!"

"*Boys?*" John says.

"You're acting like children," she says.

"Nathanael's right," Matthew says. "Jesus' words were plain."

"You were gone by then," Zee says.

Matthew looks pained. "So now it's a matter of whose testimony is more credible?"

Mother Mary covers her face with her hands.

"Now look," Simon says. "You've upset our rabbi's ima."

"I only made an observation," Zee says.

Young Mary feels the need to break in. "I made a mistake leaving camp. I was wrong. I'm sorry I relied on my own observation—my own understanding—so heavily. Jesus said he will be back."

The Marys and Ramah leave the men, heading for the women's campfire.

Chapter 51

# EYEWITNESSES

*Jotapata*

Philip has no idea what the hair-triggered Andrew might do without him along. He's intrigued by the young fisherman, admiring his passion if not his temper. Philip is fully aware of Andrew's older brother's penchant for enthusiasm too, but at least Simon evidences some latent leadership qualities. If he could only harness these, he might prove invaluable. As for Andrew, he himself needs harnessing.

Despite the urgency of the journey and the vitriol Andrew expresses with every step, it's clear when they arrive in the city that he's intimidated by all the Pharisees and Sadducees and the cacophony of recitations. His hometown of Capernaum was apparently nothing like this, and he seems to look to Philip for support.

"Don't worry about them," Philip says. "They're here for God—or to preen. You don't get in the way of either."

"Where should we go first?"

Philip can hardly believe it's a question. Where else does Andrew think they'll find Jesus? "Jail. Come on, it's this way."

Philip moves through the din with indifference. He's heard it all before. That's what had been so refreshing about John the Baptizer. Sure, he revered the Scriptures, but he also preached a new message, preparing the way of the Lord Messiah. In seconds, Philip realizes Andrew has lagged, still apparently in shock at the imprecatory nature of the orators. He beckons the former fisherman. "And they say *we're* extreme."

They hurry past a crowd in the square who seem enamored of a woman and her companion. "Look at him!" she's saying. "He can stand! It was faith that delivered this man a miracle."

Philip tells Andrew, "Now, that's more like it."

But as the speaker and her companion come into view, Andrew pulls Philip to a stop. "I know her! And him! It's Tamar and … and Ethan, the former paralytic!"

The woman is hypnotically stunning, her brilliantly colored raiment setting off her ebony skin and exquisite jewelry.

Philip says, "Who cares? We have a rabbi to find."

A man hollers from the crowd, "We heard he consorts with Samaritans!"

"I cannot personally confirm that," Tamar says, beaming. "But it wouldn't surprise me."

"Who cares who he ministers to? I was paralyzed for twenty-three years, and I stand before you now on two feet!"

"They're talking about Jesus," Andrew whispers.

Another calls out, "But is it true he claimed the authority to forgive sins? Who on earth can do that?"

As if she was hoping someone would ask, Tamar says, "The kind of person who can tell a paralyzed man to stand, and a miracle happens in front of dozens of witnesses."

"It could be witchcraft or sorcery!"

Ethan says, "Witches and sorcerers require payment for their services!"

"And he gave freely," Tamar adds.

"Then why is he in hiding?"

"We don't know," Ethan says.

"He told a leper he healed on the road to keep that miracle a secret," Tamar says.

"Then why are you telling people?"

"He gave *us* no such order. I believe that he will make himself more known soon. I can sense it in my spirit!"

Andrew breaks away from Philip and mounts the platform. "You!" Tamar says. "You were there! In Capernaum!"

"Can I talk to you?" Andrew says quietly.

"This man can attest!" Ethan says. "He was a witness!"

"Where is he?" someone in the crowd demands.

"You know this Jesus of Nazareth?" another says.

"Is he here in Jotapata?"

"Tell them!" Tamar says.

Andrew steps close. "Please!" he says. "Come with me—both of you." He leads them off the platform and gets in their faces as Philip looks on. "You must stop drawing attention to Jesus!"

Tamar looks stunned. "How can we not speak of what we have seen? How can *you* remain silent?"

"The Romans!" Andrew shouts, voice cracking, unable to continue.

"Oh, no!" Tamar says. "What happened?"

Philip says, "We'll tell you all about it. Why don't we go somewhere a little more private?"

As they follow Philip and Andrew away, people in the crowd demand to know where they're going.

## Chapter 52

# FUN

*Roman Authority headquarters, Capernaum*

Cynical as he has grown over the years, Atticus still serves Rome earnestly and with a certain passion. Sure, he's had his eyes opened, especially in the last decade, to the realities of graft, corruption, political motives in high places, and all the rest. And it would be easy to invest the final quarter of a stellar career burnishing his pristine reputation. But he can hardly be more revered or—he has to admit—more rewarded for his role.

These days he labors dawn to dusk—and sometimes into the wee hours—out of a sense of duty, of calling. He knows he could coast into a twilight of esteem. But it makes him feel better to continue to earn the reputation it took him so long to build. No, he's not the wide-eyed recruit who believed Rome deserved its powerful, dominating role in the world. Yet he still believes in its ideals—if privately dismissing the deity of the emperor.

His own monologue to Primi Gaius on the journey to arrest Jesus of Nazareth, however—intended only to impress upon the celebrated guard that the assignment should be looked upon as much more than just another task doled out by Praetor Quintus—has made even Atticus stop and think. He used his vaunted coherence and persuasiveness to gain Gaius's attention, but, he realizes, he had not once exaggerated to make his point.

This so-called miracle worker is different from the numerous charlatans Atticus has encountered in his long tenure. He's seen magic tricks before—so many that he could see most of them coming and predict their influence on the masses. Some of these characters proved so skillful at their legerdemain that by pure power of suggestion they could convince the unwitting they had been healed, restored, whatever. When first Atticus heard the rumors of Jesus' influence, he had no reason to believe the man was unique. How long before his healings wore off and people claiming to have suffered for years, and were now whole, would slide straight back into their miserable status quo? Yes, Atticus had even seen the deaf and mute appear to hear and speak until the novel hysterical euphoria wore off.

But now the things Atticus has seen for himself cannot be disputed. He isn't a believer himself—in this man or the father he often refers to. Nor does he buy into the Roman gods, though he knows enough of the lingo to succeed in pretending to when the occasion calls for that. But the very incidents Atticus rehearsed to persuade Gaius of the potential danger—or perhaps the veracity—of this man's claims continue to haunt his thoughts.

Following Gaius and Jesus in to see the praetor could easily have become one of those hallmark events in both their careers. It appears Gaius can't hide his pride in having executed this warrant by the book, but Atticus is thrilled to be along for other reasons. First, the slimy praetor himself might meet his match for once in the Nazarene. How many times has Atticus seen Quintus so condescend that his sarcasm alone seemed to leave victims in puddles on the floor?

If this preacher is anything close to what his rabid followers believe, and if he maintains the same collected persona he has exhibited in every public venue so far, well … Atticus is grateful merely for a front row seat to the coming tussle of personalities. If nothing else, Jesus will not lower himself to Quintus' depth of character. How might the praetor respond to, for lack of a better term, indifference to his power, his position, his authority? Above all, how might Jesus counter Quintus' ineffable pride? Atticus can hardly wait.

He can't deny the confidence boost it gives him to breeze past the midlevel clerks who browbeat into submission common men—even Pharisees—who wish an audience with the praetor. They mince-step in with figurative hats in hand, begging for the favor, only to be looked down upon and quickly dismissed.

As Atticus follows Gaius and the detainee, however, they don't even pause to identify themselves as they sweep past lesser guards and bureaucrats. Naturally everyone knows of this appointment, and Gaius makes quick work of unbinding Jesus—a visual designed to assure the praetor that all is under control. Guards leave Quintus's office as the three approach, and Atticus can't miss the whispers.

"Primi …"

"Atticus …"

"Jesus …"

This brief confab, whatever the result, will spread throughout Capernaum in minutes. But that is the question: What might be expected? Will the praetor rail on Jesus? Warn him? Sentence him? Have him immediately carted off to a dungeon? What will happen to the burgeoning sect if both the crazy Baptizer and the miracle worker are behind bars?

As Gaius leads the prisoner in, Atticus lays a hand on Jesus' back—if for no other reason than to indicate he has been involved in the apprehension. Atticus moves past them and stands to the back and side of Quintus, who appears nothing short of impressed—and giddy. An underling drying the praetor's feet is quickly dismissed.

As Gaius and Jesus stand before him, Quintus says, "Did he resist?"

"No, Dominus," Atticus says, affecting a respectful tone as compared to their last meeting.

"And his followers?"

"Peaceful," Gaius says. "And compliant."

"Have a seat," the praetor says, pointing to a chair. Jesus sits, and Gaius stands at attention behind him. "Leave us," Quintus says. Gaius appears hurt but immediately complies.

Jesus looks to Atticus like a normal local, yet there's a quiet confidence about him. He maintains Quintus's gaze. The praetor affects a toothy grin, as if he can barely contain himself. "Jesus of Nazareth!" he announces. "We finally meet!"

"Here I am," Jesus says, plainly not as excited about this as Quintus appears.

Quintus reaches for a cup of olives and pops one into his mouth. "I thought you'd be sort of—"

"Taller?" Jesus says.

"—crazier looking."

"Ah …"

"You know, wild hair and animal skins."

"Glad I could disappoint you," Jesus says.

With an olive bobbing in his cheek, Quintus points and says, "The first story I ever heard about you"—he spits a pit into a cup—"I didn't believe it."

"That's usually how it goes."

"Oh, it wasn't about religion or preaching or god. It was about fish."

"Ah, another common theme of mine."

The praetor turns to Atticus. "It was an impossibly huge catch. It settled the largest debt in Capernaum's ledger." He turns back to Jesus. "Oh, did you meet Atticus? He's *Cohortes Urbanae*. They're like Caesar's personal detectives. Mostly in Rome, but they go wherever. He's especially interested in you." Apparently expecting some response, the praetor stares at the arrestee. Finally he says, "Have you ever visited the Far East, Jesus?"

"I have received visitors from there but never been there myself."

"They eat their fish raw. Peel off the scales, cut off the heads and tails, and"—he affects a shiver—"take a bite!"

Jesus appears to pretend interest. "That's quite something."

"They eat all the flesh and spit out the bones."

"Of course."

"If Simon had not settled his debt, that could have resulted in my demotion. That was flesh." He leans forward and loses the smile. "You create a public disruption that results in damage to property, a stampede, and a blight on my personal reputation—hmm, bones. You seduced the single most brilliant and effective tax collector in the entire Upper Galilee, also bones. And now, the most tenured *Cohortes Urbana* in the history of the Roman Empire tells me he personally witnessed you disarm a Zealot sicarii. Well, that's flesh."

Quintus' smile has returned, and he leans to face Atticus again to emphasize his point. "That's flesh."

"Sorry to have caused so much confusion for you over flesh and bone," Jesus says.

"Confusion?" Quintus says. "No. No. If your race weren't so repugnant and odious, I'd offer you a job!"

Despite the praetor's grin, Jesus says, "I cannot take that as a compliment."

"Jesus, this whole thing is very simple. You seem to be splitting your time between creating headaches for Rome and victories we could not achieve ourselves."

"That's a little reductive," Jesus says.

Atticus speaks up. "You've doubled your following since leaving Capernaum. Then again, you returned to his senses a violent man who had been terrorizing Jericho."

"But word of your *miracles,* or whatever," Quintus says, "has spread all through Syria. And they start coming over here. Do you see my problem? I don't know whether to eat you or spit you out, to stick with the fish metaphor." Again he wrenches around to address Atticus. "But we're probably past that now." Back to Jesus. "I'm saying I don't know what to make of you."

"That's going to be a lot of people's problem with me."

Quintus leans forward again, serious as a centurion. "No more bones, Jesus. Follow me? No more draining my talent pool, creating spectacles, crowds. No more meddling, hm?"

"I cannot promise any of these things."

Atticus wonders whether anyone has ever spoken to Quintus this way, especially in light of his warnings.

"Then I cannot promise you won't stop breathing."

Again, Jesus appears to take this at face value. "Well," he says, "it sounds like we're clear on what we can and cannot promise."

This appears to amuse Quintus to no end. He bursts into giggles. "Honestly! Jesus of Nazareth, I like you! We're on the same team. Just don't make me kill you."

"I won't make you do anything," Jesus says. "But my Father, on the other hand …"

"I don't know what that means, but let's leave on a high note. I think we have an understanding here. You're free to go."

Jesus looks as surprised as Atticus. He stands and turns to leave.

"Oh," Quintus adds, "sorry about your cousin, by the way." Jesus turns back to face him. The praetor continues, "Marching himself into Herod's court and moralizing was not a very wise or brave thing to do."

"He knew what he was getting himself into," Jesus says.

"Do you? Know what you're getting yourself into?"

"It was a privilege to speak with you today, Quintus."

The praetor looks pleased, as if he believes it. As Jesus exits, Quintus tells Atticus, "Well, that was fun!"

"So nothing about him concerns you?"

"If it did, I wouldn't have let him go. He'll be a nice diversion for the people for a while."

Atticus grabs an olive from Quintus' desk and chuckles on his way out.

## Chapter 53

# FALSE PROPHECY

*Town square, Jotapata*

Shmuel and Yanni find people in an uproar. "What are you all doing here?" Shmuel says.

"We were hearing stories about a man from Nazareth," one says.

"From an Ethiopian woman and a man who claimed to have been healed."

"Where have they gone?" Yanni demands.

"They all disappeared with a curly-haired man."

"They knew they were going to be exposed, I think."

"In what direction?" Shmuel says.

A man points toward the jail. "Beyond those colonnades."

Yanni pulls Shmuel away. "Hurry!"

"Brothers," an elderly priest calls out. "Wait!"

He's accompanied by a younger Pharisee. "Are you looking for a man who performs healings on Sabbath?"

"Yes," Yanni says, looking surprised and suspicious. "Who are you?"

The older man says, "Has he invoked the title 'Son of Man' from the prophet Daniel?"

"How did you know? You witnessed this? Is he here?"

"We're from Wadi Kelt," the elder says.

"Why haven't you filed a report?" Shmuel says.

"We did," the younger says. "But we're a small town. He healed on Sabbath in our synagogue, and it got even worse from there."

"And there are women among his followers," the old man adds. "Three, to be precise."

"Tell us everything," Shmuel says.

• • •

*Just across the way*

Andrew wishes Philip would stay with him while he explains to Tamar and Ethan why it's so crucial to stop drawing attention to Jesus. But John the Baptist's former disciple peels off to visit the jail nearby where Jesus would be held.

In truth, Andrew wishes just about any of the other disciples were along too, frustrated as he is at their lack of action. Even his brother would be of enormous help. But Andrew has never been one to wait for backup, nor is he known for patience. While he admires the fervor of Tamar and certainly understands Ethan's ardor, he races through a recitation of all that's happened—from the scandalous healing in the synagogue on Shabbat to Jesus' arrest.

"But claiming to be Lord of the Sabbath or even the Son of Man are *religious* scandals," Tamar says. "What does Rome care?"

"We don't know why he was arrested," Andrew tells her and Ethan. "Rome may feel threatened as word spreads. I don't know. But you can't do this. Not now."

"I can't keep silent about what I know inside," Tamar says.

"Don't you understand what I'm explaining?"

"I'm not a child!"

"I'm telling you it's dangerous!"

"More than you know," a man says.

*Who's this now?* They turn to a stranger in civilian garb.

"Don't be alarmed," the man says. "My name is Yussif—"

"You're a Pharisee from Capernaum," Andrew says, panicky. What could this mean?

"I spoke harshly to you at the house of Matthew," Yussif says.

That's the least of Andrew's problems now. "Don't worry about it," he says.

"I'm not," Yussif says. He turns to Tamar and whispers urgently, "You're being sought for questioning."

"For what?" she says.

"Testimony about Jesus of Nazareth."

"I told you!" Andrew says.

Yussif continues, "One of Nicodemus's former students, a man named Shmuel, has come in search of you. He will twist your testimony to make an argument against false prophecy."

"False?" she says.

"I personally do not care about your convictions, and as a woman, your testimony is worthless anyway. But what Shmuel wants is information about another healing—and Jesus' background."

Tamar shrugs. "We both grew up in Egypt—"

Yussif recoils. "I-I-that's even worse. Andrew, get her out of here."

"I don't trust you," Andrew says. "Why are you helping?"

"That's my business. But so that you'll do as I ask, I believe my rabbi, Nicodemus, saw something remarkable in your master. Shmuel is threatened by what he can't comprehend. Worse, he's ambitious. Shmuel does not honor Nicodemus's teaching." Yussif stares at Ethan, as if just noticing him. "You are the paralytic man Jesus healed!"

"Yes."

"Both of you must leave this place!"

Ethan tells Tamar, "You should go with Andrew."

"But what will you do?" she says.

"I'll lie low, disappear until things go quiet."

She's near tears. "And what if things don't go quiet?"

He smiles. "I hope they don't. But it's a good idea we separate for now." He turns to Andrew. "Take her with you."

*With me?* Is he allowed to just add newcomers to the group? "I don't know if—"

"I *do* want to follow Jesus," Tamar says.

*Knowing Jesus ...* Andrew shrugs. "We will talk to him."

"Go now," Yussif says.

Just then Philip appears. "Jesus is not here," he says, then notices the stranger. "Who are you?"

When the others just look at each other awkwardly, Philip says, "Okay then. Fill me in on the road."

## Chapter 54

# "OUR FATHER …"

*The disciples' Jotapata campsite*

Zee finds it ironic that he and Simon have drawn guard duty at the same time—each standing, torch in hand, at either end of the camp. As most of the disciples and the women somberly prepare to bed down in their respective tents, Zee imagines the other Simon is as qualified a guard as anyone else in the group, except perhaps Big James. Zee no longer carries a weapon, and Simon, though small, is wiry and strong and conceals a blade.

Zee expects no trouble, but he's been as anxious as the rest about Jesus. Do the Romans already have enough on him to incarcerate Jesus? Zee hasn't seen him break any Roman laws—at least intentionally. No question he flouts pharisaical laws, and admittedly that has resulted in some unwieldy crowds. But the Romans would have to stretch to actually charge him with anything.

Mother Mary tidies up the area where she and the other women cooked dinner. Matthew writes in his journal. John and

Big James tend the small fire outside their tent. Simon appears to be scanning the dark horizon at the other end.

This is a bizarre way to stand guard, Zee decides, illuminating themselves. They might as well paint targets onto their tunics for any interloper with plans to create trouble. But part of him wishes someone would try. He has never been so prepared for hand-to-hand combat with so little potential for the same.

A silhouette at his edge of the camp picks up a glint from the moon and appears to approach. Zee immediately recognizes the gait. "He's back!" he shouts, and the others quickly emerge and follow Zee into the darkness. He jogs into a clearing, torch aloft. "Teacher, are you hurt? What happened?"

"Well," Jesus says, "I suppose I should not be surprised that *you* would spot me."

His mother hurries past Zee and into Jesus' arms.

"Hi, Ima," he says, lifting her in an embrace.

"Rabbi!" Simon shouts, having raced all the way from his post. "Are you safe? Did anyone follow you?"

"Yes, I'm safe, and they just wanted to talk."

Zee is amused that they all just stand gawking, Matthew with a huge smile. "I'm very happy!" Matthew says.

Jesus chuckles. "I'm glad, Matthew."

"Just talk?" Simon presses.

"Quintus wanted to talk, yes, but the Romans don't see me as much of a threat—which is fine."

"Hopefully that'll change soon," Zee mutters.

"So, what were you doing out here?" John says.

"Praying, John. Remember, there's a big event to prepare for."

"Rabbi," Big James says, "with all due respect, you couldn't have first told us that you were back? You were grabbed by Roman soldiers with weapons! We were all worried sick."

"Did I not tell you that I would be back and to keep

planning? You're all going to have to learn how to do this, regardless of what's happening, good or bad. Things are going to get only more difficult. You can't just shut down when you're fearful. What are you going to do when I'm no longer here?"

"Yes," John says. "We are still figuring this out."

"But we can do better," Simon says. "W-We will do better."

"Rabbi," John says, "Philip says your cousin gave his followers a prayer, in addition to the daily traditional prayers. Perhaps you could do the same for us?"

"Yes," Big James says. "I'd like to learn more about what you're saying when you're out alone."

Jesus suddenly looks pleased. He points at them with both hands. "Now," he says. "Now you're behaving like true students. This is what I like to see. And prayer is the first step in getting the mind and the heart right. It's why you see me go to it so often."

"So," Simon says, "teach us—to pray like you do. Please."

Jesus appears to study them a moment. "When we pray," he says finally, "we want to be sure to start by acknowledging our Father in heaven and His greatness. So you can say, 'Our Father in heaven, hallowed be Your name.' And we always want to be sure to do God's will and not our own. So we say, 'Your kingdom come, Your will be done, on earth as it is in heaven ..."

• • •

*Two hours later*

Matthew has fallen into a deeper sleep than he can remember, warmed by Jesus' prayer and teaching, but mostly relieved that the Master is all right. Is that a hand on his shoulder, or is he dreaming?

"Matthew. Matthew!"

"Rabbi?"

"Sorry to wake you."

It's no dream. Matthew sits up. "Are you in trouble?"

Jesus shushes him. "Don't wake the others. Nothing is wrong."

"Why did you wake me and not them?"

"I've been forming fragments of teaching in my mind for some months now in preparation for the sermon. I'm ready to organize them."

*And he needs* my *help?* Matthew wonders. "I'll get my writing materials. But you've just returned from detention. Will these teachings make things worse?"

"I'm here to make things better, not worse, Matthew."

"I mean for us. For all of us who love you."

Jesus appears to hesitate. "No promises. Let's go."

"It must be tonight?" He'd been sleeping so peacefully! *But how could I have asked such a thing? Who would reject such a privilege?*

"The time has come," Jesus says.

Matthew cannot get out of bed quickly enough. As Jesus steps away to wait for him, Matthew gathers all his materials, straightens his garments, and crawls out of the tent. He has no idea, nor does he care, where Jesus might lead him tonight. He has given his entire life to follow this man, and he will follow him anywhere.

# PART 8
# Beyond Mountains

Chapter 55

# THE LAND DEAL

*A rocky desert wilderness*

Husham, a burly man in his early sixties, never refers to himself as a landowner, though he is one. No, the moniker would make more of him than he sees of himself. Yes, he owns land, but the bulk of it is barren, sandy, virtually godforsaken. And he is a man of God. But mostly he is poor. When a man is rich in acreage but meager in shekels, what is he?

Husham can't help but feel like a failure. His family loves him and knows he has their best interests in mind. But it has been harder and harder to keep food on the table and a roof over their heads. He does his best, but life is hard.

So here he stands on his most-vast parcel of land. And useless as it is, he has never dreamt of letting it go. Until now. Standing before an obviously wily businessman and his seemingly eager young assistant, Husham has no illusions. The entrepreneur wants this land. Basically wants to steal it, despite his seemingly earnest approach at persuasion.

What should Husham do? What can he do? Centuries of

tradition tell him one does not sell land—even desolate properties like this one. It simply isn't done. He leans on his walking stick, as conflicted as he can be. His heart tells him to keep the land in the family. His head tells him a cash sale is best for his current crisis—feeding that family. Husham has spent most of the initial part of this negotiation rhapsodizing about this place, and that hasn't at all been a bargaining tactic. He means it.

"Forty talents," the well-dressed businessman says with a smile. "And you can keep the western ridge for whatever it is you love so much about it."

*The western ridge?* Of course he'll keep that. That was never on the table. Husham crosses his arms and gazes into the distance. "It's a beautiful view of the sunrise."

"You can't eat a sunrise," the man says. He plainly knows how to strike where it hurts. And he still bears that obnoxious smile, as if he's Husham's best friend. What kind of an example of respect is this to his wide-eyed apprentice?

"Believe me, I know," Husham says. He studies the man, trying to get a read on him. "What is your lineage?"

"We are here to talk price, not family history."

"This *is* about my family. Your tribe?"

"Simeon," the man says, as if forced to admit it.

"These acres have been under the tribe of Reuben for forty generations. I'm not about to surrender them to the little brother."

This makes the man laugh. "We can talk about ancient birth order all you want, but it won't put a meal on your family's table."

True. Husham must sacrifice this heirloom, but he cannot give it away. "Fifty-five talents."

"Forty-five," the man says immediately. "And we'll send a team of servants to help you move."

*Why is he so eager?* "What is it you want from this land? All rocks. Barely anything grows here."

"That's right. But things that *do* grow, what happens to them? Eventually—what?"

"They die," Husham admits.

This seems to be the apprentice's cue. "We're here to cut tombs into these rocks for the middle class."

*Make a cemetery of it?* "All the way out here?"

"Only the wealthy can afford tombs close to the cities, and more and more of the middle class are dying deep in tax debt."

"Right," the businessman says. "Left with no money for a proper burial, these families are surrendering their beloveds to paupers' graves."

"We're here to provide an affordable solution," the apprentice adds. "Even if it's far away, it's better than a pit, entwined with other disintegrating bones."

"What's to stop me and my sons from carving the tombs?" Husham says.

The businessman spreads his arms. "Why haven't you? Do you have the tools? The expertise? Capital for hiring laborers and dozens of stonecutters?"

"Fifty talents," Husham says.

"Forty-seven, final offer."

"Forty-nine. Suppose you find copper and lead when you dig?"

"I said forty-seven. You can contact me tomorrow when you change your mind." He turns to leave.

"Wait," the apprentice says. "He has a point. The land could be worth more if there's something underneath, like he says. Copper or salt. He's not wrong."

Finally, someone who listens, understands.

The businessman turns back to face him and sighs deeply.

"Our business has a reputation of doing things the right way. I'd be willing to part with a few more talents, on the off chance there is something valuable under all this rock."

"This is all part of the Promised Land," Husham says, "no matter how it looks to you."

"Forty-nine. More than ten years' wages, Husham. Let's draw up the covenants."

Husham covers his mouth and scans the horizon, taking it all in.

"What's wrong?" the businessman says.

"That word," Husham says. "*Covenant.* I was thinking about the promise made to Abraham. And all the other promises."

"You can talk to your rabbi about that. For now, let us close the covenants and toast a fair deal for everyone."

Husham hesitates. Is he really going to go through with this? He solemnly taps his stick on the ground three times, indicating agreement. The deal is done.

## Chapter 56

# NO MISTAKES

*Jotapata countryside*

Zee completes his morning jog, finishing strong. He enters the disciples' campsite to find the brothers Big James and John respectively sawing logs, splitting them with an ax, and Andrew stacking them. Zee bends at the waist, panting. "You three are going to wake the whole camp with your chopping."

"Put a shirt on, man," John says, "before the women get up."

"They're already up. I heard them studying in their tent."

Andrew straightens from his work. "Why do the women feel so strongly about studying? Isn't it enough to just listen to our rabbi?"

"When would they do that?" Big James says. "He's never here."

Zee picks up a thin strip of wood and shadow swipes it like a weapon. He misses his vigorous group training, but as long as he can stay active …

John points at him. "You know, your obsession with exercise smacks of Hellenism."

Zee scoffs. "You would compare me with the Greeks? I'm

just trying to stay ready. What if the Romans change their minds and do to Jesus what they did to the Baptizer, Andrew and Philip's old rabbi?"

"Can you please not bring that up?" Andrew says.

"The mind and the spirit are more important than the body, Zee," John says.

"Is that so? How can you have a healthy mind if you don't have a healthy body?"

"I'm talking about emphasizing one over the other!"

"Try eating a whole bush of poisonous berries, and then tell me how your mind is doing."

Simon appears from his tent, squinting, hair a mess. "What's with the chopping?"

"Oh!" his brother says. "Did we interfere with sleeping in?"

"Your sails are still full, I see, Andrew." Simon pours a cup of water over his hands for the ritual washing and whispers, "Blessed are You, Lord our God, King of the universe, Who has sanctified us with His commandments and commanded us concerning the washing of the hands."

Thomas and Philip emerge from the woods, smiling and bearing fruit. "Breakfast, boys?" Philip calls out, and they toss each man an apple.

Everyone prays in unison, "Bless are You, Lord our God, Ruler of the universe, Who creates the fruit of the ground."

As if he's just noticed, Simon mutters, "We have plenty of wood, guys."

"And a stack for the next travelers," Big James says.

"This week is going to be our last here," John says.

"It is?" Simon says.

"Yes, Rabbi told me last night."

"He told everyone," Andrew adds.

Simon looks around. "Where's Matthew?"

"He went away early this morning with Rabbi," Zee says.

"Why does he always take Matthew?" Big James says.

John stares at Simon. "And since when did you start caring about Matthew's whereabouts?"

"Big Thunder just asked the same thing."

"You didn't ask about everyone else who's not here," Andrew says.

Philip appears concerned about Andrew. "Did you sleep okay?"

"He was like this when I woke up," Simon says.

Zee explains, "Jesus sent Little James, Thaddeus, and Nathanael ahead to find a location for the sermon."

"All right," Simon says. "Do we all know what we're supposed to do?"

"I don't know, Simon," Andrew says. "Maybe listen?"

"Keep talking to me like that!"

*These brothers,* Zee thinks. "I know we'll need security at all four points of the compass."

"We know how to execute that, Zee," Simon says.

"The crowd is going to be bigger this time," Big James says, "the way the word is spreading."

"What do we do with hecklers?" Zee says. He has a few ideas.

"Well," Philip says, "the odd Pharisee used to come to these things. They used to be all over John's sermons."

"John would heckle *them*," Andrew says.

"I just said 'used to,'" Philip says.

"Jesus can handle Pharisees," Simon says.

"We need to get this right, huh?" John says. "No mistakes."

• • •

Not far away, in one of the women's tents, Mary Magdalene is writing on parchment and making a stack. Ramah slowly reads from the Psalms. When the younger woman sounds stuck, Mary prods her with the next word.

"How do you have this memorized?" Ramah says.

"I have been memorizing the rest of that song of David. I need more words, more tools. I can't let it happen again."

"Mary, you've got to stop dwelling on—"

"Go on. 'Your eyes saw my unformed substance ...'" And as Ramah continues, Mary finds herself overcome with emotion.

In the next tent, the newcomer Tamar tells Jesus' mother, "You and Mary have been so good to me."

"Of course. We're happy you're here."

Tamar can hear Ramah struggling with the text. She leans close and whispers, "Um, do we all have to learn to read?"

"No. Mary's father taught her long ago, and Ramah just wanted to learn. I think they felt left out. Maybe your being here will take the pressure off."

"Well, I'm willing to learn, if that's what it takes."

From outside they hear, "Shalom! I come bearing apricots!"

"Ah!" Mother Mary says. "It's a good day today." She leads Tamar out. "Shalom, Thomas!"

He hands her two pieces of fruit. "These are a delight!"

Tamar and Thomas greet each other, and he gives her two as well. "Is Ramah coming out?" he says.

"Uh, no," Tamar says. "I don't think so. She's pretty intent on studying."

"Oh," Thomas says, looking disappointed.

"Mary is writing leaflet notices and invitations to the sermon." She steps close and whispers, "And sometimes crying."

"She went through something bad," he says. "I think she just needs time."

Tamar nods and looks toward the other disciples, loudly bickering. "And what about them?"

Thomas shrugs. "In the most generous explanation, I'd call that love."

Tamar laughs aloud. "That does not look like love to me."

"Well, they all love our Rabbi and want to follow him the right way. They just can't agree on what that right way is."

"Hmm. Well, thank you." She reaches for the rest of the fruit. "I will take these to Ramah and Mary."

"Oh, and tell Ramah that Philip found apples, but I wanted to bring her apricots because I know they're her favorite."

"I will pass that along," Tamar says with a smile.

## Chapter 57

# ILLUSIONS

*Jotapata public house*

The business entrepreneur sits across from his young apprentice as they enjoy drinks. He's celebrating the land transaction with old Husham. "It was perfection! You played your part so well! And didn't you think my look of annoyance with you was the best I've ever given? Sophocles, Euripides, Aeschylus—they would kill for our acting skills."

The younger man doesn't seem to share his enthusiasm. "It certainly was a kind of tragedy."

"For him, sure. But for us? A triumph! All tragedies have winners and losers."

The apprentice can't argue with that. "He *was* the one who brought up potential minerals."

"Yes! And then you acknowledged the possibility of salt—without giving anything away—and I conceded the value. We came off looking like good guys."

"Hmm," the younger man says, still apparently conflicted.

"We bought a salt mine for the price of a country plot!"

"But did you see his tears?" the younger man says.

"That's common. People have emotional ties to land."

"So we grow callouses on our eyes?"

"Hey, lighten up! We just made the best sale of our lives."

That seems to silence the other man briefly. Finally, he says, "He did make a tidy profit on land he didn't know would ever be valuable."

*Now he's thinking. We did that old man a favor.* "He'll never have to work another day in his life. You know, when I brought you on, they neglected to tell me that you did not have a sense of humor."

"I do have a sense of humor."

"But you are about to become a very wealthy man. Once our miners find the salt, we're going to live like kings."

"Kings of what? There's only one true King, in heaven. Everyone else—even Caesar—is enjoying only illusions of power and wealth. Sooner or later we all become dust."

"There's that sense of humor," the businessman grumbles. "Hey, I'm not oblivious, okay? I know that's right. But we have so few opportunities to get ahead in this world."

"Opportunity? It was a calculated deception. And it didn't—it didn't feel good."

"We used what God gave us! And now we'll have greater choices. We'll live better lives. More devotion! Finish your drink."

But the apprentice is apparently not finished. "Man was formed from earth, and eventually he returns to it. The time in between—there has to be more to life than that."

"You're an orphan *and* a poet."

"I told you not to call me an orphan!"

"Hey, okay. I'm sorry. It's been a long week. Let's take some time off to rest."

"What I need, boss, is a life I can be proud of. Don't you

want to do something that will really matter, that will be remembered throughout history?"

*Wow, where is this coming from?* the businessman wonders. "I appreciate your ambition, I really do. And I see potential in you. I see it every day." He pulls out a purse full of coins and slaps it on the table. "Here's an advance. Let's take a few weeks off. Rest, go for walks, do something new, hm?"

The younger man hefts the purse. "Really?"

"Why not? You're the one who said there's more to life than making money."

"Thank you. I don't know what to say."

• • •

Nearby, Nathanael leads Little James and Thaddeus through the foothills. Jesus has told them the type of venue he's looking for, if only they can find it. "How about the knoll east of the Nahal-Kur river?" Nathanael says.

"But a knoll won't be high enough for people to hear and see him," Thaddeus says.

"And trees to the south obstruct the view of the Galilee," Little James says. "Which he specifically requested."

"Why does he need a view of the sea?" Nathanael says.

"I think he wanted to be high enough," Thaddeus says.

"What about the hills north of Korazim?" Little James says. "There's plenty of height. His voice would carry."

"Too steep a climb," Nathanael says.

"And too far for the people from Tiberius and Magdala," Thaddeus adds. "He said to keep it within a day's walk."

"Maybe we're just looking too far north," Little James says.

"What did he request?" Nathanael says. "A grove of juniper or gum trees on the backside where we could camp the night before?"

"It's like he already knows the place," Thaddeus says.

"Yeah," Nathanael says. "We just have to find it."

As they reach the Korazim Plateau moments later, they crest a ridge, and a treelined mount comes into view. A short wall separates them from a vast pasture, and a weather-beaten stone sign warns, "No trespassing. Violators will be prosecuted."

As they draw closer, Nathanael hollers "Shalom!" to a woman shepherd.

"We mean no harm, sister! We're here on friendly business!"

She approaches cautiously.

"Behind you," Nathanael says, "is that a good view of the Galilee?"

"Go away!" she shouts.

"That's not very friendly."

"Excuse me," Thaddeus tries. "Are you the owner?"

"It's closed to visitors!"

"It's very important that we speak to the owner!" Little James says.

She turns her back and walks away.

"This is probably the spot," Thaddeus says.

Nathanael can't believe it. "What? Why? It's completely repellant."

"Exactly," Little James says.

Nathanael still can't envision it, but he trusts his mates. As they head back the way they came, he speculates aloud, "I wonder if one of us approached her alone, we might at least get a meeting with the landowner?"

"Worth a try," Thaddeus says.

"Surely you've dealt with his type, Nathanael," Little James says.

"I was thinking of one of you ..."

But they both look at him expectantly.

Nathanael does not find the woman shepherd much more sociable when only he approaches, but at least she doesn't evade him. She promises to tell her boss, owner of the land, what they are proposing. "I'll tell him before he heads to the public house, as he does every day."

"Public house?" he says, wondering if it's the type of establishment a rabbi's followers should frequent. "Do you mean a tavern, a gaming hideaway?"

"No!" she says. "You and your mates will find refreshment there, but it's a respectable place, open to all."

## Chapter 58

# SPECULATION

Shmuel has scored a meeting for himself and Yanni with the legendary Shammai and now worries whether he's up to the task. The man was president of the Sanhedrin for years before Hillel's son, Shimon Gamaliel, took over. But Shammai's strict view of Torah doctrine dominates the governing religious body. Young Gamaliel and Shammai are the two most-powerful voices in Judaism, and they are at odds. It's widely known that Rabbi Shammai detests what he considers Gamaliel's radical, worldly revisions to the Law. In fact, the Sanhedrin and, it seems, all Pharisees, have split into the School of Hillel and the School of Shammai. For now, the latter seems to hold sway.

Shmuel and Yanni are ushered into the great man's richly appointed office and sit across from his huge desk. Together they spill their story about Jesus of Nazareth, Shmuel depending on his associate to be sure they leave nothing out. But the old man is hard to read. He appears to have a gift of listening—excellent eye contact, physical cues that he might actually be hearing and understanding—but he remains silent until they finish.

"That's it?" he says finally. "That's your whole story?"

"Everything we know for certain," Shmuel says, "established as fact by eyewitnesses in accordance with the Law."

Now he's done it. Shammai appears amused, smiles, then breaks into laughter. Shmuel cannot understand how so serious a matter has come across as somehow humorous. He looks to Yanni, who appears just as stunned and tries: "We could offer speculation, but we wanted to honor your time, Rabbi, with only confirmed facts."

Shmuel adds, "I know I can't prove it's the same person, but the pattern's too striking to ignore."

The old scholar grows serious. "It doesn't *need* to be the same person. That's what's wonderful. I will have Gamaliel dragged for this."

"To be fair," Yanni says, "it was the secretary who called the charges minutiae, not Shimon Gamaliel himself."

"Secretaries don't put words in their rabbi's mouth—it's the other way around. Minutiae. My congregation and students will foam at the mouth when they hear this. Make a written record of your conversation with Shimon's secretary—every word. And file it with the clerk of the special counsel for false prophecies at the Archive. It must be signed and dated by a ranking Levite. Do you understand my instructions?"

"Yes," Yanni says. "But why all the exactitude?"

"Because when this Jesus of Nazareth attracts enough followers, and enough detractors, it will get Rome's attention—not just ours. And then everyone will know."

"Know what, Rabbi?" Shmuel says.

"That Shimon was well aware of these offenses and dismissed them. His obsession with reforming God's immutable Law will be exposed for the negligent, lazy, dangerous abomination it is."

"Not just Shimon," Shmuel says, eager to gild his point. "We opened a case with the Sanhedrin, and Nicodemus dismissed it as 'immaterial.'"

Shammai nods. "Nicodemus. I've long suspected the lamps were going dim in that house, if you get my meaning."

"Well, I don't know about that ..." Shmuel says, but a surreptitious nudge from Yanni stops him.

"Spread the word," Shammai continues. "Tell every scribe, Pharisee, Sadducee, Essene, priest, teacher, and Levite you know."

"Why, Rabbi?" Yanni says.

"First, the facts." He glances at his notes. "Self-identifies using a divine title from the prophet Daniel ..."

"Son of Man," Shmuel says.

"Claims authority to forgive sins. Violates Shabbat on multiple occasions, *and* commands others to do so. Eats with tax collectors and sinners."

"Degenerates!" Yanni throws in.

"Now, the speculation you mentioned?" He pulls out a fresh sheet of parchment and looks up.

Shmuel is hesitant to speculate, at least formally, and Yanni remains awkwardly silent too.

"Spit it out. I don't have all day."

Shmuel scrambles to think what might impress Shammai most. "One of John the Baptizer's students is among his followers. And there are rumors of a second."

"Delicious," Shammai says, scribbling. "We'll never be pestered by that freak again."

Shmuel thinks of something else. "In Capernaum there were women of ill repute seen at table with him in the tax collector's house."

"You're telling me women are among his followers?"

Shmuel hesitates. "You asked for speculation."

"Keep going."

"He consorts with Gentiles," Yanni says. "Specifically the Ethiopian woman, who knew his name and his origin."

Shmuel feels they've gone too far. "The last is very vague and small," he says.

"Nothing is too small," Shammai says, "when it comes to fidelity to God's Law."

Shmuel covers his embarrassment with another tidbit. "The praetor of Capernaum ordered Jesus detained. When I spoke with his office, they made mention of the Fourth Philosophy."

"The Zealots?"

"It was just a passing comment."

"He must be out of his mind!" the old rabbi says. He stands. "You must make these confirmed facts, and your inferences from them, made known far and wide. But never mention that Shimon or Nicodemus dismissed the case. The gullible masses will defer to their supposed wisdom. But then, when we reveal dated documentation showing that Shimon had early warning and did nothing, the house of his wretched father Hillel will fall. And the House of Shammai will rise."

This is way more than Shmuel could have expected, and again he fears excess. Have they put in motion a scheme that will irreparably damage the Sanhedrin? "Rabbi Shammai," he says, "respectfully, we didn't come here today seeking to influence either school of thought. We came looking for someone who would care that a false prophet is deceiving our people."

"If that was your intent, you have succeeded. Everything you've shared with me will make an appearance in my next Shabbat sermon."

Chapter 59

# SYMMETRY

*Outcropping overlooking the disciples' campsite*

On the one hand, Matthew feels more at peace than ever before in his life. On the other, he still sometimes feels unsure of himself, wholly at a loss for what to do. He has not once regretted his decision to entirely turn his back on his former life and follow Jesus. Indeed, he would follow the Rabbi anywhere. And in his presence, he feels—no, believes with all that is in him—that his life is complete, his purpose, his future secure.

It's when Matthew is with the others—when Jesus is off by himself somewhere—that he is out of sorts. In a strange way, he admires even his former acquaintances—the four fishermen with whom he conducted business as a tax collector. They hated him, sure, as did most fellow Jews. But he sees in them now a hint of what Jesus must have seen in them in order to surround himself with them. Simon is a born leader—impetuous, yes, but strong-willed and unapologetic about his faith. His brother, Andrew, has a temper that manifests in passion.

And the brothers John and Big James—they're opinionated both, which serves them well with the assignments Jesus doles out.

Those four cannot hide their feelings for Matthew, for some reason unwilling to see that he's no longer the person he was. Neither are they, and he can see that. Why this is not reciprocated, he does not know. It's as if they're demanding an apology from him, and deep inside he feels he owes that. But he can't so much as inhale to try to express his regret before one of them—usually Simon—tells him to save his breath, that he doesn't want to hear it.

Matthew cannot deny that he is enamored of Mary from Magdala. He doesn't know if this is a romantic attraction, because he isn't sure he'd recognize that if it was. All he knows is that he loves to be in her presence, to hear her voice. He cares about her, cares for her, and he certainly agonized over her in her time of distress. She's kind to him but also a bit distant. Treats him as a younger brother. Shows patience. Maybe he does love her; he doesn't know.

But right now, since before dawn when he and the Rabbi began working in the Master's tent, Matthew is with Jesus and all seems right. They sojourned up here at the break of dawn, and he found a broad rock where he could spread a blanket and lay out all his writing tools—an inkpot, several styluses, and a supply of writing tablets fashioned from lime-wood and cut into thin sheets. Matthew had learned to create his own inks for keeping records in the tax booth, blending carbon and gum arabic with water. Others of his diptychs had wax bases in which he could engrave without ink.

He sits reviewing the many paragraphs he has meticulously recorded the last couple of hours, glad for the break. Jesus, as he has done many times already, moseys to the edge of the rocks to peer down at the camp. He stands with his back to Matthew, hands clasped behind him. "Matthew, come look."

Matthew grabs a fresh tablet, just in case, and joins him.

"Mary finished the notices," Jesus says. "They're leaving to spread the word."

As the disciples set out in pairs, Matthew says, "I hope they can find a way to work together."

"What do you mean?"

"They can't seem to agree on a single thing lately. Me included sometimes."

"Oh, I've noticed. In some ways, it's to be expected."

"But not desired," Matthew says. "Surely."

"No, but it's what's bound to happen when you start something that's open to all, truly all people. Zealots. Even tax collectors." He chuckles. "People who have been through tough times. People both hesitant and skeptical. As well as bold and confident. People hungry to learn, as well as those learned and knowledgeable." As the men disappear and the four women set out, leaving the camp empty, Jesus says, "Let's get back to work."

They head back to Matthew's ersatz rock desk, and Jesus says, "How many sections are we up to?"

"Nineteen," Matthew says, and for some inexplicable reason, the odd number nags at him.

"Feels a little incomplete, huh?" Jesus says.

Glad for the chance to plead his case, Matthew says, "There is something about twenty that is more symmetrical. You could always shorten it to eighteen."

"Brevity is usually preferred." As Matthew settles before his copious notes, Jesus stands over him. "Which section stands out to you the most?"

Dare he say? Well, it's obvious and certainly will come as no surprise to Jesus. "'Do not be anxious about your life,' of course."

"Are there any sections that concern you?"

Matthew hesitates. Now he really feels out on a limb, because, yes …

"Give me your honest opinion," Jesus says. "I know *I* don't have to say that, but—"

"The whole truth?"

"You know I won't be offended."

Matthew speaks cautiously. "It's all—very striking. But, if I do the math, in terms of good news and bad, it seems there's not a lot of—good news. Like this: 'Anyone who looks at a woman with lust has already committed adultery.' Doesn't that make everyone an adulterer? And this: 'If your right eye causes you to sin, gouge it out.' Wouldn't that lead to an entire population of people walking around with only one eye?

"Oh, and this one: 'If anyone were to sue you and take your tunic, let him have your cloak as well.' You've also got trees that bear bad fruit being cut down and thrown into the fire. 'The gate is narrow and hard that leads to life.' 'Depart from me, I never knew you.' Do you realize how heavily laden your sermon is with these kinds of ominous pronouncements? I haven't even named half of them."

"It's a manifesto, Matthew. I'm not here to be sentimental and soothing. I'm here to start a revolution."

"Well, 'Love your enemies and pray for those who persecute you …' isn't exactly—"

"I said *revolution*, not *revolt*. I'm talking about a radical shift. Did you think I was just going to come here and say, 'Hey, everyone, just keep doing what you've been doing for the last thousand years, since it's been going so great'?"

Matthew recognizes the sarcasm, which he knows he wouldn't have not so long ago. But while he can't argue with

Jesus' logic, there is something else. "Also, there's your beginning and end."

"What about the beginning?"

"My concern about the beginning is more logistical. Right now, your opening line is, 'You are the salt of the earth.' I'm worried, particularly if it is windy, or if the crowd is larger than we expect, that people near the back will hear, 'salt the earth,' and it will immediately call to mind a negative connotation."

"The Punic Wars?"

"Yes, when Rome destroyed Carthage, they sowed the city with salt to make it barren and to curse anyone who would rebuild upon it."

"I share your concern about the opening line," Jesus says, "but for different reasons. I think the sermon needs some sort of introduction, an invitation into what—as you have rightly pointed out—will be a complex and, at times, challenging set of teachings."

"What does 'You are the salt of the earth' even mean? I'm not good at metaphor."

"Salt preserves meat from corruption, Matthew. It slows its decay. I want my followers to be a people who hold back the evil over the world. Salt also enhances the flavor of things. I want my followers to renew the world and be part of its redemption. Salt can also be mixed with honey and rubbed on the skin for maladies. I want my people to participate in the healing of the world, not its destruction."

Matthew looks up from his torrid scribbling. "Then why not just say that?"

Jesus laughs. "C'mon, Matthew, allow me a little poetry, huh? Not everyone is like you. Some people like a little flavor. Read the songs of David or Solomon. I'm not going nearly as far with metaphor as Solomon."

"I'm reading him next."

"Well, good luck. He's probably *whoo!*" Jesus mimes an over-your-head move.

"Yeah."

"I told you. These things will make sense to some and not to others. I don't want passive followers. Those who are truly committed will peer deeply into it, looking for truth. But I do agree with you—we shouldn't begin with salt. You make a valid point. Good work."

Jesus heads back to the edge. Matthew rises and follows. "You could just flip it with the next image: 'You are the light of the world. A city set on a hill cannot be hidden.'"

"I could."

"Or, 'Whatever you wish that others would do to you, do also to them.' That one's inviting."

Jesus gazes down the mountainside as if his mind is miles away.

"Master, may I ask why you keep coming down to look at the camp? They've all gone, haven't they?"

"They have," he says sadly. "I'm going to need time."

Chapter 60

# WON OVER

*Jotapata public house*

To Nathanael's delight, the place does look respectable. In fact, the patrons are largely well-dressed men, and snippets of conversation he overhears tell him many are discussing business. He and Thaddeus and Little James find the landowner in question and invite him to join them at a table near a window. He seems pleasant enough, but guarded, perhaps even suspicious.

"My sister-in-law told me your plans. Frankly, it doesn't sound like a good idea."

"We have measures in place for crowd control," Nathanael says.

"And," Thaddeus says, "we can set aside some of our men to assist your goatherds and shepherds in keeping the animals corralled on the other side of the mount."

"But I don't like preachers," the man says. "And I don't care for crowds. You're not even offering to pay for the use of my land."

"We have no significant money to offer," Little James says.

"We may be able to secure a loan," Nathanael says, feeling the pressure of time. They need this space, and if it's just a matter of money …

"May?" the landowner says.

"We have some people in our group who are skilled at negotiation," Thaddeus says, and Nathanael tries to signal him to keep his voice down. The two at the next table—a middle-aged man and a young companion—have stopped conversing and appear to listen in.

The landowner perks up at Thaddeus' comment. "Skilled at negotiation? Why didn't you bring them?"

Nathanael knows why, but he's not about to get into that. "Sir, do you know of any neighboring pastures similar to yours, someone else we could talk to?"

"Look, I only came here because she said you'd pay for my drink if I heard you out, and I have." The landowner reaches for his shoulder bag and begins to rise. But he sits back down when the older man at the next table interrupts.

"What about product association? If this man is as important as they say, and the sermon is as significant as they are predicting …"

"I just don't care about some vagabond teacher," the landowner says.

The younger man addresses Nathanael. "This is the man who has healed many, yes? The one we've been hearing about?"

"Yes!"

The elder continues, "Think of all the pilgrims who see him as more than a teacher. How many did you say? Hundreds? Perhaps thousands?"

"Multitudes," Nathanael says.

The young man adds, "Thousands of people having

life-changing experiences on your land—perhaps even experiencing miracles."

"Yes," the older says, "what happens when those pilgrims go to market for supplies? I mean, all those travelers. Well, they associate your products with the feelings they had on that day. People from all over …"

Little James chimes in, "Your milk, your cheese, your wool, huh?"

"Your name will be the only name they can trust," the stranger adds.

The landowner's countenance softens, and he looks to the three disciples. "Multitudes?"

They nod.

"Fine. But if I find one piece of trash left behind, I'll sue for damages."

"You have our word," Nathanael says. "We'll leave it better than we found it."

"Good," the man says as he stands and leaves.

"I can't believe it!" Little James says with a grin.

"Did we just get the land?" Thaddeus says. "I think we just got the land!"

"We got it!" Nathanael says.

Thaddeus picks up his cup to toast the two strangers. "How can we ever thank—"

But they've gone.

• • •

Outside, as they head away from the public house, the businessman drapes an arm around his apprentice's shoulder. "You see, boy? I have not led you to ruin. Life is a negotiation."

"Hey, you were right."

"Opportunities are everywhere, staring us in the face. And

the only difference between us and most people is that we have the tools to take advantage."

"I'm learning."

"And I'm telling you, I don't want to be in business forever. I just want to make enough money to make my own choices. I'm like you—I believe there is more to life than deals and land titles. Hey, you know what would be really interesting? To see this preacher in person."

"I'm really glad to hear you say that," the apprentice says. "I want to see him too."

Chapter 61

# THE OPENING

*Western Galilee*

The disciples and the women are as busy as they've ever been. They pass out flyers on the road, throughout the countryside, and in villages and towns, nailing notices on walls in markets, public squares, even at fishing wharfs. Many strangers, who have either seen and heard Jesus or are aware of him, ask for extra handouts and assist in publicizing the coming sermon on the nearby mount.

Nathanael supervises the fashioning of a fabric backdrop that opens to an ascending progression of broad stones that create a temporary raised platform where Jesus can best be seen and heard. Nathanael has carefully drawn several schematics, which the others follow to build the wood and rope framework for the apparatus. Much as Jesus seems energized by crowds and individuals, it will be good to allow him a bit of seclusion behind the backdrop before he begins on the day in question.

Meanwhile, Matthew sits before all his notes and writing supplies on the outcropping that overlooks the Jotapata campsite. He's tidied up the writing of all Jesus has recited for him, and he's made more legible much of what he's had to scrawl quickly. The Rabbi politely refused his offer to use the notes while speaking. "I will not need to be reminded of all I have been contemplating for days."

Still Matthew remains nervous. Jesus paces several yards away, praying—but not loud enough for Matthew to make out what he's saying. With each passing day, the Master has seemed more burdened, as if the weight of the world is crushing him. Perhaps this burden will lift after the sermon is preached. Matthew can hardly wait for the multitudes to hear it, but even more he's excited for his new friends to take it in. While his focused mind has never been agile enough for metaphor and subtlety, having been over this material as many times as Jesus himself has burned it deep into his heart. He senses the profound nature of it. And the Teacher is still honing the beginning and the end. What majestic form might that take?

• • •

Simon leads several of the others back to camp from their canvassing work—Andrew, Big James, John, Zee, Thomas, Ramah, and the younger Mary. Simon checks Jesus' tent, then Matthew's. Privately he contends with envy. How he wishes Jesus would choose him as a confidant. He feels loved, yes. Trusted too. And, for the most part, included. Except for now.

"They're still gone," he tells John.

Andrew overhears. As they all gather, he says, "Have we been advertising something that might not happen? What if he never comes back?"

"We go to sleep and he's not here," Big James says. "We wake up and he's not here."

"Correction," Zee says. "When *you* wake up, he's not here. I've seen him leave with Matthew every morning for the past week."

"I think he's just trying to get it right," Mary says.

Ramah looks puzzled. "Can he get anything wrong?"

"I mean get it right for the people."

"What if we've all been misled?" Thomas says.

"How can you say that?" Ramah says. "You saw what happened at Cana!"

"Everyone!" Simon says. "Calm down."

"I'm sorry," Thomas says. "I'm just nervous."

Simon wants to be the voice of reason, though he has his own doubts. "We're all tired from a long day. We need to rest for tomorrow and go meet the others at the mountain early to help set up."

"What if no one shows up?" John says.

"What if *everyone* shows up?" Mary says.

"Either way," Big James says, "Simon is right. We should rest."

"You think I'm going to get a wink of sleep?" Thomas says. "I just want to make sure I've done everything I can for him."

Ramah gazes at him. "You always do."

Simon whispers to Andrew, "He'll sleep well now."

• • •

The day wanes, and Matthew lights a lamp so he can keep working as Jesus continues to pace in the distance, gesturing, rehearsing. Matthew's eyes grow heavy. He sits with his back to the rock for just a moment's repose. Just a moment.

He dreams of a hand on his shoulder.

"Matthew."

It's not a dream. He rouses. "Rabbi."

"I've got it."

"The opening?"

"Yes."

"What is it?"

"A map."

"A what?"

"Directions. Where people should look to find me."

*What in the world is he saying?* "Okay," Matthew says. "Give me a moment." He sips from his water sac and rubs his face. Grabbing a diptych and a stylus, he finds Jesus at the edge of the plateau, again gazing down at the disciples' camp. "I'm ready."

But apparently Jesus is not. At least not yet. His countenance appears woeful in the fading light, and Matthew follows his gaze to the central fire below, where the disciples gather. It's clear they're arguing about something—again.

"Rabbi?" Matthew says.

And the man Matthew has come to know and believe is the Messiah begins a haunting recitation so melancholy and evocative in its tenderness that he can scarcely take it in. All he can do is his duty and make a record of it.

• • •

"Blessed are the poor in spirit," Jesus says, his mind returning to Nathanael weeping under the fig tree, pleading with God to see him. "For theirs is the kingdom of heaven."

Jesus reflects on precious Andrew, sobbing in frustration and fear at the news that his former rabbi, John the Baptizer, had been captured. "Blessed are those who mourn, for they shall be comforted.

"Blessed are the meek," he continues, thinking of Little James and Thaddeus, "for they shall inherit the earth.

"Blessed are those who hunger and thirst for righteousness …" He's reminded of the beloved Sons of Thunder, John and Big James. "… for they shall be satisfied."

Jesus thinks of Ramah and his own mother ministering to young Mary when she returned to him. "Blessed are the merciful, for they shall receive mercy."

He remembers Thomas and Ramah the day they said

goodbye to her father. "Blessed are the pure in heart, for they shall see God."

Jesus recalls how, in the midst of all the squabbling, Philip is the voice of reason. "Blessed are the peacemakers, for they shall be called sons of God."

Reflecting on his own fearless cousin, Jesus says, "Blessed are those who are persecuted for righteousness' sake, for theirs is the kingdom of heaven."

• • •

Jesus turns to face him, and Matthew looks up from his notes into a face of deep compassion. "Blessed are you when others revile you and persecute you and utter all kinds of evil against you falsely on my account. Rejoice and be glad, for your reward will be great in heaven."

*How can he know a man's innermost thoughts and feelings and pain?* Matthew realizes that the Rabbi has spoken truth to his very soul, the most loving and affirming statement anyone could ever utter to him. "Yes," he says, smiling. How can he do other than rejoice and be glad?

And yet that persistent part of his brain won't leave him alone long enough to bask in this glow. "But how," he says, "is it a map?"

"If someone wants to find me," Jesus says, "those are the groups they should look for."

*That makes sense,* Matthew decides, *even to me.* "And then?"

"You are the salt of the earth."

Perfect, Matthew decides. Even the metaphor works. He cannot suppress a grin, and yet neither is he embarrassed when tears follow. If he cannot cry in the presence of one who loves him so …

## Chapter 62

# COLOR

*The mount*

With all the disciples and the women busy behind the draperies separating them from the expanse where the crowd—if there is to be one—will gather, Jesus paces several steps away, rehearsing. "Therefore, do not be anxious about your life—what you'll eat, what you'll drink, about your body, what you'll put on …"

"Jesus!"

It's the blessed voice of his own mother. If it were anyone but her, he would tell them to wait until after the sermon. She's standing with the other Mary, Ramah, and Tamar. "Yes?"

"Please come. We'd like to show you something."

Surely this can wait. "I'm preparing, Ima."

"Fine. We'll come to you." She says it with such delight, he cannot deny her. But it's not just her. All four women approach, each bearing a bolt of colorful cloth. His mother looks him up and down, taking in his simple off-white tunic. "This is no good."

"What? Why not?"

"You'll blend into the rocks."

Tamar adds, “To the people in the back you’ll be a disembodied voice coming from a slate quarry.”

*And what would be so wrong with that?*

“You need a pop of color,” Ramah says.

“I know what the prophecy says about my appearance. Is this your attempt to change it?”

His mother nods, and Mary Magdalene steps forward, holding her cloth up to him. “Blue,” she says, “the symbol of peace, like the water and the sky.”

*She means well. They all do. But …*

Tamar follows and drapes hers over his shoulder. “Red, a symbol of passion, blood, sacrifice, love.”

*She can’t know how prescient she is.*

Tamar backs away as Ramah approaches. “Purple. Royalty, kingship.”

*If only more than my most-devoted followers agreed.*

His mother presents hers. “Gold. Warmth, wisdom, light, the sun.” She steps back. “Well?”

“Well,” he says, “we have no glass or still water to peer into for a reflection. And even if we did, I can’t tell you how little I care about how I look.”

The women giggle but clearly will not be dissuaded. So he calls for a vote. “Ima?”

“Blue, the symbol of peace. Our Prince of peace.”

“Ramah …”

“Purple. Because of the night I first met you. Grapes. Wine.”

*That* is *a precious memory.*

“Mary?”

“Purple also. Royalty.”

“Tamar?”

“Blue, it’s a calming color. Softens your hard edges.”

*That’s a new one.* “I have hard edges?”

"You've been known to say hard things," Mary says.

"Ha! Just wait."

• • •

From the other side of the expanse of drapery comes the sound of countless footsteps. Simon consults with his brother, who tells him, "Thomas says we're up to three thousand people!"

"At the rate people are showing up, it will be four thousand in no time."

"Should we even tell him?" Andrew says.

"I don't want him to be surprised when he comes around to his place."

"Is he capable of surprise or being thrown off?"

"Oh, this is not good," Simon says. "If more people show up or if one more thing goes wrong, this could be a disaster."

"Am I allowed in?"

Simon whirls to find Eden. He rushes to her, having had no idea she was coming. They embrace. He so hopes the day is a success, especially with her there. And how he would love to smother her with kisses. "Later," he whispers. "Where's Dasha?"

"She's with Zebedee and some of the others. They secured a place at the front."

*What a special day this could be for her, too*. Simon is grateful his mother-in-law is up to it.

"Eden!"

It's Jesus.

"Yes?"

"Get over here! I need a tie-breaker."

Simon hates to surrender his beloved's attention to anyone. Except to Jesus himself, of course. He senses her joy at being summoned.

Chapter 63

# THE MULTITUDE

The businessman and his apprentice find themselves among thousands as they crest the mount. "This is even bigger than I thought," the older man says.

"Oh, I had a feeling," the younger man says.

"You had a feeling." He wonders where they can land and still have a view of this preacher. "I want to see him."

"I want to find a place where we can at least hear him," the apprentice says.

"I'll come and find you," his boss says. "I won't be long. See if you can find one of his followers, one of the men we met. Let them know we can help them. They clearly need it." He sees a few people welcoming various members of the crowd. "They look like they're with him." He approaches one. "Excuse me, son! May I have a very brief word?"

"Certainly. I'm Philip. How can I help you?"

• • •

On his own now, the apprentice murmurs, "This is amazing." He's heard so much about this preacher. Is it possible the rumors are true? So many cannot be denied. These are more than just stories of miracles, of healings. They're eyewitness accounts, even testimonies of the beneficiaries themselves. Relatives and friends swear their loved ones have been cured of lifelong maladies. The young man cannot help but long for this to be true.

The miracle worker seems never to have failed to heal someone. Even one misstep would prove he's not who people hope he is—the Messiah himself. Could it be? It is almost too much to hope for, and yet the young man has wished for this, dreamed of this, his whole life. He has struggled to live right, to do right, to follow the teachings of the Torah. His boss has persuaded him to stretch the truth, but always with some rational justification. No one's been hurt, have they?

Still, his conscience nags. He wants to live a life of purity, not one of finding a way to assuage his guilt over white lies and half-truths. What might this vagabond teacher have to say about such things?

A one-legged man hobbles along on a crutch, a blind woman on his arm. "Excuse me!" the apprentice says. "Do you know where I should stand to hear him?"

"To hear the teacher from Nazareth?"

"Nazareth?" the young man says. Has he heard correctly? Surely such a famous person cannot be from there.

"He performs miracles," the man says.

"They are saying he could be the One," the blind woman says.

"We're not going to miss a word," the man adds. "You could do a lot worse than to follow us."

Just what he wanted to hear. "That's kind. Thank you."

But when he follows them, they seem to head away from the action. Are they both blind?

The woman says, "You know, Barnaby, today is one of those days when it's definitely better to be blind than deaf."

"Oh, Shula . . ." the lame man says.

"I'm sorry," the young man calls after them, "but if we're moving to where we can hear the teacher, why are you going this way?"

"We'll get back there," Barnaby says. "We're just going to say hello to some old friends before the show."

"It's not a show, Barnaby," the woman says.

"It was a show at Zebedee's house!" he says, cackling.

The apprentice has no idea what they're referring to, but he's intrigued with whatever connection they have to these people and this event.

• • •

Atticus, the *Cohortes Urbana*, steps from a clearing and stops, scanning the massive crowd. He wouldn't have missed this and has to admit it's drawn many more pilgrims than he dreamed possible. He has a job to do, an obligation to Caesar himself, but he can't deny he's become obsessed with this assignment. At first confident he would find the Nazarene just another in a long list of pretenders, at the very least he's found the man the most convincing and elusive of his career. The Messiah? That may be something the Pharisees will have to determine, but the recipients of the man's influence are certainly convinced.

A horse sidles next to him and stops, the Primi Gaius on its back. The men glance knowingly at each other. Dotted among the commoners, all over the hillside, stand Roman guards in their red finery, as well as Pharisees in their black and white vestments. Atticus is tempted to broach with Gaius the subject of Jesus' authenticity, but he dares not reveal his own uncertainty.

• • •

John and Zee try to control the crowd at the front, shouting for everyone to step back. "No more pushing!" Zee hollers. "This is the line!"

John yells, "Five cubits back, everyone! Please!"

"And what if we don't?" a man demands.

*This is all I need right now,* John thinks and puffs his chest to take charge, only to face his own teasing father.

"Abba!" he blurts, and they embrace, laughing and clapping each other's backs.

"You think we'd stay home and miss this?"

John spots his mother, and she rushes to him. "Ima!"

She pulls back from his hug. "You look skinny."

"No, I'm—"

"Are you eating?"

"Yes, yes, I'm fine."

"Where's James?"

"He's on the other side. I actually have to go there now."

"Okay," she says, beaming. "Go!"

As he backs away, he points. "And no heckling, you two."

"No promises!" his father bellows.

"Zebedee!" John's mother scolds.

John can only shake his head.

• • •

Mother Mary and Jesus stand alone, she again straightens the blue sash Eden chose in the end.

"What are you thinking about, Ima?"

"Your father," she says, her voice thick. "How he never got to see any of this."

"My father? Which one?"

That elicits a chuckle. "You know what I mean."

"I do miss him," Jesus says, lip quivering. "But I'm glad you're here."

She locks eyes with him. "I am proud of you."

"Maybe wait to say that until after I'm done. In case I mess up in front of such a big crowd."

She shakes her head. "Whatever you say will be beautiful."

He smiles. "It is pretty good, actually."

They share a laugh.

How grateful he finds himself at his heavenly Father's choice of a mother for him. Naturally, it's no surprise that God would appoint a woman of such character. But for her to have shown such devotion at such a young age! And now, in her late forties, she has become a woman of such depth—even joy in the face of trials—that it seems everyone who comes into contact with her reveres her. She is the ultimate friend, confidant, counselor.

"Master," Simon says, his eyes bright. "It's time."

Jesus presses his forehead to his mother's and recalls with deep affection their conversation nearly twenty years before. She had searched frantically for him when she feared he had become separated from their party leaving Jerusalem, only to discover he had been about God's business in the Temple.

"If not now …" he prompts her.

"When?" she says.

• • •

Nathanael notices Barnaby and Shula come around behind the curtains, followed by a young man. "We heard some guy's gonna tell jokes on a hillside or something?" Barnaby yells.

"They're not jokes!" Matthew says, while everyone else laughs and rushes to greet their old friends.

Nathanael stares at the young man. "Wait! It's you! You're the man from the public house. You're—"

"I just followed them. I don't actually know what I'm doing here."

"Come on over! Please, stick around. Simon! This is the man who got us the mount and the pasture! Convinced the landowner it was worth his while."

"Aah, good work! I'm Simon."

"Judas," the young man says, shaking his hand.

"Welcome, Judas. I'm sure you're gonna love this sermon."

"Oh, I wouldn't miss it."

Simon pats him on the back and hurries off.

As the crowd of clearly more than five thousand now appears restless, Simon fears they can wait no longer. As he approaches Jesus again, he thinks this Judas seems a nice-enough fellow—bright-eyed and eager. And if he is the one who helped secure this location … Simon wonders what Jesus might make of him. Another chosen follower?

Simon hates to interrupt the rabbi and his mother. But he's been assigned to keep things on schedule. "Shall we?" he says.

• • •

Mother Mary tugs at Jesus' sash one more time. He strides toward the blowing curtains. Though she knows without question he is following his call, doing the Father's bidding, the mom in her wonders if addressing such a massive crowd is the right thing to do. Up to now, his fame has spread, yes, but it has seemed manageable. What will happen when thousands tell others how profound they find him?

And he will be profound, she's sure. At least he is only

preaching today. No healing is planned, as far as she knows. If only this spectacle can remain somehow low-key. But she knows better. Rome is represented. The Sanhedrin. Who knows who else?

Jesus avoiding the ire of the government and the Temple seems less possible every day, and Mary does not want to dwell on what that might mean for him. Her nephew is behind bars already.

• • •

As Jesus follows Simon toward the makeshift stone stairs from which he will speak, his mother gives him one last smile of love and pride. He slowly passes everyone he cherishes. Pensive, smiling, supporting, eager, they stand motionless, as if trying to communicate with him with their eyes, and he takes the time to look each fully in the face.

The younger Mary, who once hid behind an alias but whom he called by name.

Ramah, the vintner, who left her home and her father to follow him.

Precious Matthew, still clinging to his notes.

Thaddeus, whom Jesus first knew as a common laborer.

Little James, cheerful and tireless despite his physical ailments.

Nathanael, the gifted architect he saw in agony under the fig tree and who has designed this very venue.

A young stranger standing behind the others, a man with curious eyes and an earnest bearing.

Beloved Simon, now with his arms wrapped proudly around dear Eden, who gazes upon Jesus with a look of gratitude for all he means to her, her mother, and her husband.

Philip, his cousin John's former disciple who has so quickly become a mentor to Jesus' followers.

Tamar, the beautiful Egyptian believer who shrinks from no one, loyal to the end.

Jesus is soon flanked by the brothers John and Big James, the Sons of Thunder who vow to protect him at all costs.

Thomas, the angst-ridden caterer who has abandoned a lucrative career without a second thought.

Simon the former Zealot, who appears zealous still.

And at the bottom of the steps, Simon the fisherman's impetuous little brother, Andrew, never afraid to speak his mind.

Jesus solemnly mounts the stairs, his message bursting in his heart. He steps through the handmade draperies and scans the colossal crowd, slowly beginning to sit, their outer reaches rimmed with Roman guards on horseback. He's aware of the Pharisees as well.

But he has come to speak to the people, and the great weight of the responsibility washes over him. He plans to change minds today, speaking in paradoxes that could turn their worlds upside down. One heart at a time.

THE END

# ACKNOWLEDGMENTS


Mere thanks seem paltry compared to what I owe:
My assistant, Sarah Helus
My agent, Alex Field
My editors, Larry Weeden and Leilani Squires
Steve Johnson and the Focus team
Carlton Garborg and the BroadStreet crew
And my lifetime valentine, Dianna